"A beautiful, haunting tale that tugs you in as past mistakes are explored and forgiven and the future forged with honesty and bright new hope. With characters you'll want for friends, a charming island setting, and a love story that will leave a smile, this is a story to be savored long after the last page is turned."

—**Catherine West**, author of *The Things We Knew*

Praise for *The Red Door Inn*

"*The Red Door Inn* is a heartwarming story of second chances, restoration, and hope."

—**Fresh Fiction**

"A compelling and consistently entertaining read from first page to last."

—**The Midwest Book Review**

"The characters are endearing, and their emotional and faith journeys elevate this novel and make it truly meaningful."

—*RT Book Reviews*

Praise for *Where Two Hearts Meet*

"*Where Two Hearts Meet* is one of the sweetest, most endearing contemporary romances I have read this year and, dare I say, in a long while."

—**Straight Off the**

"*Where Two Hearts Meet* will melt your own h each story-turning page."

—**Jenny B. Jones**, award-winning auth and the Katie Pa

"A delightful, yummy tale of faith and the lovely Red Door Inn."

—**Rachel Hauck**, *New York Times* bes ng author

Books by Liz Johnson

The Red Door Inn
Where Two Hearts Meet
On Love's Gentle Shore

ON LOVE'S GENTLE SHORE

A NOVEL

Liz Johnson

Revell

a division of Baker Publishing Group
Grand Rapids, Michigan

Published by Revell
a division of Baker Publishing Group
P.O. Box 6287, Grand Rapids, MI 49516-6287
www.revellbooks.com

Printed in the United States of America

Library of Congress Cataloging-in-Publication Data
Names: Johnson, Liz, 1981– author.
Title: On love's gentle shore : a novel / Liz Johnson.
Description: Grand Rapids, MI : Published by Revell, a division of Baker Publishing
    Group, [2017] | Series: Prince Edward Island dreams #3
Identifiers: LCCN 2017001829| ISBN 9780800724511 (paper) | ISBN 9780800728885
    (print on demand)
Subjects: | GSAFD: Christian fiction. | Love stories.
Classification: LCC PS3610.O3633 O5 2017 | DDC 813/.6—dc23
LC record available at https://lccn.loc.gov/2017001829

Published in association with Books & Such Literary Management.

17 18 19 20 21 22 23   7 6 5 4 3 2 1

For my dad, who hasn't gotten
to visit the island with me yet.
No matter how far I travel,
I'm sure of your love.
Thanks.
I love you back.

1

She'd thought it was safe to come back to the island. She'd thought it was safe to come home.

She'd been wrong.

It wasn't even safe to pick up lunch.

Natalie O'Ryan ran suddenly sweaty palms down the front of her crisp ankle pants and swallowed the lump that had settled at the base of her throat. The bell over the front door of Grady's Diner had barely finished its reckless cry when every head in the open room turned in her direction. She stared down the curious gazes, some in faces she'd known her whole life. They sported a few more sun spots, a handful of new wrinkles. Dark hair had turned gray, and cheeks had hollowed with age.

And every eye was sharp with assessment.

That hadn't changed a bit.

The tourists turned back to their fish and chips, clearly finding her unworthy of their distraction.

But the locals—the women of the ladies' auxiliary and the men of the Lions Club next door—continued their open-mouthed gapes.

She'd thought perhaps no one would recognize her. A foolish hope, maybe. But she'd carried it nonetheless. It had been in her pocket like the prayer stone Mama Kane had given her when she was eight. Whenever her heart had begun to pound on the long flight from Nashville to Toronto, she'd rubbed at that fantasy, her thumb wearing the skin on her index finger raw. Every time her breath caught in her throat as they soared over the island she'd called home for more than half her life, she'd hugged her neck pillow like it could conceal her from all of these knowing eyes.

It hadn't worked.

The flush-cheeked child inside her tugged on her arm, begging her to pull a 180 and disappear like she'd done all those years ago. But she shook her arm as though she could physically dislodge the urge to flee.

She wasn't entirely successful at that, but she also wasn't the same child she'd been. Managing to plaster a smile into place, she marched across the tile floor. Weaving between brown tabletops surrounded by matching chairs that looked like they'd been stolen from the church's basement, she grabbed for the lapels of her tailored jacket and tugged them together over her chest.

The nosy glances followed her every step. But they hadn't turned into behind-the-hand whispers.

Yet.

"Is that little Natalie O'Ryan?"

As if they'd all been waiting on the confirmation, tongues set off wagging, followed by stage whispers filling the air until even the children in booster seats craned their necks to get a look at North Rustico's very own prodigal daughter.

Natalie licked suddenly dry lips and forced herself to

search out the owner of the voice. She'd have known it anywhere. It was the last one she'd heard before leaving the island nearly fifteen years ago.

"Hello, Mrs. Burke."

The matriarch was a fair bit older than Natalie's mom, even though her daughter, Bethany, had been a grade behind Natalie. In part because the Burkes hadn't had children until they were in their late thirties. But mostly because Natalie's mom had been barely seventeen when she gave birth.

Mrs. Burke nodded stiffly, an attempt at a smile elbowing its way across her face in fits and starts. It never reached the wrinkles at the corners of her eyes, but she tipped her head in greeting, showing off box-blonde hair and a style that hadn't changed in all the years Natalie had known her.

"This is quite a surprise."

Like she had as a nine-year-old, Natalie moved to shove her hands into her pockets and hunch her shoulders against the intrusive stares, but she stopped halfway there. She wasn't a child anymore.

And her J.Crew pants didn't have pockets.

Squaring her shoulders, she schooled her features into what she hoped was a very pleasant expression, which she bestowed on all three women at the table. "It's good to see you again, Mrs. Burke."

It wasn't.

But she'd learned to keep some things to herself.

"Natalie? Natalie!"

At the call, she spun toward the counter, where she was nearly blinded by a smile that reached ear to ear. "Aretha?"

The woman, Aretha Franklin—no relation to the singer, as she liked to remind folks—nodded as she scurried across the floor, unashamedly bumping into chairs. But her eyes never wavered, and they felt like a warm embrace—a missed embrace. Reaching out both hands, Aretha swept Natalie into her grip and squeezed like this might be the fulfillment of her life's dream.

"I didn't believe it when Marie said you'd be coming."

Natalie returned the gentle grasp, careful of the paper-thin skin and the simple diamond on her left ring finger. Ever since Russell had proposed with a rock that rivaled Gibraltar, she'd become especially aware of every other ring.

But she couldn't ask about Aretha's rock, so she stumbled back to her last sentence. "Marie?"

"At the Red Door."

Natalie's eyebrows bunched. Right. Marie and Seth, who owned the inn. The one that was new to her hometown. So were Marie and Seth, for that matter. But Russell hadn't known that. So he'd plowed forward, booking the inn for as many of their wedding guests as it would hold and hiring Marie to help make the final arrangements for the wedding.

A sharp pain in her chest sent her hand to her collarbone, and she tried to wipe away the discomfort.

But there was no wiping out the truth.

There were more than just final arrangements to make for the wedding.

The dress. Rings. Guest list. Groom. Those were all she had lined up.

Everything else—flowers, food, cake, decorations, and more—was going to have to fall into place in the next six weeks.

The unchecked items on her mental to-do list flashed like the neon sign of a Nashville honky-tonk, and her head spun. The air thinned as though she'd hiked fifteen thousand feet, and a sudden rope around her chest rubbed her lungs raw.

Aretha pressed a hand to her wrist, the wrinkled fingers warm and softer than wedding dress satin. "Honey? Are you all right?"

Natalie forced a smiling mask across her features—one she'd donned a thousand times. It was the collected concierge, the proficient professional. No matter the situation, she could handle it. Sneaking a subtle breath that did little to fill her lungs, she nodded quickly. "Yes. Of course."

The wrinkles around Aretha's eyes crinkled, her gaze knowing, unbelieving.

Some things never changed.

Aretha had perfected that look long before the first time she used it on seven-year-old Natalie.

"I came over to pick up lunch for Russell." She flipped a hand over her shoulder in the direction of the inn. "He's checking into our rooms."

Eyes flashing with delight, Aretha followed the motion of her hand. "Of course, Adam's brother. We've all been so eager to meet him."

Right. Because everyone here knew and loved her soon-to-be brother-in-law, despite the fact that she'd met him exactly three times. And that she downright disliked him.

Well, that wasn't entirely true. He seemed a nice enough sort. Her grandma would have called him a good seed. Hardworking and not predisposed to finding trouble. In their three years together, she'd never seen Russell as happy as he'd been when he introduced his little brother—his long-lost brother. He hadn't offered her the details, and she hadn't pressed for them. But there had been a rift between them until Adam showed up a year before.

Adam had been pleasant and jovial. And he was dating one of her former schoolmates, Caden Holt. He was also the reason she was back on the island.

Which put him at the bottom of her list.

"When Adam told us that Russ was going to have his wedding here and stay at the inn . . ." Aretha's eyelashes fluttered like a teenager in love. "Well, it was more than we'd dared to hope for."

Natalie leaned forward at the note of wistfulness in Aretha's voice. It tugged at her heartstrings, as though there was some deeper meaning to Adam's suggestion that they stay at Rose's Red Door Inn for their wedding and Russell's acquiescence to island vows.

Still, the ceremony could have been in a lovely country barn outside of Nashville. Several of the musicians Russell had worked with over the years had even offered their property. Middle Tennessee at its finest. Verdant green pastures. Stunning wooden beams. Colorful wildflowers.

And no unpleasant memories.

Yes, Nashville would have been better.

But Russell had been so pleased when he told her he'd agreed to have their wedding in North Rustico. He'd thought it would make her happy.

And rather than risk making a scene over his forty-dollar steak, she'd opted to plaster a smile into place and get through the rest of their date. After that he'd been too thrilled, too pleased with himself at doing such a thoughtful thing, for her to tell him she didn't want to go back to the island. For her to tell him there were more reasons for leaving than she'd hinted at early on in their relationship.

She rubbed at a sudden throbbing at her temple and squinted against the fluorescent reflection off the pale tile flooring.

In her old stomping grounds, there would be no ignoring the childhood that had chased her off the island, across the border, and all the way to Music City.

Suddenly a ruffled shock of white hair appeared at Aretha's side. It belonged to a man with a map of wrinkles that would take a lifetime to navigate, but his eyes were kind, the easy line of his mouth hinting at a smile that was never far gone.

Aretha grabbed his hand, her fingers sliding between his easily. "This is my husband, Jack Sloane. Jack, this is Natalie O'Ryan."

Natalie's stomach gave a good bounce. "Husband? You got married?"

"Three years ago this October."

Jack added his silent nod, his grin no less satisfied than his bride's.

So the ring wasn't for show.

Natalie couldn't wrap her mind around the announcement, and she managed only a slow series of blinks. Her hands were more frantic, suddenly too big, fluttering about at her sides and searching for those nonexistent pockets.

Aretha had been alone since forever. Her antiques store was off-limits to most of the area's teenagers, but her story was well known. If Natalie's family had been the most popular topic for gossips in the Crick—North Rustico to outsiders—twenty-five years ago, then they'd only inherited the title from Aretha, whose husband had taken off for parts unknown long before Natalie's dad took to the bottle. And other women's bedrooms.

Natalie cringed at the memories, the ones that seemed to trail her wherever she went.

But Aretha and Jack didn't seem to notice. Their sly glances and the subtle brush of their elbows kept them both distracted by something infinitely sweeter than the bitterness rising at the back of her throat.

After a long moment of silence, another voice interrupted them.

"Natalie O'Ryan! Pickup!"

The familiar face at the pickup window was topped with a white hat that looked like it hadn't been washed since she'd made her first trip to this counter.

Some things never changed.

"We'll see you soon, honey," Aretha said.

Natalie turned to the counter and leaned her forearms along the smooth grain of the pine. A white sack with two matching Styrofoam containers appeared at her elbow beside a matching bag as she looked under the overhang.

Harrison Grady stared back at her with his one good eye, the patch on the other nearly as worn as his hat and apron. His brown gaze was almost too intent for just the one eye, and she shivered under its weight. When he finally spoke, his voice was filled with as much gravel as ever. "I saw your name and said, 'It can't be our little Natalie. Back from away.'"

She tried for a smile at the words she was sure were supposed to be endearing, but it refused to show up.

If she'd really been their little Natalie . . .

Well, no one had loved her half as much as they loved talking about her parents. Except maybe the Kanes, who owned the local dairy and invited her into their home for more meals than she could count.

She'd spent a fair bit of the flight praying she wouldn't see them this summer. Any of them.

"Harrison." She tipped her head in greeting. "Still frying up the burgers, I see."

He crossed his meaty arms over a barrel chest and nodded. "What else would I be doing?"

Because no one in this town ever did anything except what they were expected to do. Little boys grew up to be fishermen like their dads. And little girls married those little boys.

But not Natalie.

Her path was about 1,500 miles away, and she'd get back to it as soon as the wedding was over.

Harrison sucked on his front tooth before adjusting his eye patch, and she couldn't keep her mind from straying to all the ways she'd imagined he'd lost his eye. No one seemed to know. But it hadn't stopped her and little Justin Kane from speculating.

"How long you in town?"

"Six weeks and four days."

"That's awfully specific."

She snatched one of the white bags on the counter. "Just long enough for the wedding."

"Wedding? You're getting married?"

Apparently Aretha hadn't blabbed about her plans to the whole town. Not that she'd ever been one to pass tales over the back fence. But old suspicions died hard.

When Natalie didn't respond to Harrison, he just kept the questions coming. "Why didn't you say you were getting hitched? Who you marrying?" He gave her a half smile. "I always figured you'd end up with Justin."

She nearly choked on her own tongue, the cough rattling her shoulders and beating up on her lungs.

Justin.

She hadn't heard his name in a while.

Had almost hoped she wouldn't hear it again. At least not here on the island. Certainly not in relation to her pending nuptials.

After all, he was the Kane she most wanted to avoid.

"You've got his lunch there anyway."

Her fingers suddenly forgot how to work, and she dropped Justin's lunch to the floor. The rustle of the bag and crack of Styrofoam against linoleum pierced the room. Every head in the restaurant spun in her direction. Again.

She cringed as she ducked to pick up the bag. If the sloshing bottom of the plastic was any indication, something had spilled. And would be all over her if she wasn't careful.

Holding it out by the twin loops, she shot him an apologetic look. "I'm sorry. I'll pay for the replacement."

Harrison took the remains of the lunch and shook his head. "No problem. I've got it covered." With a nod he indicated the sack that had been closest to her elbow. "That's yours."

Flames licked at her neck, and she swiped a hand over them in a vain attempt to settle her nerves. Trying for a low chuckle, she settled for a too-high laugh as she snuck a peek at the diners. Most had returned to their meals, although there was still a tourist family staring a little too hard, a little too long.

Squaring her shoulders, she turned a tight smile back to Harrison. "I insist."

His squint suggested that he remembered a time when she couldn't afford to buy one meal, let alone two. So she flashed two colorful twenties in his direction, which brought just the wide-eyed glimmer of recognition she'd been hoping for.

"Maybe you don't need to tell Justin that I ruined his lunch."

"Who ruined my lunch?"

The voice was deeper than she remembered, thick like honey over almonds. Like the years had taken something from him too. But it couldn't steal the island lilt and the touch of humor she'd always known.

Yet no amount of levity in his tone could keep his words from wrapping around her chest and squeezing until there wasn't enough fresh oxygen in the world to keep her breathing.

With a shaky hand, she dropped the money on the counter and grabbed her lunch. No matter how long she stared at Harrison, his gaze never wavered from a spot over her shoulder.

There would be no curling up and rolling out of the restaurant unnoticed. She hunched her shoulders just to make sure.

The weight of the gaze on her back didn't shift.

Nope. She was stuck. And she was going to have to face him.

It had been a ridiculous dream that she could dodge him all summer in a town the size of a postage stamp.

Even more so when she considered that anyone who remembered her would remember *them*. There hadn't been a Natalie without Justin. Or a Justin without Natalie.

Not until he'd stayed. Not until he'd let her leave. Alone.

Irritation burned in her stomach, and she tried to physically push it down. But no amount of smoothing her blouse was going to calm the tumult inside. No amount of anything could save her from this moment.

Might as well get it over with.

Squeezing her eyes closed, she turned as Justin let out an audible gasp. When she blinked, he was frozen, his jaw hanging slack, dark and foreboding like the whiskers on his chin.

"Natalie?" There was a judgment in the single word, a condemnation that sounded like it tasted of not-yet-ripe raspberries. Maybe he was angry.

Even if he had no reason to be. After all, he was the one who had changed their plans.

He was the one who hadn't followed through.

He was the one who'd left her alone.

So he had no reason to be mad at her.

The force of his steamed breathing grated on her, shredding her nerves and binding her up until her own breathing turned hard, furious. The rush of anger gave her the courage to meet his eyes.

Blue. So blue they still put the sky to shame.

If time had aged his voice, his face hadn't been dealt the same hand. His skin was as smooth and tan as ever, the five o'clock shadow darker, coarser now. And his black hair was longer, pulled back into a short ponytail.

He'd asked his mom to cut it every other week when they were kids.

The memory must have flickered across her face in the form of a smile because he flinched at the same time, his glower turning fiercer.

"Natalie?" He seemed to need to confirm her identity before lashing into her.

And she had no doubt he would lay out all of his grievances.

Only it wasn't her fault. He could be as mad as an unmilked dairy cow. It didn't change the facts of the past.

But now, face-to-face with that past, she did the same thing she'd done fifteen years ago.

She ran.

2

Justin Kane slammed the back door hard enough to rattle the old toys in the farmhouse's attic. He followed that with stomping feet that sounded like they belonged to a fuming teenager rather than the man responsible for keeping the longest-running family-owned dairy in the county in the black.

"A cow step on your foot?"

His mother's voice carried from the kitchen to where he stared at the ceiling in the mudroom. It was a little too light. A little too nonchalant. She knew what was going on.

He crossed his arms, fisted his hands, and held himself just on the brink of slamming his head against the wall. Of course, that would only amplify the thunder beating against his temples. "No." He hadn't been stepped on. It just felt like that.

"I suppose you heard about Natalie then."

"How long have you known?" He nearly bit his tongue off. The traitor. He didn't want to know how long his mom had been keeping secrets from him. Especially not where Natalie O'Ryan was concerned.

But mostly he didn't want her name said in this house.

"Aretha told me she ran into Natalie at Grady's."

He cringed before easing his fingernails out of his palms. But he didn't make a move toward the kitchen door, the white frame with four triangular windows open only far enough to allow a breeze and the sounds of home cooking through.

And the smell of something sweet like cinnamon and sugar.

"Did you see her there?"

The question poked to life the image of Natalie's freckled face and the halo of red curls that swished around her shoulders. A flash of bitterness washed over him, overriding anything sweet coming from his mother's kitchen. So he answered her question with one of his own. "How'd you know I was at Grady's?"

"It's Wednesday, dear."

Of course. Because his life was completely predictable.

"Did you know she was coming back?"

Something slapped against the side of a plastic bowl, and her pause spoke volumes. Maybe she was a traitor.

"I'd heard a . . . murmur."

"You mean a rumor."

"I wouldn't call it that." She might not, but the rest of the town would. Natalie most certainly would. At least the Natalie he'd known so many years before.

Crossing an ankle over his knee to untie his boot, he yanked on the lace until the bow morphed into an angry knot. His blunt, callused fingertips fumbled against it, only managing to bumble it more. Hopping on one foot, he thudded a shoulder against the whitewashed board wall and bounced against the cement basin. Pain shot through his hip and up his side, and he groaned as he leaned against the work sink.

"You okay in there?" His mom appeared at the open door, her face only just making the turn around the corner.

Lowering his still-booted foot to the floor, he looked up at her. He must have looked more rotten than he felt because her features immediately wilted like a dried-up tulip. Lips puckered and cheeks sunken, she shook her head and walked into the mudroom. "Oh, hon."

He held her off with a single raised hand. "I'm fine, Mom." The words didn't even waver, and he took more than a little pleasure in salvaging his dignity—whatever was left of it anyway.

"She looked so pretty. Her hair as red as Anne's ever was."

His eyes snapped back to his mom's face, and the chagrined smile that played across her lips told him everything she hadn't said aloud. But it did little to heal the hole in his back where she had certainly stabbed him.

"When did you see her?"

She crossed her arms over her midsection, poking out one hip and cocking her head to the side. "Not that it matters." Which roughly translated to, *This matters most.* "I passed her on the road. I was driving over to Aretha's, and she was walking toward Grady's."

Sweat peppered his forehead, and he swiped at it with the back of his wrist, cursing any physical reaction he still had to Natalie. "And you couldn't take a minute to warn me?"

"Well, I didn't know exactly when you'd be there."

"You didn't guess that it would be at the same time I always go to Grady's on Wednesdays? Or the same time I always break for lunch?" He bit off the last word, trying to stem the bitterness that sprang up with each syllable.

"It's not like Harrison sends me your schedule."

He snorted. "I wouldn't put it past him." Undoubtedly the man had a knack for making his mom happy. "He'd rat me out faster than you could smile in his general direction."

A pink blush crept along her cheeks, but she rolled her eyes and pressed her hands to her hips. "This isn't about Harrison Grady."

"Right."

No. Wait. He wanted to snatch the word back as soon as it popped out because he knew exactly where his mom was headed, and he wanted to be as far from that path as possible.

Too late.

"This is about Natalie. And you." Her eyes were as blue as the ones he saw in the mirror every morning.

"No it's not. There is no Natalie *and* me. There's only Natalie." He waved his left hand at the edge of his wingspan. "Way over here. And this is me." Reaching as far as he could with his right hand, he wiggled his fingers to draw his mom's attention. "See? No *and* about it. Our lives are so separate I haven't thought about her in a dozen years."

Now it was her turn to snort. It wasn't delicate or soft, exactly what he'd come to expect from a farmer's daughter turned farmer's wife turned farmer's widow. She didn't have time to hide her feelings or play a part that wasn't real.

"I think there's a lyric book under your bed that would prove that's a lie," she said.

He scowled at her. This was why grown men shouldn't live with their moms.

But he didn't have a comeback or half an argument to stand on. It was true.

So he turned his attention back to his boots. Leaning his

rear end against the wall, he grabbed the heel of his left foot with one hand and the toe with the other. Then he yanked.

"Oof!" His boot didn't budge, but his ankle popped under the abuse, shooting fire up to his knee.

Elbows still protruding and hands clamped on her waist, his mom stared at him, her gaze swallowing his pitiful position. "What did you say to her?"

He shot her another glare through a lock of hair that had escaped the rubber band that usually kept it out of his face. Her face was expectant, eager. She was serious. His stomach plummeted into the stupid boots still on his feet. Brushing his hair behind his ear, he dropped his gaze and shook his head.

"What's that mean? You didn't—you didn't talk with her?"

Another quick jerk of his head and he pinched the bridge of his nose between two fingers.

"Did you not see her? No. Of course you saw her. But you didn't go up to her? You didn't get a chance to. You only saw her from a distance." The tone of her words danced upward, as though she could speak the story into reality. Any other scenario seemed impossible.

"No. I saw her. Face-to-face."

Like it was on a hinge, her mouth dropped open. It was enough. He knew the question she couldn't ask. *What happened?*

He'd been asking himself the same thing for the last four hours. What had happened?

He'd seen her hair from behind, but he'd sworn it was only his eyes playing tricks on him. Clearly the summer sun had left an orange glow around everything he saw. The woman in front of him in line didn't have a head of waves so lusciously red and topped with a golden halo.

It was his worn-out memories that had made him imagine Natalie. That butted him in the gut like a protective mama cow and forced out his breath.

The minute he'd walked into Grady's he'd started telling himself it wasn't her. He'd told himself he was imagining her back in town like he'd done a thousand times over the years.

But every time he tore his gaze away, it fought its way back. He stared at his hands but then suddenly found himself counting the ripples from the crown of her head to her shoulders. When he tried to look around the dining room, he found Stella Burke and followed her gaze straight back to the woman talking with Harrison at the counter.

"Maybe you don't need to tell Justin that I ruined his lunch," she said.

He would have known her voice anywhere, and it turned his insides to soggy toast. Still, something in him begged for the torture of confirmation, and he'd asked for it. "Who ruined my lunch?"

Pinching his eyes closed now didn't stop her face from flashing through his mind. Stricken. Shocked. Furious. Before he could even identify it, every emotion that had torn through him swept in her eyes first, as if he was always a step behind. Like that time they'd had to learn to dance in grade six. No matter how long he watched his feet, he couldn't find the beat. But he'd had no trouble finding her toes.

"What did she say? Did you invite her over? Is she coming for dinner?"

His mom's questions jerked him from memories a whole lot older than that afternoon, and he grimaced. "No. I didn't say anything."

Eyebrows bunching together, she frowned. "Excuse me?"

He opened his mouth, but snapped it closed when she held up a hand.

"I heard what you said. I just can't believe it. What did she have to say?"

Again, he shook his head and bit his lips into a thin line.

"Nothing?"

"She—I didn't know—there was some confusion about lunch orders."

She raised her eyebrows until they nearly disappeared behind the bangs she'd worn for as long as he could remember. They weren't as dark anymore—more accurately, they were salted with a liberal dose of white and gray where once her hair had been as black as his.

"It all happened so fast, and it's not like I had a speech prepared. What would you say if your former best friend, who skipped town without even telling you she was leaving, showed up?"

"Hello."

Typical. His mom picked the sarcastic option.

But if she'd been there, she'd have been just as tongue-tied. She wouldn't be quite so glib about this whole situation. Because Natalie hadn't just run out on him. She'd left behind a lot of people who really cared about her—especially Mama Kane.

A low growl in the back of his throat surprised him, but he shrugged when his mom cocked her head to the side in question.

Natalie had hurt a lot of people, and he wasn't eager to write it off or welcome her back to town with open arms. She'd have to offer something a whole lot better than those freckles, a pert little nose, and angry eyes to get back into this town's good graces.

And her eyes had been angry. Filled with bitterness, like he'd ruined her lunch instead of the other way around.

Like he'd left town when he promised to stay.

Nope. That was her too.

Every memory from a lifetime of friendship enjoyed and then destroyed wrapped around his lungs, cutting off his air and making his head spin. He doubled over at the waist and redoubled his efforts to get his blasted boot off. Wedging the toes of his right foot behind his left heel, he pressed as hard as he could, clenching his jaw against a choice word or two as his ankle wrenched inside the protective leather.

All at once something popped, and the shoe flew across the mudroom, thudding into the far wall before bouncing to the floor right back at his feet. He stooped to pick it up and set it in the row of shoes neatly placed between the floorboards and a multicolored rug before taking off his other one with a lot less drama.

Without looking in his mom's direction, he plodded into the kitchen and forced himself to ignore the rich cinnamon scents wafting from the oven. Habit prodded him to open the stainless steel door and indulge in a real sniff of the dessert. But not today.

He kept walking, moving through the kitchen's warmth and into the dim coolness of the hallway that led to the back stairs. His first stocking foot was on the lowest step when he heard his name.

"Justin Anthony."

Anything other than an endearment meant business. Two names meant trouble.

Backpedaling, he slipped into the kitchen, his gaze searching for anything to land on. But the simple white cabinets, gray Formica countertops, and matching tiled backsplash weren't enough to garner more than a passing glance. Finally he took a real look at his mom.

Sweat had formed curls at her temples, and she ran a not quite steady hand through her hair. The lines around her mouth, which were so often shaped by a wide smile showcasing all of her slightly crooked teeth, were tight, the corners of her lips tugged into something that hinted at a frown.

It formed a lump in his throat, and no matter how hard he swallowed, it wouldn't dissolve. So he pushed the words around it. "Mom? You okay?" He reached out his hand, and she grabbed it with a quick squeeze just as an egg timer dinged.

Dropping his fingers, she slipped on oven mitts, opened the oven, and pulled out a bubbling blueberry cobbler, its purple juice dripping over the edge of the white dish.

"Marie Sloane called today." Her tone was taut, at odds with the innocuous announcement. It sent the lump in his throat straight to the pit of his stomach.

"Uh-huh."

"She was wondering about the barn. The old one."

Naturally. Because the owner of the town's only bed-and-breakfast wasn't interested in the seventy-five dairy cows inhabiting his new barn.

But the old barn was just that—old. It was missing a section of wall where a hurricane had swept away the boards a few years ago. Several of the crossbeams could stand to be replaced. And the outside desperately needed a coat of paint. The roof was sound enough, though. Sound enough to house a plethora of uninvited critters anyway. But ugly enough to make him grateful it wasn't in the dairy's roadside pasture.

"What's she want with the barn?"

Mama Kane replied to his question with one of her own. "Did you talk to her about using it for an event of some sort?"

He scrunched up his face, searching for that memory and why his mom had brought it up after an almost-argument about Natalie O'Ryan. "I guess so."

Marie had sought him out at church weeks ago. Her eyes wide and flashing with excitement, she had barreled across the lawn, waving toward him. Caden Holt tried to stop her but then let her go with a quick nod. He had a sudden urge to run. Anywhere would be better than on the end of Marie Sloane's razor focus. But when he looked around there was no escape. Bethany Burke's blonde hair whipped over her shoulder as she shot him a predatory smile from his right. To his left, the ladies' auxiliary contingent circled. He wasn't looking for Marie, but she was still the best option.

When Marie made it to him, she heaved a loud breath and doubled over, one hand on his arm, the other on her stomach. Then she stretched away from him so far he couldn't believe her back didn't pop. "Oy. I've got to quit eating so many of Caden's cinnamon rolls. But I'm just hungry all the time. You know what I mean?"

He didn't have a clue what she meant, but arguing with her wasn't going to hurry this conversation along, so he nodded. "Can I help you with something?"

Her eyebrows danced twice. "Caden told me you have a building at the dairy that you're not using."

He froze, terrified to confirm it and even more so to deny it, because there was a determination in her eyes that was not going to be denied. His gaze flicked past her ear and landed on Seth Sloane, who Justin could swear gave him a shrug that seemed to suggest it wasn't worth putting up a fight.

If Seth and his uncle Jack were to be believed, Marie had nearly single-handedly wrestled the old house along the harbor into the shining, thriving inn that it had become in just three seasons. According to the rumor mill, she was also battling some kind of court case back in the States. He didn't listen long enough to pick up any particulars, but he'd gathered enough to know she was more force of nature than neighbor.

Of course, the whole town adored her.

He nodded slowly. "The old milking barn."

"Is that the one by the gorgeous cliff?"

Gorgeous was a generous term for the steep drop into the water. But it did have some nice views of the ocean and enough surrounding red cliffs to satisfy even the most ardent Anne fan. "Sure."

"What would you think about renting it out?"

"What kind of livestock?"

Her dark lashes blinked in an otherwise immobile face, confusion finally easing as her whole face erupted in a smile. White teeth flashing and laughter lacing her words, she said, "The human kind."

"Human?" Clearly. He should have known. She wasn't a farmer. She worked with people. But he still couldn't wrap his head around why she would want to put people in his old barn. That's why she'd spent months renovating the inn. If they were running out of space already, there was room on the inn's property to expand. Why would she want his barn?

"You know. People."

He nodded mutely, her answer doing nothing to solve his own confusion.

By some miracle she read the shrug of his shoulder accurately, her smile going even wider. "For events."

He bit his tongue to keep from parroting her last word, and she seemed to understand that he still didn't have enough information.

"Some of the inn's guests are coming to the island for special events, and I'd like to be able to offer them a few location suggestions. Of course, you'd be paid for the space and any of your time. But there aren't a lot of venues large enough for bigger events on the north shore—especially not near the Crick."

"What about the community center?" It popped out before he really thought about why he was suggesting an alternative. After all, he had no real use for the barn, and he could sure put some extra cash to good use.

Maybe it would be enough to get him into a real recording studio.

As soon as the image of the barn flashed into his mind, he shook off the idea of renting it out—and whatever dreams that might finally afford him. It would cost more to refurbish the barn than it would to tear the place down. Besides, the dairy didn't exactly run itself. He couldn't just abandon his responsibilities on the farm to focus on an outdated outbuilding that might bring in a couple hundred bucks.

Marie nodded slowly. "The community center is nice, but you can only fit six round tables and a small dance floor in it. That's not big enough."

"For what?"

"Oh, you know. Bigger events." She waved her hand around between them, her smile turning secretive.

Actually, he didn't know what bigger events she meant,

but he shook his head for another reason. "I don't think so. It's an old barn. Mostly gutted, but it's not in good shape."

The light in her eyes dimmed for the briefest moment. "Well, Seth and I can help you with that."

"You don't even know how much work it needs."

"We'll figure it out. Seth was a contractor, you know."

He'd heard that. And seen the new gables on the old inn. Seth wouldn't have any trouble with the barn. But why his barn? He squinted at her, trying to read her reasons in the features of her face. Instead he saw the set of her jaw and the line of her mouth.

From across the yard Seth caught his eye again and followed up with a nod that seemed to say, "Give in now. You're not going to beat her."

Justin kept his chuckle to himself. Maybe it wasn't worth it to fight Marie over the barn. She'd probably get a close survey of the sagging walls and tired wood and walk away, so he shrugged. "Sure. If you really want to take a look at it. Just call the house," he said.

But that conversation had been weeks ago, and she hadn't said anything more about it. He'd assumed it was a passing interest, no more than a flippant thought. All of her event suggestions had been vague at best.

That didn't stop a bucket of dread from gnawing its way into his belly and settling in like it was paying rent.

His mom crossed her arms over her chest and tipped her head in his direction. "Marie wants to come by and take a look at the barn on Friday."

"All right. Can you show it to her?"

"I'll be at the farmer's market selling cheese all day."

Of course. "Then let's do it later this week."

"Or you could take care of it, since you agreed to it in the first place."

He sighed. Just because she was right didn't mean he wanted to give in, even if he could rearrange his schedule. And his best friend and right-hand man, Dillon Holt, could probably take care of midday chores for one afternoon. But it would mean throwing off his schedule. "Mom, you'd be much better at it than I would."

She harrumphed. "Probably. But still not my problem."

Arguing with her was about as effective as arguing with Marie, so he let out a tight breath. "All right."

"She's bringing a guest from the inn with her." She held his gaze, hers intense and filled with trouble. "They're looking for a place to hold a wedding."

Like a cow had kicked over the bucket in his stomach, dread splashed out until it reached the ends of his fingers and the tips of his toes.

He didn't need her to go on. The truth was as plain as the blue-and-white lighthouse on the edge of his property.

And it sucked all the air out of the room.

"It's Natalie's wedding."

3

Natalie was pretty sure she'd never tasted anything as good as Caden's blackberry drizzle muffins—made from locally grown berries, fresh lemon zest, and a heavy dose of island sun. The sharp flavors tasted like her childhood. Like running barefoot through the back pasture and dodging bellowing cows. Like picking ripe blackberries until her fingers were stained purple and her teeth crunched the seeds.

She popped the last bite into her mouth, letting the sugary frosting dissolve on her tongue, and leaned back with a sigh.

"I told you." Across the breakfast table, Adam's smile turned into more of a smirk as he dug into his second muffin. Apparently extra sweets were one of the perks of being the chef's boyfriend.

Maybe that included extended family too. After all, they were about to be family. Six weeks and two days and counting.

Her thumb found the band of her engagement ring and wiggled the enormous diamond, which caught the light shining through the windows behind her. The sparkle was nearly blinding, but she couldn't seem to tear her gaze away from it, even as Russell reached out and pressed his hand over hers. His squeeze was gentle. She tried to return his smile, but her lips felt numb.

Clearly a result of too much sugar after dieting for the last six months. Her wedding dress didn't have an elastic waist, and she was going to have to be careful or she wouldn't fit into it on the big day.

"You weren't lying," Russell said. "She's very talented. And she works with Jerome Gale, you said?"

Natalie was only familiar with Jerome Gale as Canada's premier chef because he'd hosted an event at Nashville's performing arts center the winter before. It had been some sort of foodie haven with demonstrations and tastings and enough wine to float a cruise ship. Every guest at the Heritage Hotel where she worked had asked her to get them tickets.

Every guest had been disappointed. The tickets had sold out in a matter of hours.

Despite her lack of knowledge about the Canadian food scene, she recognized how prestigious Caden's work was, so she leaned an elbow on the table and nodded in Adam's direction.

"Yep. During the school year she teaches an after-school program for students in low-income communities in Toronto, which she designed and started with Jerome." Adam's Southern drawl came out as he bragged on Caden. "And it's expanding next year. They've had so much interest that they're adding a second section in another part of the city."

Suddenly the blonde at the center of their conversation strode out of the kitchen and straight to their table. She stood behind the empty chair directly across from Natalie, resting her hands on the curved section of dark wood.

A strand of hair had escaped her French braid, and she tucked it behind her ear. "Natalie, it's so good to see you again." Caden's eyes shone so brightly that Natalie couldn't doubt her sincerity.

But it didn't deflate the balloon expanding in her chest. It was one thing to be back on the island with people who hadn't been around when the O'Ryans nearly set the town's gossip mill on fire. It was entirely different to be face-to-face with someone whose hand-me-downs she'd been forced to wear.

Bile built in the back of her throat, and she swallowed it, which only set her eyes to burning. Perfect. She was about start crying because one time Mrs. Holt had slipped her a bag of clothes after Sunday school, and even though they were two sizes too big, she'd worn them. Because they were clean. And they smelled like sunshine instead of liquor and regret.

That was a rabbit hole she couldn't afford to go down. That led to her mom and dad. Two faces she would not be seeing on the island. Two figures she didn't need to think about.

Time to find her concierge mask.

Letting out a quick breath through her nose, she bit her lips together and dropped her gaze to where Russell still held her hand, comforting and stable and all the things she'd never known when she lived on the island. When she looked back up, she plastered a smile into place. "Thanks. It's good to see you too."

"What have you been up to? Adam said you're in Nashville with—" Suddenly her eyes grew rounder, and her mouth pinched closed, regret blanketing her features.

Natalie knew that look.

It was always the same when someone let slip that they'd been talking about her. Or her parents.

And that happened a lot. People talked, and then suddenly seemed embarrassed about it when they were caught in their web of gossip. But Natalie had nothing to be ashamed of now.

Scooting to the edge of her seat, she leaned her elbows on the table and turned up her smile. "Yes. I've been in Nashville for fifteen years already, and I'm the concierge at the Heritage Hotel downtown."

Caden nodded enthusiastically, but it was clear that she didn't—couldn't—understand what her title meant. Apparently Russell picked up on that too. "It's the best hotel in town. It's a beautiful old building, but they've remodeled it into luxury accommodations. All the celebrities stay there when they visit, and they all count on Natalie to help make their trips special."

A warm flush reached her cheeks, and she squeezed his hand. He was always quick to speak highly of her, but she had wondered once or twice if it was because it made *her* look good or because it made *him* look good.

"That's wonderful." Caden beamed like she really meant it. "I'm not at all surprised. You could talk the teachers into changing their lesson plans or convince Harrison to give out free burgers when we were kids. You're so good with people."

Natalie wasn't quite sure if Caden herself believed that last line. Maybe it was a jab at all the animosity between her and the people of North Rustico. Or maybe Caden just chose not to remember the way it was.

Natalie didn't seem to have that luxury.

Russell continued. "Her boss was pretty disappointed when Natalie requested a leave of absence this summer." He winked at Caden. "But when I promised to hold my label's Christmas party at the hotel this year, he agreed to the time off."

"Is it good to be back?" Caden asked.

She attempted a response but sucked in an unexpected breath instead, and it caught in the back of her throat. Sputtering and coughing, she chugged half a glass of water as Russell thumped her back.

"Okay, babe?"

By the time her gasps ended, every head in the room was turned in her direction, and she hunched into her chair. But there would be no disappearing. "Fine. Yes. I'm good."

The air hung thick with silence until Caden nodded toward the empty plates on the table. "How was your breakfast?"

"Perfect." Adam snuck his arm around her waist, tugging her a few steps closer to him and smiling with a warmth that even Natalie could feel.

Even though they'd been dating for almost a year, Caden's cheeks turned pink and she brushed at his hand, which stayed rooted on her colorful apron.

Russell squeezed Natalie's hand again, and she tried to read his feelings in his features, which were so similar to his brother's. The sharp lines of his jaw met at a cleft in his chin, but where Adam seemed to always wear a five o'clock shadow, Russell looked like he'd shaved just a few minutes before. No matter the time of day. And the smooth planes of his face showed no particular emotion. His dark eyes were no more help in deciphering the reason for his grip.

Only the easy curve of his lips hinted at his happiness.

But it was enough. He was glad to be on the island. He was with his brother. Seeing his brother happy. It was enough to make Russell happy.

So it was enough to make her happy.

Except for a persistent bubble in her stomach, which she wouldn't quite label as such.

"So, Adam tells us that you teach cooking classes," Russell said.

Again, the red in Caden's cheeks burned bright, but it couldn't outshine her smile. "Yes. I've been teaching teenagers for a little over a year, and I'm starting classes for guests here at the inn next week."

Russell sat up a little straighter, bending forward at his hips. "For adults?" His gaze flicked to Natalie, and it matched his mischievous smile.

Oh no. No. This wasn't good. Not even a little bit.

She shook her head hard, but his grin only grew.

He knew she couldn't cook.

Didn't cook.

Didn't try.

Some things—like kitchens—weren't in her purview.

And she hadn't even pretended they were when they first met.

A cooking class would succeed in doing exactly one thing: putting her lack of skill on display for everyone to see. Which sounded about as fun as being stung by a jellyfish.

Natalie tapped his arm to get his attention at the same moment Caden confirmed the classes. "They'll be in the afternoons on Wednesdays and Saturdays, and you can sign up with Marie. We'll limit it to three couples per class, and we'll be cooking a few local favorites like potatoes and lobster."

Caden's little shudder on the last word drew Natalie's attention, and a memory appeared from deep in the recesses of her mind—Caden at the annual lobster cook-off and fund-raiser, cringing as she tore apart an orange claw. Her eyes had filled with tears as Bethany Burke poked fun at her. Until Justin scowled and waved his fork at the most popular girl in school, sending a stream of butter onto her sweater. "Leave her be or else." The threat and the fork were better than a sword at shutting her up.

Natalie had only been there because Mama Kane insisted she go. "Someone has to keep my son in line. And you've won the lottery."

"Or lost," Natalie muttered.

Mama Kane laughed until she doubled over, her giggles bellowing to the ceiling and rolling down the walls. It had only been funny because they both knew it was a lie.

"Well, sign us up." Russell's words hung out there like underclothes on the line, too embarrassing to take down after someone else had pinned them up for the whole town to see.

He must have caught the terror in her eyes and read it as uncertainty instead of the debilitating fever that made sweat pepper her neck. "Come on. It'll be fun."

With stiff shoulders, she managed a half shrug. It wasn't necessarily agreement, but Russell didn't need that.

"We said we'd do some fun things this summer. A pre-honeymoon and all that."

Adam's eyebrows hitched, and Caden's stare turned questioning. "Pre-honeymoon?" she said.

Russell nodded as though it was the most normal thing in the world. "Sure. It's a honeymoon before the wedding. My label is dropping some big albums in August, and I need to be in the office, so we're having our vacation before the wedding."

The confusion on the faces on the other side of the table

eased, but Natalie couldn't help but dissect what they were almost certainly thinking.

Exactly how much of the honeymoon are they having?

Sure. She was thirty-two years old. And it was none of their business. But that had never stopped this town from talking about her—closed doors or not.

Maybe that was why she had insisted on her own room at the inn—always insisted on her own room, actually. Or maybe it was the way her mother had always looked at her and said, "If you hadn't come along . . ." Like Natalie was the reason she'd been stuck in a small town and stuck with Rick O'Ryan.

Or maybe she insisted because of that time in junior high school when she'd overheard one of the newly married Sunday school teachers gushing to her best friend about how thankful she was she'd *waited*.

Whatever had prompted her to tell Russell she wanted to wait, he'd agreed. And this wasn't the moment to be hashing it out even in the corner of her mind.

Natalie had nothing to regret.

Except his flippant use of the word *honeymoon*, and whatever rumors that might stir up in small-town minds.

"What day do you think?" Russell tapped the back of her hand with his thumb.

Neither. But that wasn't an option.

"Wednesday?"

She nodded. "That sounds fine."

Caden's smile doubled in size, setting off two incandescent dimples. "Wonderful. I'll have Marie put you on the schedule."

"Have me put who on what schedule?" Marie Sloane wasn't

particularly tall, but her presence filled the room as she sashayed up to the table. The lines around her mouth testified that her life hadn't been easy, but there was a joy deep in her eyes that pricked at the back of Natalie's neck. She held an empty serving tray in front of her midsection, her slender fingers and thin arms clearly weighed down by the ornate silver platter.

"Natalie and Russell are going to take my cooking class next Wednesday."

Marie's smile matched her chef's. "Perfect. I'll put you on the calendar, and we'll add the cost to your bill."

"Good deal." Russell pressed his palm to the tabletop. "Now, my brother promised to show us around this place."

"Actually, could I steal Natalie for a moment?" Marie caught Natalie's gaze, her smile faltering for an instant. It wasn't particularly noticeable, and the men didn't stop their side conversation.

Still, Natalie's insides took a painful nosedive. Maybe brides had a sixth sense about these things. When the default wedding planner asked for a private conversation, something had almost certainly gone wrong. And if something went wrong—if anything went awry—she was sure to be the topic of every whispered conversation behind fluttering hands.

Fear bubbled in her throat, and she squeezed her eyes closed against the urge to slide under the table, forcing herself to find control.

Whatever it is, it's okay. We still have time.

The firm voice in her head was familiar—one she used often. But it was enough to get her eyes open and the concierge smile in place.

If Marie noticed her moment of panic, she said nothing,

so Natalie pushed her chair back and rose. "Of course." To Russell she said, "I'll meet up with you both later."

"We'll wait for you."

She risked another glance at Marie, whose generous lips were pinched with the smallest hint of the strain that echoed in her eyes. "Don't worry about it. I'll call you when we're through."

A consummate hostess, Marie waved to the men, squeezed Caden's arm, and led the way to the hallway on the far side of the kitchen. A door at the back wall opened to a tight office with just enough room for a wooden desk and rolling chair.

Marie didn't bother to close the door behind them, and Natalie took that as a good sign. Even if it was more likely because there wasn't room for them to both fit into the closed office.

"I have some bad news." At least Marie didn't beat around the bush.

"How bad?"

"The community center is double-booked for the day of your wedding and is backing out."

Natalie could do nothing but let her mouth hang open for the longest ten seconds of her life. She couldn't manage to blink so was privy to every moment of Marie's pained expression and distress-filled eyes.

"I'm so sorry." Marie's forehead wrinkled with the pain it must have taken to explain the situation that she hadn't caused. After all, they'd been working together over email for months to secure all the necessary arrangements for the wedding. Marie had always erred on the side of overly professional—double-checking every reservation and confirming every request.

Natalie's boss at the Heritage Hotel would have loved having a Marie in his sales and special events office.

But all of Marie's skills hadn't kept trouble away.

Invitations had been sent out, and wedding guests had already booked flights and paid deposits on rooms at the Red Door and nearby cabins. More than a hundred and fifty guests were about to descend on North Rustico, filling every rentable room within a ten-mile radius for several days before and after the wedding.

They all expected a ceremony at the church and then a big party at the community center. Even if they had to spill tables onto the lawn to fit all the guests.

Now they had no place to host the party. No place to entertain their guests.

And no way to avoid a scandal.

Finally Natalie found her tongue and used it as soon as it worked. "But the invitations went out weeks ago. And we have a contract. And . . . and . . ." She searched for any argument to make her case. "We paid a deposit."

Marie nodded. "I know. I told her all of that, but she wouldn't budge. She said it had been rented months before you signed the agreement with them." With a shake of her head and a shrug, she sighed. "At least Stella agreed to refund your deposit."

"Stella? Burke?"

Marie's lips puckered to the side, her nod barely a confirmation but enough to set off the alarms in Natalie's chest. The clanging inside made it down her arms until her hands shook no matter how hard she clenched them.

Perfect. Of course Stella was the one scheduling out the community center. She was probably still president of the ladies' auxiliary too.

And she was still out for retribution—for something that was as much Natalie's fault as the family she'd been born into.

But logic had never been Stella Burke's strong suit. No, her specialty was revenge. And holding on to bitterness.

Natalie forced out a slow breath as Marie pressed a hand to her arm. "Do you have a history with Stella?"

"Ha." Her laugh was breathless at best. Hostile was probably more accurate. "Marie, I have a history with everyone in this town." Exactly seventeen years of embarrassing memories churned inside her. "It's no coincidence that our location has become unavailable at the last minute."

Maybe she'd expected Marie to pull back or act shocked, but she didn't. Instead wild curls shook around her shoulders in a slow dance. Marie leaned in, her gaze narrowing. "Oh, I have a few of those relationships too. But here's the thing. I'm on your side. So is Caden. And Seth and Adam too. Not to mention your handsome fiancé. You're not alone."

Something inside her swooped. Maybe it was a flush of joy at the mention of Russell.

More likely it was the strange feeling of not being on her own.

Not since she'd left the Crick—and Justin—behind had anyone spoken words like that to her.

She'd been doing life alone since her best friend had abandoned their plan. Not even Russell spoke words like that over her.

Suddenly someone switched on the faucet, and her eyes gushed with tears so fast she couldn't knuckle them away before one escaped down her cheek.

"I'm sorry. I'm—this is all a mess."

Marie chuckled and squeezed her arm. "Honey, this office has seen more than its fair share of tears. Weddings are hard. Lots of moving parts and people and emotions. But we're going to figure this out."

Weddings. Right. Marie thought Natalie was a mess because she'd lost the reception location, and if Stella Burke had any say in things, she'd most likely lose the church for the ceremony too.

Marie hadn't seen her unspeakably awkward run-in with Justin at Grady's the day before. She didn't know about more than twenty-five years of memories. She didn't know about a childhood of climbing trees under the island sun.

She definitely didn't know that the second-to-last step up to the lighthouse creaked and that Justin had always stepped on it extra hard to make sure he didn't surprise her.

And that he'd always known where to find her—and when she most needed him to.

Most of all, Marie didn't know that Justin had understood that leaving her alone would hurt the worst. And that he'd done just that late one June night.

She blinked hard as the tears kept coming, washing down burning cheeks.

Marie grabbed both of her hands, careful of the three-carat diamond on her finger. "It'll be all right. I have an idea."

Natalie sniffed against the tide from within. "You do?"

Leaning forward, Marie let a secret smile trickle into place. "How would you feel about getting married in a barn?"

"A barn?" Something inside her tried to warn her to run for cover, but she could manage only the insipid repetition. "Like a barn, barn?"

"More like a renovated barn. It's seen some weather and

needs a few new boards. Maybe a little paint. But we'll clean it up and add some island decorations to balance the rustic setting."

She tried to imagine the picture Marie painted, but instead her mind conjured only one barn. It had been old even when she was a child. But that couldn't be the one.

Papa Kane had said it wasn't fit for man or beast. That's why he'd built the new one. Or at least started on it.

"It has one of the prettiest views on the north shore. All jagged red cliffs, summer wildflowers, and ocean as far as your eye can see." Marie's voice drifted like a daydream.

Natalie's heart seized.

There was only one barn on the island that refused to give up such prime real estate. She was shaking her head before the thought even fully formed. "No."

"But you haven't even seen it." Marie's eyes grew wide. "We'll make it perfect. We can put the right touches on it. Make it match your taste."

"It's not a good idea. There has to be another option."

Marie lifted her shoulders as her nose wrinkled. "What did you have in mind? Where could we set up fifteen round tops? Grady's?"

"What's wrong with Grady's?" She meant it as a challenge, but the words fell flat. They both knew that the town's restaurant couldn't hold seventy-five people comfortably, let alone a hundred and fifty of the music industry's finest.

Marie rolled her eyes just enough to suggest that Natalie should be serious.

"Okay. Fine. Not Grady's. What about the Lions Club?"

"They require a membership. And you'd have to cut your guest list in half." Suddenly Marie pressed her hand to her stomach, a twinge in the corner of her mouth catching Natalie's attention. "And before you suggest the beach, who are you going to hire to keep the birds at bay?"

Rats. She had been about to suggest a waterfront reception. But Marie was right. Between the birds, dragonflies, and mosquitoes, her guests wouldn't have a moment of rest. And forget the cake. It would attract everything with wings for miles.

"We have to come up with another option." Even as she said the words, she feared they were impossible. Still, her voice was stronger than usual. Harder.

Marie didn't appear to be intimidated. "Won't you at least take a look at it? Just think about it, and—" Suddenly her face turned white like a veil had dropped into place. Her eyes became glassy, and she pressed a hand over her mouth.

"Are you all right?" Natalie began to reach out but quickly jerked her hand back when Marie waved her off.

Marie held up a finger to indicate that she just needed a moment, but suddenly her shoulders shook and she squeezed past Natalie, ducked into the hall, and disappeared down the back stairwell. Natalie's stomach gave a sympathetic swoop, and she pressed her hands to her face, forcing her thoughts to Marie's last words.

Think about it, indeed. What did she have to think about? She had exactly one option for the reception.

The old barn at Kane Dairy.

Her stomach sank as she sagged against the doorjamb. She was going to have to see him. Again.

And this time it would be on his turf.

4

Justin cranked the wheel of his truck, and his tires spit mud and grass as he skidded to a stop beside Marie's little sedan. The pasture hadn't seen much use in a decade. But he couldn't bring himself to repurpose the land or tear down the first building his grandfather had added.

A gust of wind picked at loose shingles, slapping them together as he kicked open his door and slammed it closed behind him. A section of peeling paint along the front of the barn rippled under the sun's brilliance, and he frowned. Hands on his hips, he surveyed the adjacent wall. The salt water and wind had bleached patches at their whim, and small holes along the foundation were clearly entrances for whatever rodents had been seeking shelter. Then there was the section of roof that had been shredded by the last hurricane. It wouldn't stand up to a light drizzle, which was why he'd sent one of his hands to clear out any remaining straw.

The old girl was barely stable. And ugly as all get-out.

There was no way Natalie would agree to have her wedding in this barn.

That was enough to put a smile on his face as he stepped

through the open door from the sunshine to the darkness. Blinking several times, he tried to adjust to the dimness, but all he could see were the dust motes dancing in the beams of light coming through the holes in the roof.

He rubbed his eyes with his fists, and they finally cleared enough to make out the silhouette of a slender woman in the far corner, her face turned up toward the exposed beams and cathedral ceiling.

"Justin, thanks for meeting us."

He spun in the direction of the voice, only then seeing a second figure. Marie.

Which meant that the other half of "us" was . . .

Lungs constricting and acid backing up his throat, he swung his gaze back to the other woman. She met his stare, her eyes blue and fierce and holding back a thousand brutal words.

"Natalie." He hadn't meant to say it out loud, but somehow her name made it through his gritted teeth.

Marie's eyebrows rose, her eyes lighting with surprise. Then she shook her head and laughed ruefully. "Of course you know each other. You probably grew up together. I keep forgetting that this was your home long before I showed up."

Natalie's smile to the other woman was kind, forgiving. But as her attention moved to him, it turned to steel, cutting into his chest and beating at his heart.

He could go. He could up and walk away.

Just like she had.

The urge to take off only grew stronger with every rise and fall of her narrow shoulders. Her slim-cut jacket didn't do much to add to her nearly nonexistent intimidation factor. It was hard for her to look like she was in charge when she barely reached his shoulder. When they were kids, he could nearly touch his thumb and middle finger around her arm above her elbow.

She was just as skinny now, but the flash in her eyes was new. And it struck at him like an axe to rotted wood.

Whoa.

He grabbed at his chest, as though to hold in whatever her searing gaze had let loose. But there was nothing on his flannel shirt except for a mud stain it had sustained years ago.

"Justin." Her chin dipped in what appeared to be a conciliatory nod. Only her gaze never left his and never let up. The ire in her voice was thicker than peanut butter on a sandwich.

What had her so riled up? *He* was the one who had been wronged. *She* was the one who broke their pact.

Clearly she hadn't gotten the notice about that.

It didn't matter that they'd spit on their palms and shaken hands to seal their deal when they were twelve. It sure as fire wouldn't have made a difference if they'd agreed to it the day before she left.

They'd said forever. Always. Together.

But she'd disappeared. And now she had the audacity to show up on his land. In his barn.

For her wedding.

He fought the sudden urge to spit on the cement floor. But his mom had taught him better than to be so uninhibited in front of a lady. And everyone in town knew Marie was just that.

"This place is perfect." Marie's sudden outburst drew both of their gazes. She inhaled through her nose like she couldn't get enough of the smell of musty hay, wet wood, and the memory of a thousand cows. "Don't you see it?"

He shook his head at the same time as Natalie, who apparently caught his motion and immediately froze.

With a sweep of her arm, Marie introduced them to her vision. "Twinkle lights hanging from all of the beams across the ceiling. Fifteen round tables over here. White tablecloths with mini milk bucket centerpieces. The head table right under this beam with strings of light hanging behind the bride and groom. Caden's most delicious cake on a table in that corner." She tiptoed away from the main entrance. "And over here all of your loved ones swaying and spinning on the dance floor to the music of the island. Can't you just see the fiddle player along that wall, beside a man with a guitar, stomping his foot? Of course, it'll need a good cleaning and a bit of touch-up work. Some paint on the outside and a rich cherry stain on the internal walls and exposed beams. Maybe a coat of paint over the floor." She offered a secret smile. "And a bit of airing out."

Understatement of the century. No amount of *airing out* was going to erase the current bovine perfume.

Justin crossed his arms over his chest, displeased with the picture she painted. Mostly with how pleasant it sounded and how he could immediately hear the music deep in his chest, the urgent tempo of the jig filling him with island pride.

But this couldn't be the place they wanted, and he was pretty sure that Natalie was going to say as much any minute.

The sharp ring of a phone echoed in the wide-open space, and Marie jumped to find it in her purse. As soon as she looked at the screen, she said, "Excuse me. I'll be right back." She strode out of the barn with all the poise of a princess.

Only when she had fully disappeared did he realize Marie had left him alone with Natalie. Swinging back to face his former best friend, he tried to read her expression, to see if she'd managed to put out some of the wildfire that had been raging just moments before.

No such luck.

With a glance over his shoulder, he contemplated following Marie into the fresh air. Only she'd obviously stepped outside because she wanted some privacy.

Which left him face-to-face with a fireball.

Maybe they could stand here in silence.

Her snarl turned into a growl. "What on earth is wrong with you?"

Maybe not.

He pressed his thumb to his chest. "Me?"

"You see anyone else around here?"

"Whoa. Hold your horses, lady. I'm not the one snapping like a hungry dog."

Her nostrils flared, and her pale eyebrows almost reached her hairline. He hadn't thought the line of her mouth could get any tighter, but it nearly disappeared before she snapped again. "Lady? Dog? Which is it?"

"Whoa, whoa, whoa." He held up both hands to ward off her attack, but there wasn't a motion known to mankind that could stop her from slamming her hands against her hips and taking a menacing step in his direction. "That's not what I said."

"It is what you said."

"Fine. But it's not what I meant, and you know it." He moved to shove his fingers through his hair, but they caught in his ponytail, and he ripped the rubber band free, shaking his hair loose over his collar.

"And what's with your hair?" The corner of her narrowed

eyes twitched as her glare intensified. But her voice hovered on the edge of a whisper. "You always hated it long."

"Well . . ." He searched for an explanation that wouldn't sound as juvenile as the truth about why he'd let it grow long. But he didn't have one. "People change. I'm allowed to change."

And he had. So had she.

Natalie's slim slacks and lightweight jacket were far from the too-big overalls she'd worn in childhood. And the girl who had sworn she didn't have time for makeup had become a woman who wore her lips pink and her eyes shaded by long black lashes. Maybe she wore blush on her cheeks too, but he couldn't tell for sure, as her whole face was red.

She'd changed her mind about some things.

And he'd grown out his hair.

Big deal.

Her gaze swept over him, pausing at his chest, sending a flutter all the way down to his toes. That's right. It wasn't just his hair that had changed. Fifteen years of running a farm had broadened his shoulders and replaced his spindly limbs with muscles he was proud of.

And he wasn't upset that she was noticing those muscles now.

"Maybe people do change. But you hated it when it got in your face."

He flicked the rubber band under her nose before reaching behind his head, taming his unruly waves, and securing them back in place. Out of his face. Which he really did hate.

If he flexed his arms in the process and she happened to notice, well, that was just too bad.

Her jaw twitched when she clenched her teeth, the steam coming from her ears practically visible. "Fine. I don't care what you do with your hair. I don't care what you do at all." She threw her shoulders back, her neck long and lean. The freckles there were as enticing as ever.

The urge to count every last one of them was a kick to his gut.

Forget her loathing for his hair. Mostly he hated that he'd noticed she'd turned into a woman. And he'd never found her more beautiful.

Which was saying something, given the surge of teenage hormones that had pretty much ruled his life during his last two years of school.

"That's not what you said the last time we talked."

Her jaw dropped. "At Grady's?"

"We didn't talk yesterday."

She nodded, like he needed her to confirm his assessment of their interaction. Like he didn't remember how she'd beat a hasty retreat the moment they'd locked eyes.

"The last time we talked. At the lighthouse."

Natalie opened her mouth. Closed it. Opened it again. But no sound came out. Like a fish searching for water, she puckered her lips and shook her head. A denial for sure.

"I know you remember." Massaging his temples, he tried to release some of the thunder building up there. "We spent an hour talking about our plan."

"Yes. We had a plan." She sounded like he was holding a knife on her. "We were going to leave."

"No. We were going to stay together. The plan was always to stick together."

"Yes. Away." Her arm shot out, finger pointing toward the

ocean. "We were going to get off this island. Together. And you never showed up."

He threw up his hands to stop her rant but only invited her to continue. "Me? I didn't show up?"

"Yes, you! Don't try to play dumb here. We said the day after graduation. Don't act like you didn't have the map highlighted and your guitar packed."

He opened his mouth to deny her words, but she wasn't wrong. Things had just . . . changed. "You knew I couldn't go. I told you. We agreed. We'd stay here. Together. And then you just disappeared. You didn't even stick around for the *funeral*!"

The outburst knocked him back on his heels, heat rushing to his face and sudden tears stinging his eyes.

They had to be about his dad. He'd cried over that loss.

But never once over the girl who had left.

Natalie deflated, her shoulders sagging and mouth drooping. "I'm sorry I wasn't there." Her words were mollifying, but her tone didn't even hint at giving up the fight. "He was a good man."

"I know—" He bit off his words. It wasn't right to yell about his dad's finer qualities, which had mostly been soft-spoken. Stopping just short of stabbing his fingers through his hair again, he scrubbed his face with a flat palm. "You said you were going to stay."

She sighed, the air leaking out of her. "I couldn't. Things were . . . complicated. You *knew* that."

"Yes. But I couldn't leave. *You* knew that. My mom couldn't run this place on her own. And Doug and Brooke weren't old enough to step up."

"And you were?" Swinging her arm like she might backhand him, she cried, "You were seventeen years old!"

"I was old enough."

"But you had dreams. *We* had dreams."

"Well, you found a new dream, didn't you?" He flung his hand around the empty barn that he still pictured with Marie's wedding decorations.

By the flash in her eyes, he knew she'd understood. "I—" She clamped her mouth shut, glared at him, then at her shaking fists. "You have no right. You're the one who changed the plan."

"And you agreed to the new plan."

"Your dad wasn't the town drunk."

"My dad"—he heaved a great breath just to gain the strength to finish the thought—"was dead."

Her face twisted like he'd thrown boiling water on her, and she opened her mouth, clearly ready to lay into him.

A sudden movement in the doorway diverted her attention, and they both turned toward it to find Marie there, her eyebrows raised and arms crossed. Her presence was like a blanket over a flame, cutting off the oxygen and extinguishing the fire.

At least the verbal part of it.

The anger and heat in his belly raged as volatile as ever.

With a glance between them, Marie said, "Did I interrupt something?"

"No." Natalie jumped on the word faster than a frog on a fly. She might have a few more choice words for him, but she wasn't about to say them in front of anyone else. That would constitute a scene. Maybe one worthy of gossip.

A lot of things about her had changed—like those too-shapely-for-her-own-good legs—but he'd wager the entire farm and his family's legacy with it that her aversion to being the topic of public scrutiny hadn't changed.

She'd move heaven and earth to stay out of the local gossip mill.

He shook his head. "We were just rehashing old times."

If the look that crossed Marie's face was any indication, she didn't buy his line any more than he did. But when he caught Natalie's eye, something akin to gratitude flickered there.

Good. At least she recognized that she owed him for something.

"That was Seth on the phone," Marie said, obviously ignoring the strain between him and Natalie. "I need to get back to the inn."

"Sure," Natalie said, stepping past him.

"But first, the barn. What do you think, Natalie?"

She twisted a strand of her hair tight at her ear and pursed her lips, staring hard at Justin. "I think it stinks in here."

It wasn't entirely clear if she thought it was the barn that stunk or him. But he managed to refrain from sniffing the inside collar of his shirt, which he hadn't changed after his morning chores. Maybe he was the one who smelled bad.

"Good. Fine. So you'll find another place for your . . ." He couldn't make himself say the word, so he flicked his hand around, searching for a replacement. "Thing."

Regret flashed across Natalie's face, followed quickly by something that looked like she'd bit down on her tongue. Hard.

Marie frowned. "I don't know where else we can go."

"Why not the community center?"

Although he'd directed his question to Marie, Natalie responded, her tone low and tired. "Because Stella Burke decided it had been double-booked. Even though we reserved it months ago."

He shook his head, trying to work out the connection, but everything he remembered about Mrs. Burke and the O'Ryans was years old. Sure, there had been some bad blood, but that couldn't still be a problem.

It just couldn't. The whole town had moved on. He was sure. Almost.

Maybe.

Rats.

If indeed Mrs. Burke had set out to make Natalie's life miserable and ruin her wedding, there was only one thing to be done.

Rubbing his temples with his thumb and forefinger, he bowed his head and prayed for another idea. Any way to fix her problem without having to be personally involved.

None came.

"I can get rid of the smell."

"You can?" Marie's eyes lit up. "And we'll work with you to do the repairs and repaint?"

He risked a glance at the woman who had been about to tear his head off not ten minutes before, but her expression was stone. He couldn't tell if she wanted him to agree to it or was doing her own praying that he'd turn them down.

"Well, I can work with Seth on some of the major stuff—the roof and cleaning the barn out. But you'll have to take care of whatever cosmetic changes you want."

Oh, Lord, please don't let her want it. Any of it.

Marie traipsing across his property a couple times a week wasn't ideal, but it was livable.

Having Natalie show up whenever the thought popped into her head was liable to leave him so distracted he'd be trampled by hungry cows and covered in spilled milk.

Natalie stared into the expansive ceilings and crossed her arms over her chest. It was clear she wanted to have her wedding in his barn about as much as he wanted her here.

But when she finally opened her mouth, it was with a resigned sigh. "We'll take it."

Oh, man. This summer couldn't get any worse.

5

"Are you going to take me to see your childhood home today?"

Natalie jerked her attention from the rich, melt-in-your-mouth salmon quiche to Russell's innocent expression across the table for two. "My what?"

"You know. Where you grew up. Your home."

Home.

That was a loaded word if ever there was one.

The one-story pale green house she'd lived in for almost eighteen years wasn't home. It was a residence. A place where she slept in a little twin bed and, as a child, hid in her closet when the yelling grew too loud. It was the place where she climbed out of the window, making a mad dash for the lighthouse on the Kane property.

It was the place where she prayed over and over again that her parents might become like Mama Cheese Sandwich and Papa Kane.

Maybe if they had, it would have become home.

It wasn't.

"No. We don't need to go there."

Honestly she hoped that the house had been torn down. Thirty years ago the wind had howled through cracks around the windows, and the outside paneling bowed under the weight of the salty spray off the bay. And it had only gone downhill from there. Maybe a winter snow had finally caved in the leaking roof, leaving it wholly uninhabitable.

"Sure we do. I mean, that's part of why we're here. So I can learn more about where you came from, get to know more about your past."

She didn't recall agreeing to anything like that, and the very idea made her palms sweat. Wiping them on her cloth napkin, she tried for a smile. "Well, you've already met some of my old classmates like Caden. And I could take you into the national park. You'll love it. It's beautiful."

He nodded. "That sounds great. Maybe tomorrow. Today I want to see North Rustico the way you saw it."

No. No. No. No.

She wasn't about to show him what it was really like growing up here.

He thought she was a composed professional from a regular middle-class family. And that's what he was going to keep thinking. Until the last ring was on her finger. Until they were safely back at his loft in downtown Nashville. Until she was back at her job and he was so invested in a new record that he'd forgotten he ever asked to see her home.

Not that she wanted to lie to him. At all. That wasn't the way to start a marriage. At least not from what she'd witnessed in other relationships.

But the truth might just end the marriage before it even started.

Picking her words carefully, she said, "Of course. It was small-town life."

"Right. But it couldn't have been just like the small town I grew up in, in east Tennessee."

"No." She dragged the word out, still hunting for the right phrase to appease his curiosity but shift his focus onto something else. Anything else. "PEI is surrounded by water, so we had beaches."

Russell threw his head back with a laugh that drew the smiles of the neighboring table of Canadian visitors with the towheaded son.

Natalie wiped her hands on her white napkin until it was limp and damp. The quiche she'd enjoyed just a moment before turned to a solid lump in her stomach.

"We had a river and a few lakes. My childhood wasn't completely devoid of water." His eyes sparkled with the humor that had made her agree to that first date. "I think I can handle waiting a day or two before we go to the beach. Show me around the Crick first."

"Sure. But . . ." Something. She had to come up with something. Now. "Wouldn't you like to see . . ." She mentally ticked off all the other tourist traps in the area. The boardwalk. Kayaking. Lobster fishing.

None of those were enough to distract him.

Come on, Natalie.

She rolled her eyes at herself, wishing not for the first time that her mind was twice as fast. And then, before the thought had fully formed, she blurted out the only thing that might work. "Wouldn't you like to see the site for our reception?"

As soon as it was out there, she longed to reel it in. Especially when the corner of his mouth lifted into a grin. "The barn you visited the other day?"

She nodded, all the while calling herself every name she'd heard through the years. *Stupid. Idiot. Good-for-nothing.*

She could have—should have—said the church. They needed to meet with Father Chuck before the ceremony anyway, and the weather was perfect for a walk to the picture-perfect white-steepled building where they'd say their vows before moving to the barn for dinner, dancing, and an evening of fun.

Instead she'd invited him to the scene of her near knock-down fight with Justin only days before. It made her stomach roll to think about how she'd spoken to him. She hadn't intended to raise her voice or even hint at how much he'd hurt her. After all, she'd dealt with it. Years of counseling couldn't be wrong. She'd moved on.

Except, face-to-face with him, she wasn't quite so sure. Which had been abundantly clear when the very worst version of herself had flown out of her.

She'd get to relive every regrettable word the moment she stepped back into that barn, because she'd gone and invited her fiancé to visit it.

"Of course I want to see the barn. Marie said there's some work to be done. Maybe we could take inventory of what needs to be done and decide if we'll need to hire anyone."

"Oh, I'm sure that Marie and"—Justin's name nearly slipped out, but for no earthly reason she kept it inside—"the guy who owns the barn will handle that."

He shrugged and tore into the spice muffin in front of him, then sighed like he'd found the best thing to ever come from the island. She swept a forkful to her mouth and immediately understood why. Caden had a way with local flavors. A way of making Natalie want to sink into them and forget everything else she'd ever known from this scrap of red land.

"I'm sure they will. But it doesn't mean we can't offer our input."

She nodded, hoping that her flashing teeth would cover the internal battle she was fighting. She should have just told him she'd show him the old house. And then shown him someone else's. Or found an empty lot and said that the house had met the same fate she'd hoped it would.

Except that was one more lie. Another falsehood she'd end up having to cover up. Another half-truth that would require her to watch not only what she said but what everyone else said.

As far as she was concerned, Russell could spend the whole summer with his brother. Adam didn't know her and didn't know about her past. He wouldn't inadvertently say something about Rick or Connie O'Ryan that would tip Russell off.

Adam was safe. Marie and Seth maybe were too.

The rest of the community, not so much.

She couldn't let Russell out of her sight. But not because she was lying to him.

It wasn't a lie. Not really. Not *technically*.

Her stomach churned, and the ridiculously delicious muffin suddenly turned to stone. Pressing a palm against her middle, she glanced at Russell to make sure he was still enamored with his pastry.

He hadn't noticed a thing. Now or every other time she'd had this war within.

No matter how many times she told herself it wasn't a

lie—she hadn't spoken a single untruth about her family—a gnawing deep inside told her she was wrong. Lies of omission were still lies. Just because she'd deftly diverted any discussion from the topic of her family didn't mean she'd been honest with Russell. And any relationship required honesty. That was elementary Sunday school stuff.

But still. She wasn't hurting anyone. And if she fessed up now? Well, there was a lot at stake. Abandonment by her fiancé. In front of the whole town. Reclaiming her position as everyone's favorite topic of conversation.

Her cheeks burned, and she grabbed her glass and chugged the chilled orange juice.

Some things were worth a little white lie. And she was going to keep telling herself that until the boulder in her stomach disappeared.

"Good morning. Can I get you anything else?"

Natalie looked up into Caden's blue eyes, which reflected the bright smile across her face. It was welcoming and warm, and a change from the other mornings they'd spent at the inn. She was so used to seeing Marie that Caden threw her off.

"Where's Marie today?"

Caden glanced toward the kitchen as her eyebrows pulled down. She rubbed her hands together, her smile faltering. "She's in the back, taking care of some paperwork. I'm sure."

The last was an add-on that made Caden sound anything but sure.

Where was the inn's hostess? They didn't have an appointment to talk about wedding plans today, but inviting Marie along to visit the barn might keep her from reliving that regrettable interaction with Justin.

"So what are you going to do with Adam taking off tomorrow?" Russell asked Caden, laying his napkin down beside his plate.

His expression was entirely relaxed, the opposite of the knot forming around Natalie's lungs. "Adam's leaving?" She barely managed to keep the squeak out of her voice.

Caden didn't look too upset. "He'll be in New England for a few weeks, working on an article and meeting with some of the editors he freelances for. And then I'll finally have some time to work on lesson plans for the fall semester." She let out a girlish giggle. "He's rather distracting."

Russell laughed too, as though he knew a thing or two about his little brother. But Natalie couldn't force herself past his leaving. "Article?"

"He's a travel writer, and he's reviewing a new inn in Connecticut."

Of course. Natalie knew he was a writer, but she hadn't considered that it might take him away. Who was going to distract Russell if Adam was gone? She'd been counting on the brothers making up for eight years of lost time this summer. Tuna fishing with Captain Mark. Biking the Confederation Trail. Relaxing on the porch over a game of checkers.

Her plan for keeping Russell busy while she put the finishing touches on the wedding was merely a daydream if Adam wasn't around.

She needed a new plan. A better plan.

Fast.

Natalie smoothed her fingers across the lace overlay covering the blue tablecloth, while trying to force her face into an expression that didn't look completely terrified.

"So what are you up to today?" Caden asked.

"We're going to take a look at the barn where we're having our wedding reception."

"So you'll see Justin—"

"Kane." Natalie cut Caden off, her hands flipping in her lap as her gaze darted back and forth between Caden and Russell. "At Kane Dairy. I'm sure he'll be far too busy to meet with us."

"Don't be silly. He'll make time for an old friend like you."

Brilliant. She'd stepped right into that.

Russell's eyebrows shot up. He wasn't exactly the jealous type, but there was a hitch in his breathing that spoke to more than basic curiosity. "Old friend?"

Caden shot Natalie an appropriately chagrined smile. "Have fun today." Scooping up their empty plates, she ducked back into the kitchen.

"Oh, you know how it is in small towns. Everyone knows everyone."

"Well, let's go then." Pushing his chair back, he stood and hurried to pull out her chair too.

She rose a little slower, a little more thoughtfully. "Maybe we should wait until Marie can join us."

"Do you need her help with something today?"

Biting the tip of her tongue, she shrugged. "Not exactly." Not unless she counted silencing the voices of too recent memories.

"Then let's go. I'll pull the car around."

Natalie grabbed at his elbow, wrapping both of her hands around his arm. He stopped but gave her a strange look. She'd been made. He knew she was up to something. Or at least he knew something was up. She plastered on the most innocent smile she could find. "Or we could walk. It's a beautiful day."

Walking her fingers down the muscles in his forearm until she reached his hand, she held his gaze until the lines between his eyebrows dissipated, and with them any hint of suspicion.

They strolled through the inn, past the parlor off the foyer, and onto the porch. A row of Adirondack chairs filled the corner space and were taken by a young mother and her two boisterous boys, who bounced from one seat to another while their mom buried her nose in a paperback. Whatever she was reading was fascinating enough to keep her from noticing the tugs on her arms, and Natalie had a sudden wish to be deep in the pages of whatever book her fellow guest had discovered.

Russell squeezed her hand as they walked down the steps. Maybe it was his way of saying that if she stumbled he'd catch her.

Which would be nice. If she needed it.

But she didn't. Couldn't. Wouldn't let herself.

The air was sharp with the scent of salt and the exhaust from the boats scouring the mussel farms in the harbor on the far side of the street. While a light dusting of clouds had settled over the water, the sun made her arms tingle with life.

"So, I suppose you've walked along this boardwalk more than a few times."

She nodded slowly, not sure what he was getting at. "Sure. It's a popular place for joggers." Not that she'd ever been one of those.

Russell tipped his head toward the boards worn smooth by many steps and endless feet. Sunshine had bleached most of the original color away, and the trail was almost as white as the gazebo that stood sentry across from the inn. Lush green grass, rich pine trees, and water shone so bright, everything else faded.

Except the touch of his hand in hers.

It was warm and strong, just like the man.

"I was just thinking you must have met up with a boyfriend by that bench." His eyes twinkled with teasing. "Or at the gazebo. Or by the beach. All those dark spots must have been perfect for living out teenage angst."

"Huh. You think?"

His chuckle came from somewhere shallow in his chest, an echo of others she'd heard before, but he didn't press the issue.

Letting out a little sigh, she stepped toward him, pressing her arm against his, more than sensing the tension in his muscles. Maybe he needed her to paint a better picture than the one he'd conjured. "There weren't too many nights along the boardwalk." She winked at him, her smile subtle but true.

Dark brown eyes flashed in her direction. "But it's so beautiful here."

"It is." She couldn't argue that point. There was no need to pretend otherwise. "But do you really wish I'd gone looking for dark corners with high school sweethearts?"

With a laugh and a shake of his head, he said, "Of course not."

"I haven't been here since I was seventeen."

His brow knotted. "Why not?"

Oh, now she'd done it. She'd all but opened the door to talk about why she'd really left. The whys she'd rather forget.

A man from a Tennessee town no one had ever heard of with big dreams to change the music world could understand the need to leave a small town. While her need didn't stem from exactly the same motivation as his, she couldn't deny that it connected them.

"I guess I didn't have a reason to come back."

He accepted that with a nod, and they continued their stroll, but even at a crawl it was possible to make it from one side of North Rustico to the other in a second. When she looked up, the blue-and-white sign of Kane Dairy hung from its post just off the road. The farmhouse was as clean as ever, every window scrubbed and the white exterior walls gleaming in the sun. The new barn had an attachment—a small shop—that she hadn't noticed when Marie had driven her by it a couple days before.

"Artisan cheese and fresh bread," Russell said, reading the shingle over the door. He had tugged her off the road and halfway to the store before she even realized what he was doing. "Come on. Let's pick something up."

"But we don't have a kitchen."

"Caden does, and she'll share with us. Besides, this type of cheese probably doesn't even need to be refrigerated. Just think of it. Creamy cheese on warm bread."

Maybe she could have planted her feet to keep from being dragged inside, but it was far too late for such measures.

She'd just have to go inside. With any luck she wouldn't know the person working there. Maybe it wouldn't be Justin. He certainly had plenty of other responsibilities with the dairy.

Russell swung open the door, a blast of cool air and rich cheddar swirling around her.

Maybe it wouldn't be . . .

"Mama Cheese Sandwich."

Natalie clamped a hand over her mouth, wishing she could

put the words right back where they came from. Not because of the delighted woman who nearly hurdled the counter to reach her, but because the questions in Russell's eyes were going to demand an answer.

Before Russell could ask them, Mama Kane reached for her, pulling her into a hug with all the strength of her fifty-plus years, the embrace so tight it stole her breath and any desire to be elsewhere. Her black hair held a touch of gray, and the long braid over her shoulder tickled Natalie's cheek, but she smelled of fresh bread and sunflowers, a life spent equally in the kitchen and the outdoors. Her arms were still strong but gentle, and her embrace stirred more memories—and the emotions that trailed them—than Natalie could identify.

"Oh, sweetie!" Mama Kane pulled back just enough to press her hands on either side of Natalie's face and look directly into her eyes. "We've missed you around here."

"I've—" Her voice cracked, and she cleared her throat, pushing down every sweet memory this woman had tried to slip into her life. A thousand miles away, it had been easy to only remember the hard stuff. But in Mama Kane's arms, she couldn't deny the kindness she'd known on this farm. "Me too."

Russell gave a polite cough, and both women turned in his direction.

"Oh, you must be our Natalie's fiancé."

He extended his hand. "Russell Jacobs, ma'am. It's a pleasure."

Her gaze swept over him, assessing his crisp polo shirt and nearly creased jeans, before shaking his hand. "I'm Kathleen Kane, but everyone around here just calls me Mama Kane."

With a questioning stare and raised eyebrow, he said, "Or

Mama Cheese Sandwich. Apparently." There was a touch of humor in his tone, but it was barely perceptible beneath the weight of the unspoken query.

Laughter as rich as fresh cream filled the box of a room and crinkled the corners of Mama Kane's eyes. "Oh, that was entirely Natalie."

His gaze shifted, heavy and unbending. Natalie dug her toe into the cement floor, hanging her head and fighting the blush she already knew was creeping across her cheeks. At least this was a question she could answer. No one had teased her about her verbal flub after all the other kids started calling Mama Kane the same.

"Mama Kane used to make the best cheese sandwiches."

"Used to?" She planted her hands on her hips, a clear indication that the award for best cheese sandwich still resided at Kane Dairy.

Natalie laughed. "I'm sure you still do."

Mama Kane nodded firmly.

"She would bring them out to the town kids sometimes when we were playing." A stab of heat speared Natalie's cheeks, and she ducked her head at reliving the memory. "Whenever she showed up, all the kids would yell out her name. But one day . . . well, I guess my brain was so focused on the sandwiches that it substituted that for her name."

"And you called her Mama Cheese Sandwich."

Natalie nodded. "And then all the other kids started doing the same."

He scratched at his chin, and she could almost see the gears in his mind working out his response. Finally he said, "I like it. And I'd really like to try one of those sandwiches."

"Adam loves them too."

"Adam? My brother? How did you know?"

"News travels round here." Mama Kane shrugged. "Let me make you a sandwich."

She took the long way around the wooden counter this time, her pace much more leisurely as she opened the display, which housed a dozen types of fancy cheese and a handful of traditional flavors.

"I wish you'd come by a little earlier. Justin was here."

All the moisture in Natalie's mouth suddenly disappeared, and her tongue turned to sandpaper.

Thankfully Mama Kane didn't need a second party to keep a conversation going.

"I'm sure he'd like to see you."

Not likely.

Natalie tried for a smile but settled for a strained grimace. "Oh, I saw him the day before yesterday. When we toured the barn." She hoped her words implied that one meet-up with him was enough to satisfy her summer.

Even if she wasn't entirely sure that was true. She had at least a few other verbal grenades to lob in his direction. Ones she'd been saving for years, crafting and polishing for the moment when she could tell him why he had no right to be angry.

She was just peeking into that sack of ammunition to give them another good shine when Mama Kane whipped up. Hunched shoulders flew back and straight. With narrow blue eyes, she looked far beneath the skin.

"You saw Justin this week? I mean, you spoke to him?"

Natalie risked a glance at her fiancé to make sure he hadn't latched on to the strange intensity of Mama Kane's line of questioning and found him mesmerized by the cheese rounds. She nodded.

"Interesting." Mama Kane dragged out the word, enunciating every syllable. "He didn't tell me."

Natalie couldn't begin to imagine what that meant. Had he simply forgotten to mention the fireball that had erupted between them? Or was he trying to put it as far out of his mind as possible?

It didn't matter to her. He didn't matter to her.

Sure. That was a sound argument.

Except it was entirely a lie. And she'd been lying a lot lately. No need to start lying to herself.

"Well, I'm sure he'd love to see you tonight. To meet Russell."

Her stomach took a nosedive as she shook her head. "I'm sure he has better things to do."

Mama Kane laid out four slices of bread on a piece of parchment paper, her gaze always on her hands. "He's playing at the community center tonight. With Jordan and Penny and Alex."

Russell perked up. "There's a show?"

With a chuckle and a flip of her hand, she dismissed the very idea. "*Show* is an awfully fancy word. It's a kitchen party."

He cocked his head to the side, clearly unfamiliar with the term.

"It's local musicians getting together to play music. They used to gather around the kitchen table in the old days, but now . . . well, now there are enough people who want to hear jigs and folk songs and the like that they play at the community center a couple times a month. It's fiddles and guitars and lots of stomping feet and clapping hands. It's not a full *ceilidh* like some of the shows with step dancers, but it's fun." She wrapped the sandwiches and offered them up. "You should both come. Starts at seven."

Russell was already nodding as he accepted the lunch. "That sounds great."

He looked at Natalie to confirm, but she shoved her sandwich in her mouth and gave him only an awkward smile in response.

She should have said something.

6

Justin would have rather seen a moose stroll into the community center than the pair that walked in. They weren't holding hands or touching in any way, but he knew immediately that the man escorting Natalie into the hall was Russell Jacobs. And not just because he looked like a taller, lankier version of his brother Adam.

More because Justin's heart picked up its speed and a rope in his stomach pulled taut. Something deep and primal inside him identified the other man as competition.

Not that he was competing for Natalie's attention. He'd rather stay as far away from her as he could in a small town on a tiny island. At best he could put three kilometers between them. So that's what he aimed to do. And if she insisted on showing up on his property at the old barn? Well, he'd find an errand that needed to be run. In Charlottetown.

Yes, sir. He'd keep his distance. He wouldn't give her the chance to yell at him again. And he wouldn't be forced to think about how he might have let her down.

Except tonight.

Tonight she'd paid the twelve-dollar entrance fee along

with a line of tourists and a few friends and followed her fiancé into the second row on the middle aisle.

Right in front of him.

Tonight he'd have to stare at her all night from his spot on the stage. This wasn't a high-tech performance venue. The lights on the stage were on the same switch as the rest of the room, so all twenty rows of seats—and the church pews along the walls—were completely visible from the stage and everywhere else in the room.

He wasn't sure how he was supposed to concentrate on the music when the guy with the cleft chin had his arm around the back of Natalie's chair and was leaning in to whisper in her ear.

That rope took another hard jerk. This was going to last all night.

Perfect.

He picked up his guitar, lifted the strap over his head, and thrummed it harder than was necessary to tune it.

To his right Jordan LeSea plucked at his fiddle strings, the instrument tucked below his square jaw and bow loose in his grip. Penny Garner and Alex Folley stood just off the end of the stage at the center's back door, talking with a few friends he recognized. He tried to catch Penny's eye and nod her on the stage, but the middle-aged woman had thrown her head back in a deep belly laugh. Alex wasn't much better, his attention clearly focused on a pretty brunette from the Cavendish area. Justin had seen her more than a few times, lingering around after a show. She'd smiled shyly at him. Once. Apparently he hadn't returned the gesture, and she'd moved on to friendlier pastures.

His forehead wrinkled and his gaze narrowed as he remembered that interaction. She'd been sweet and certainly flirting with him. So why had he scowled at her?

Because that's what he did. It was how he'd responded to everyone and everything for a long time.

Since . . .

Well, he didn't want to think about that. Especially right before a show.

"You 'bout ready, man?"

He looked over at Jordan and nodded. "You?"

"Sure. But who's going to pull Alex away from that girl?"

Alex wasn't the best-looking guy in the room. With lanky limbs and ears a bit too big for the rest of his features, he looked like he'd forgotten to grow out of the awkward teenage years. But he was certainly the most charming guy in the whole town, and he had maneuvered his arm around the brunette's shoulders, leaning in just enough to keep her on the line.

The same scowl that had scared her off fell right back into place. "You do it," Justin said.

Jordan shook his head. "No way. This is your show."

"Doesn't that mean I get to delegate unpleasant chores?"

"Nope. Not enough people around here to delegate." Jordan tossed him a full smirk before turning back to tighten a string on his instrument.

With a sigh Justin hustled down the four steps from the hollow wooden stage to the tile flooring and inserted himself into the laughter there. With one arm around Alex and the other around Penny, he said, "Excuse me. I need these guys."

His gaze swept the small group, and it landed on Alex's young woman, whose deep brown eyes grew wide. Something like fear swept across her face, and she took a small step under the protection of Alex's outstretched arm.

His whole body clenched at her reaction to him, and he searched for a smile. But it wasn't there. "Let's get started and give these folks what they paid for."

Penny and Alex nodded, followed him up the steps, and picked up their instruments. They each found their mics, and Justin stood at his, giving the audience a quick scan. His mom sat in the back row next to Harrison Grady, who was leaning into her shoulder and whispering something in her ear. Funny, Harrison rarely talked to anyone except at his diner. Whatever he'd said made her whole face light up.

Before he could wonder what had made her cheeks glow, his mom turned toward the stage, made eye contact, and used her fingers to push up the corners of her mouth even farther.

Great. Not only was he scaring girls, his mom also had to make the universal *smile* motion. His face didn't feel any different than usual. Which probably meant that he'd become used to frowning.

It hadn't always been that way. Had it?

Alex cleared his throat, so Justin stepped up, strummed his guitar, and said, "Let's do some Stompin' Tom Connors."

The tourists clapped politely, but the locals let out a whoop that could have taken a less sturdy roof off. Justin forced a smile as he launched into a song about a potato truck driver from the Canadian Maritimes' favorite folk singer.

Three bars in, even the island first timers were hooked, feet stomping and hands clapping. Justin let himself relax into the song. A jig featuring Jordan's fiddle and a Maritime fishing song quickly followed, and Justin's head and heart were swept away on the familiar melodies.

In an instant the show was almost over, and he took a quick moment to point out Penny's new album available on the table by the door. "Can we do a few more for you?" he asked no one in particular.

"Do 'Good-bye, Girl'!" The cry came from the back of the room, from Father Chuck sitting beside his mom. It landed like a punch to the gut. No way was he going to sing that song tonight. Maybe not all summer. It didn't matter if it was his most requested—the song he was most proud of.

Catching Father Chuck's eye, Justin shook his head. "Not tonight."

The man elbowed his neighbor, who happened to share Justin's home. Justin attempted to keep his smile in place while glaring at his mother.

She simply crossed her arms and yelled over the low hum of the crowd, "We want to hear 'Good-bye, Girl.'"

Traitor.

She knew who it was about.

Man, the whole town knew who that song was about. It wasn't like he'd tried to hide it. Not back then. Not when the wounds were still so fresh that every breath could reopen them.

Maybe they liked his angry rant, knowing who had inspired it. Maybe they just liked that they could make him remember her at every show.

But it was one thing to write a song about Natalie. It was quite another to sing it in front of her. She wasn't an idiot. She'd know the truth by the third line.

A few more calls from the crowd egged him on. "Do it!"

Justin waved them off, looking to Penny to begin her next number. But the trouble with a kitchen party was that there was no set list. No rules. No one to say they couldn't take requests.

In fact, in any other setting, with any other audience, he'd have been happy to oblige.

But not tonight.

"Penny here has a brand-new album. Just came out last month." He waved her toward her mic, but she stayed near the back of the stage, one hand resting at her waist above her generous hip.

Come on, Penny. Don't do this to me.

He tried to speak to her with his eyes, to beg for her to rescue him.

The laughing quirk of her lips told him she understood. She just wasn't interested in saving his sorry behind. Jordan and Alex gave him matching grins.

They all knew. And they were going to have a good laugh at his expense.

Risking a glance toward the second row, Justin read the confusion on the face of Natalie's fiancé. At least one person didn't understand why a musician had been dragging his feet for sixty seconds.

But if the horror in Natalie's eyes was an indicator, she'd already put two and two together and come up with bad news for both of them. She had the song—had him—pegged before he'd played a single note.

A little boy in the row behind them leaned into his mom and whispered loudly. Feet tapped and chairs scraped against the hardwood floors. A white-haired man on a pew under the oversized window crossed his arms over his stomach and closed his eyes before his chin dipped and then jerked back up.

Every musician knew the cues of an antsy audience. He had to win them back, and if the ongoing murmurs from the locals in the back row were right, he had no choice about what to play next.

Natalie already knew he'd been angry. Their face-off in the barn was evidence of that.

She might as well hear the rest of it.

Stepping up to the microphone, he strummed an A minor chord on his guitar. The audience perked up. He shot lasers from his eyes at his pastor for starting the whole thing. The older man raised his eyebrows.

"I wrote this one a few years ago. It's a local favorite. Hope you like it." His voice disappeared like vapor, and he sucked in as much nerve as he could with his next breath as Jordan leaned into his fiddle. A haunting progression filled the box of a room.

> "Went looking for you last night
> In all our favorite haunts.
> Along the water, near the light.
> But you were gone."

He gulped in a breath as he pumped his hand up and down his guitar. Jordan and Alex joined him, the sound swelling until it felt like it could reach the waves and still have enough energy to make it back to them.

> "You didn't even bother to say good-bye, girl.
> You left without a second look.
> You left me on the hook,
> And you couldn't even say good-bye, girl."

As the words flowed out of him, he refused to look in Natalie's direction, his gaze locked on the back row. On

Father Chuck's seemingly smug grin and his mom's drooping eyelids. But a movement from the middle of the room
caught his attention. His gaze snapped to the little girl who'd
dropped her toy, and he squeezed his eyes closed.

If only he could play a venue where it was just him on a
stage larger than a double bed.

If only the lights above could block out the room before
him, and he could lose himself to the run of the chords and
the rhythm of his heart pounding in his chest.

If only he wasn't consigned to this life.

"You're nothing better than a good-bye, girl."

A jab in his back from Alex's guitar was his cue that he'd
missed the lead-in to the bridge. Forcing himself to fall back
into the music, he pushed away the if-onlys that had only
made his life more miserable.

Settling back into the song, he opened his eyes, and they
knew right where to go. Right where he didn't want them to.

Natalie's face was whiter than a lone cloud against a PEI
summer sky. Her blue eyes had nearly doubled in size, and
her lips had all but disappeared. Arms wrapped around her
middle and shoulders like stone, she glared at a fixed point
near his feet.

But her fiancé wasn't nearly as cool. Elbows leaning on
his knees and chin resting in his hands, he gave faint nods
in time with the music. And he watched the musicians not
with the detached interest of someone merely enjoying the
music, but with the assessing eyes of someone knowledge-
able. His gaze made Justin's palms suddenly feel damp and
the hairs on his neck tingle.

Finally they reached the last chorus, and Justin had to keep himself from rushing through.

The closing lines seemed to drag on forever, but finally it came to an end as Penny crooned a sweet note, and the room erupted in applause.

He gave a slight bow and prayed the show would end quickly. It did.

One more song and a solo by Jordan took them through their time, and with a wave and a word of thanks, he was off the stage and pounding a beeline for his mother. He was going to tell the back row just what he thought of them for unleashing a song he'd rather forget he'd ever written.

But before he could make it halfway across the room, a white-haired couple stopped him. "What a wonderful show. Where can we buy your album?" the woman asked.

Album?

He bit back a bitter laugh. "I'm still working on that, ma'am. Excuse me." He stepped to the side, about to make his break.

A hard hand clamped on his shoulder and stopped him cold. The fingers didn't exactly dig in, but the grip was firm. Before he even turned around, he knew they belonged to Natalie's fiancé.

And he'd never wanted to punch a pastor more.

Taking an easy breath to get his heart back to a normal pace, Justin pressed his fists into his thighs and slowly turned.

Sure enough, Natalie's fiancé dropped his hand from Justin's shoulder and held it out for a shake. Justin glanced between the man and Natalie's still oddly pale face. Maybe it was that she'd been so red, so fired up, the last time they'd spoken. Or maybe she was gravely ill. But something wasn't quite right with her.

"Russell Jacobs," the other man said by way of introduction.

Years of his mother pounding common courtesy into him showed up in a reflex. He shook Russell's hand and gave him a curt nod. "Justin Kane. Good to meet you."

"This is my fiancée, Natalie O'Ryan."

A beast inside him roared at being introduced to the woman he'd known forever. No one had to introduce them. Not when their names had practically been one word. JustinandNatalie. Not when they'd splashed their way through every kiddie pool in town and terrorized enough teachers to fill a retirement home.

It took some gall for this guy to *introduce* them. But Russell didn't know that. So Justin bit off the rising temper that seemed to rear its ugly head whenever Natalie showed up. He said only, "We've met."

Russell chuckled. "Of course you have. Natalie mentioned you'd gone to school together."

For a moment he wondered if he could shoot lasers out of his eyes, so intense was the heat flashing through him. *Gone to school together?* That's how she'd explained their history? Schoolmates. Acquaintances crossing paths.

Fine. Two could play that game.

It was infinitely clear in that moment that this was a game. One he had no intention of losing.

Forcing a big smile, he nodded. "Oh, we go way back. Man, I could tell you some stories about this one. We were practically engaged, you know."

Russell's eyebrows dipped dangerously low, and Natalie coughed like she'd swallowed her tongue.

With a half grin that he hoped didn't give away how much

he enjoyed that reaction, Justin said, "Well, that was the rumor anyway."

Natalie thumped her chest before confirming. "It was *just* a rumor. We were not engaged. We never even dated."

Her vehement denial stung, and Justin laughed to cover the flinch. "Of course not. What would our Natalie want with a dairy farmer?"

Russell's narrowed eyes suggested he understood more of the subtext of this conversation than Natalie would probably like him to, but he didn't speak into it. Instead, he clapped Justin on the shoulder again. "Well, I don't know about your dairy farming, but you're some musician. Where'd you learn to play like that?"

"PEI winters aren't good for much except sitting in front of a fire and playing music." He shrugged and then offered a real laugh. "With fifteen feet of snow and a tunnel that gets you only as far as the barn and back, everyone on the island can play at least a little."

Russell glanced toward Natalie, and Justin quickly amended his statement. "Well, nearly everyone."

She scowled, and he could hear her frequent lament. *I tried to learn.*

Well, he'd tried to teach her a few times. But that had gone about as well as his mom teaching him how to drive.

The truth of it was that while most kids on the island grew up with parents who played around the kitchen table on cold nights, Natalie's folks hadn't. They hadn't even been at the table. And when she'd first started having dinner with his family, she'd been too shy to ask why his dad's banjo had only four strings or how his mom made the old upright piano sing like the morning birds.

"She said she only ever learned half a song on the guitar," Russell said.

"Three quarters." Justin said it at the same moment as Natalie, and a familiar connection zipped between them.

So much history. So many years lost. All the years they'd missed because she'd abandoned him twisted inside.

Again, Russell's eyebrows asked questions that Natalie clearly hadn't answered. While Justin had an urge to lay out their entire history, something in him pulled up short. Maybe it was the way her eyes filled with fear. Maybe it was a loyalty born from a thousand nights in the lighthouse. Maybe it was just that he knew it would be a jerk move.

And his dad hadn't raised him to be a jerk.

Swallowing the words that were right there, he shoved his hands into the pockets of his jeans and hunched his shoulders. "Do you play?"

Russell nodded quickly before reaching into his pocket and pulling out his wallet. "Percussion, piano, guitar, and a touch of mandolin."

Justin's eyebrows rose as he pulled his hands from his pockets. Crossing his arms, he leaned away as Russell dug through the crisp leather billfold. It matched the starch of his button-up shirt, the crispness of his jeans. Even his sleek hair looked like it had been polished.

Had Natalie forgotten to tell him that a kitchen party wasn't the Met?

He glanced down at his own attire. Tan cargo shorts that were frayed at the hem. A black T-shirt that he was lucky didn't have a bleach stain on it. Gray sneakers.

And he was the headliner.

He covered his chuckle with a cough behind his hand.

Russell blended into the island about as well as a turnip in a potato field.

Russell found what he'd been looking for and pulled a white card from between the leather lips. Holding it out to Justin, he said, "I know artists in Nashville who can't sing like that."

Now his cough was real, his throat suddenly stone dry. His stomach hit his toes and his head spun as he tried to focus on the words clearly printed before him.

RUSSELL JACOBS. PRESIDENT. RJ MUSIC.

RJ Music. One of the up-and-coming labels in country and crossover music. RJ Music had Grammy winners and Billboard chart toppers. Its stable of artists boasted a judge on a reality TV singing competition.

When Justin let himself dream about the music career he'd never been free to pursue, always it involved a label like RJ.

And RJ stood for Russell Jacobs.

Justin couldn't make his tongue work. He couldn't figure out how to say what he wanted to. Mostly because he had no idea what he wanted to say. His legs were lead, his arms frozen.

He could barely blink, his mouth opening and closing quickly. But no sound came out.

"You've got a great sound. Really unique." Russell pushed the card between Justin's fingers. "Call me next time you have a show. I'd love to hear you play again."

Oh man. This had been an audition, and he'd had no idea.

He swallowed the lump in his throat, and his whole tongue almost went with it. "Thank you. I-I'm glad you enjoyed it."

"Russell!" A voice from clear across the room broke the spell that had kept Justin firmly rooted. They all looked in the direction from which it had come to find Caden waving wildly at them. "Can you come here for a second?"

After a quick shake of Justin's hand, a squeeze of Natalie's arm, and a kiss on her cheek, Russell strolled toward the far side of the room.

Suddenly the words that had eluded Justin before gushed out. "Well, isn't that something. Where did you meet a music producer and label owner?"

Defiance flashed in her eyes, like maybe she thought he didn't consider her worthy of the head of RJ Music. "You think I owe you my story after you played *that* song?" Her voice remained low, but still she shot a glance around their corner of the room to make sure they weren't the subject of anyone's attention. "I can't *believe* you."

"Me?" He threw his hands up in a vain attempt to ward off her verbal attack, his word escaping through clenched teeth.

"You could have warned me." The tip of her nose began to turn pink, and if he had to guess, he'd say that below the fierce red waves of her hair, her ears were doing the same thing.

"Warned you of what? That I wrote a song that's pretty popular on the island and I wasn't planning on playing it tonight anyway?"

"Well . . . y-yes." She waved away his argument and her weak response with a flick of her wrist. "I mean, you could have at least *told* me you wrote a song about me."

"Well, maybe if you'd warned me that you were coming back to the island, I would have."

She flinched at his words, and he wanted to take them back. He wanted to apologize but couldn't. Once the words began, there seemed to be no stopping them.

"When else could I have done that? When you didn't meet

me at the lighthouse? Or when you never called?" Low and humorless, his laugh rattled deep in his chest. "Besides, who said it's about you?"

"Who—" Aside from the slow up-and-down movement of her eyelashes, she stood perfectly still, her mouth open and silent.

"Anyway, you never answered my question. Where did you meet a music producer like Russell Jacobs?"

Instantly thawed, she swung her hair over her shoulder while keeping her glare locked on him. "At my job."

"You work for him?" He couldn't keep the shock out of his tone. Not that he was trying.

"No. I work at a hotel where he was attending an event."

"Where?"

"The Heritage Hotel." She paused like she might be done, but a light flashed in her eyes just before she offered a simmering smile. "In Nashville."

That hit him like a hammer against a nail, sinking deep into his chest, letting the air escape his lungs. "Nashville? You moved to Nashville?"

She crossed her arms, a wall between them. "You act like you didn't know."

"I didn't."

The color that had pinked her cheeks suddenly drained away, her hands falling to her sides. "I can't believe no one told you."

Nope. No one had told him that she had landed in Music City. That she'd found an in with the music crowd. That she was engaged to a man who could make Justin's dreams come true.

7

Was it possible that the barn looked even worse in the shadows?

On this overcast morning, Natalie had agreed to accompany Marie to the barn to try out several wood stains to freshen up the interior walls and beams. But now, as she spun around in the entrance of the cavernous room, it was so much worse than she remembered. Despite overcast skies that kept the corners dim, she could see enough of the splintered walls and dusty corners to think she might have made a mistake.

The sunlight that had cast a halo through the cracks in the roof on their last visit was gone, which made the room feel like a drooping felt hat. Not even the new crossbeams that Seth and Justin had installed the day before could perk it up. Seth had promised that he'd have the hole in the wall fixed within a week, but an urgent meeting in Charlottetown had sent him out of town for at least a day or two.

Marie slid her hand along the wall as Natalie shook her head. "I think I was wrong."

With a flick of her wrist, Marie set off a dull yellow glow

from the fluorescent lights above. It covered the room with a sickly blanket, and Natalie blinked to adjust her eyes to it.

"It's not so bad," Marie said.

Natalie put her hands on her hips and rolled her eyes.

"All right. It's not great. But we can make it work." Marie gave her a hopeful smile. "We'll bring in so many white twinkle lights that it'll look like the wedding of your childhood dreams."

Natalie cringed but tried to nod her affirmation. She hadn't had much in the way of childhood dreams.

But Marie didn't know that.

"If you say so."

"You're not convinced, are you?" Marie didn't wait for a response. "We can get there. I know we can. Once we stain the inside walls a rich red, the whole room will feel completely different. Then when we set up the tables, it'll have some structure. And I was thinking we could borrow some antiques from Aretha's for the centerpieces. Things that are implicitly island. Maybe a lantern or miniature lobster traps."

Okay, sure, she hadn't spent much time in her early years thinking about her future wedding, but she most certainly hadn't planned on decorating with wooden traps that had flat, netted bottoms. They were for fishing, for work. Her dad had built his fair share over the years and worked on and off on a lobster fishing boat out of Tignish. When he could hold down a job.

"Aren't they kind of . . . touristy?"

Marie nodded slowly, rubbing her chin. "Could be. But they're also a key piece of island life."

She made a good point.

Natalie stepped into a pool of yellow light and tried to

picture the image Marie had painted. It could be beautiful. Or it could be a flop.

But backing out of having the wedding here would be the biggest flop of all. Nothing would set tongues wagging like Natalie announcing another change in location. The whole town would speculate about why she didn't want to celebrate her marriage on Kane family land. And it would just serve as a reminder that Stella Burke had snatched the community center away at the very last minute.

Natalie wasn't sure if the rest of the town needed a reminder of why the Burkes hated the O'Ryans, but the memory was as fresh as an apple on a tree to her.

Plus, if she backed out now, she'd have to explain to Russell why she wanted a move. And the less she had to articulate about any connection to her childhood, the better.

They had to make this work.

Marie flipped the wall switch again. "I promise we won't ever turn these lights on again."

"Deal."

Marie smiled broadly, pressing one hand to the small of her back and adjusting her grip on a paint can in the other. "Let's see what we can make of these walls." She set down her load, stepped outside, and returned with arms full of three pints of wood stain. A cracked wooden door had been laid across two sawhorses in a makeshift table, and Marie set her bounty on it. After pulling a screwdriver from her pocket, she popped the lid off one of the stains. Her face pinched, and she suddenly stepped back, nearly bumping into Natalie.

"Are you all right?"

"Sure. It's just . . . strong."

Natalie agreed with a nod and a wrinkled nose, but she

wasn't put off enough to keep from leaning over the open container. The stain was a rich red, like the cherrywood of the buffet in the Red Door's dining room. It might smell like burned rubber, but the color made her think about the cupcakes Caden had set on the antique the afternoon before, and she couldn't hold back a smile.

"Shall we?" Marie held up a paintbrush and pointed to the adjacent wall. "I'm thinking a three-foot patch should be enough to give us a good feel for how it will cover the wood."

"All right." She took the brush and dipped it in the can while Marie pried off another lid.

Halfway through her first brushstroke, a clatter at the open door made her jump. She gasped and dropped her paintbrush. Bending to catch it, she managed to wrap her fingers around the wrong end just as the bristles met her leg, and she bit into her tongue.

Looking up from the mess all over her pants, Natalie squinted toward the entrance, where the sun had fought off the clouds and now illuminated a broad set of shoulders.

And that ridiculous ponytail.

She scowled down at her palms, red with varnish, then up at Justin. Why did he insist on showing up at the worst possible moments? So what if it was his barn? He'd told Marie to pick out the colors, and that's what they were doing.

His face was in the shadow, but she'd bet a clean pair of pants that he was scowling too.

"Natalie, are you okay?" Marie hurried over to check on her. Out of the corner of her eye, she saw Justin stoop over to pick up the armload of lumber he'd dropped in the doorway.

"Didn't mean to startle you," he said. He'd wiped all emotion from his voice, certainly a concession to Marie's presence, even if the weight of his gaze swept over her.

"I'm fine." Natalie gave Marie a firm nod to let her know no harm had been done. Pants and hands could be washed.

Justin shrugged one of those big shoulders, stretching his plaid flannel shirt. "Sorry anyway. I didn't expect company today. Didn't see your car outside."

"We parked in the back so we could scout some locations for the photographer."

Natalie didn't bother to add to the explanation, instead wiping her hands onto a clean patch of her once gray slacks. The residue on her fingers was still sticky, but she moved back to the task of painting her patch.

And ignoring Justin's presence.

And his gaze.

And especially the way her mind wanted to revisit the flex of the muscles in his forearms under the weight of the lumber.

She slapped another stroke of red down her wall, harder and louder than necessary.

Marie shot her a curious stare, but Natalie wasn't about to acknowledge it. Not with Justin only a few meters away, measuring a rotted section of wood for replacement. After setting his load onto the cement floor, he tucked a pencil behind his ear as he stretched a neon yellow tape between studs. Then he squatted in front of the wood on the floor, running the measure over it too. He marked it with the pencil before resting his elbows on his knees.

"Pretty convenient that Seth had to go to Charlottetown." The teasing tone that laced his words made Natalie's skin tingle, its familiarity both welcome and abhorred. Even if he wasn't speaking strictly to her.

Marie's cheeks turned pink as she formed a hard right angle on her patch. "I'm sorry." She offered a thoughtful frown, genuine concern in her eyes. "I know he wanted to help out more, but he had to meet with our lawyer."

Justin nodded, the grim line of his lips saying he understood. But Natalie wasn't privy to whatever reasoning Seth had for abandoning ship after only a few days of work. Despite the nudge of curiosity that poked at her middle, she didn't ask.

She never asked.

"So, have you thought about adding to your guest list?" Marie's tone had lightened from a moment before, her eyes bright and expectant.

Natalie nearly dropped her brush again, hanging on to it only by sticky fingers. She coughed and shook her head at Marie. "Guest list? It's all set."

"But the barn has room for at least fifty more guests than the community center. We could easily accommodate two hundred in here."

Natalie nodded, but a little twist in her stomach suggested that she probably wasn't going to like the direction of this conversation.

At least Justin seemed preoccupied with his tape measure and tools.

"I just assumed that you had limited your guest list because of limited space. Besides, I noticed that your list for place cards doesn't have your family on it. I'll be happy to add your parents."

She couldn't tell if it was she or Justin who gasped, but

the air in the barn suddenly sizzled. Justin had put down his pencil in favor of watching her.

Natalie licked her lips and blinked at the other woman, whose back was turned.

When she spun to load up her brush, Marie paused. Her hand froze, the bristles only halfway into the paint. She tilted her head, her eyebrows bunched, and she seemed to put some of the pieces together. "I just assumed they'd be here. Are they . . . ?"

Dead?

The question was everything but spoken. Natalie wished she knew for sure. Either way.

Her mom was definitely gone. Liver disease and a hard life. She'd received word from Aretha that Connie O'Ryan had been buried in a cemetery outside Souris on the east side of the island.

But her dad was a little more of a mystery. To the best of her knowledge he'd disappeared shortly after she had. And for ten years that had been enough.

But now . . .

She caught Justin's gaze and found a challenge there, his blue eyes bright and clear. More than anyone else on the planet, he understood. After all, he'd been the one she'd run to. When the screaming had been too loud, the bruises too fresh, her home too much, she'd run to him—to their spot.

Then he'd protected her.

Now the look in his eyes dared her to lie, to stretch the truth even a millimeter. Because he would call her on it.

With the loss of an ally in a war she didn't even know she was fighting, she sighed and looked down at her stained hands. She couldn't confirm where her dad was, but she sure wasn't going to save him a place at the head table.

"Um . . . my mom died about ten years ago. And my dad? W-w-we shouldn't expect him."

She nearly bit her tongue off. Where had that stutter come from?

In a flash she was back in second grade, being teased by the boys in her class when she tried to read out loud. She stumbled over her words at least every other line, her tongue having to fight for each syllable. Her shoulders had shaken under her too-big hand-me-down sweater, and tears had streamed silently down her cheeks when the teacher told her to sit down.

But she couldn't remember that moment without also recalling Justin on the playground, his nose bloody and his shirt covered in mud as he wrestled her tormentors to the ground and made them apologize.

She'd fought her stutter for years and had finally beat it in high school. At least she'd figured out how to deal with it so it didn't bother her in everyday life.

But this . . .

Her stomach clenched. This was a reminder of both her past and everything she'd worked so hard to leave behind.

Marie shot her a gentle smile that seemed to say she understood. Natalie refused to look anywhere within a mile of Justin. She did not need any more memories of him popping into her mind. Or another challenge to reveal the whole truth.

"I'm sorry about your mom."

Strangely, Natalie had been too when she found out. Her therapist had tried to get her to explain why her mother's passing had affected her so, but she couldn't name it then or now. It wasn't a deep ache or significant loss. It was the strange hole that came from knowing someone who had been there simply wasn't anymore.

"Thanks," Natalie said, her voice low and eyes straight ahead.

"No problem about your dad." Marie looked back at the square she'd just painted, then at the one Natalie was still working on. "What about others from town? Aretha said you had a lot of friends in town. Should we add some of them?"

"Like who?" She bit her tongue hard, hating the sarcasm in her voice. Hating it even more when Justin grunted. It was subtle enough that Marie might have missed it, but Natalie knew her words were a sharp smack to him.

Yes, Justin had been her friend, but she couldn't very well invite him.

Not after he'd played that stupid song in front of half the town. Even if the lyrics and haunting melody happened to run through her mind as she lay in bed praying for the sweet escape of sleep.

The song was explicitly clear. She'd hurt him. But she hadn't meant to. She hadn't wanted to.

And besides, he'd hurt her.

She pulled out her list of grievances against him like a worn shield. But somehow it didn't feel as complete today, as though someone had poked a sword through it.

Anyway, he'd been wrong. She had said good-bye. Maybe not in person. Definitely not conventionally. But she'd made a stop before leaving town to tell him she hoped to see him soon. And she'd made sure he knew where to find her, even if no one else had told him.

The solid thwack of a hammer against a nail shook her free of her musings, and Justin hit the wood a few more times than might have been necessary.

"What about Aretha and Jack? Or Caden?" Marie turned to the table still holding the paint cans and jammed a screwdriver beneath the lid of a closed container. "Oh, what am I thinking? Of course Caden will be there. She'll be Adam's date."

"Yes."

"What about the Burkes? Bethany must have been in school with you."

Justin snorted and mumbled something under his breath that sounded a whole lot like, "When fish quit swimming."

She actually smiled. He knew how it had been between their families.

Well, some of it anyway.

Marie shot a squinting glance in his direction but refused to be deterred. "What about Mama Kane?"

The steady rhythm of the hammer stopped, but she refused to look in Justin's direction.

"Umm . . . I hadn't really . . ."

She hadn't given Mama Kane a single thought. It was much easier thinking that the whole town had heaved a sigh of relief when the last O'Ryan left than it was to imagine anyone missing her presence at the annual lobster cook-off.

Except that Mama Kane's hug had felt like it was trying to make up for a thousand lost days.

"I'm not sure she'd like to—" Natalie stopped as soon as she caught sight of Marie, who had managed to get the lid off the third paint can. Her face had turned green, as though they'd turned on the overhead lights again. Except no one had.

"Marie? Are you all right?"

"Sure. Fine." Her cheeks suddenly ballooned in the universal sign of decidedly *not* fine.

Tossing her paintbrush to the side, Natalie rushed toward her wedding planner.

Justin beat her there. His hands were free of his tools, which she saw in his wake out of the corner of her eye. He gently cupped Marie's elbow, guiding her toward the open door.

Natalie grabbed her other arm, holding her up and urging her away from the potent scents of the mingling stains. The combination of odors made her eyes water, and Natalie cringed against it.

When they reached the fresh air, Marie gulped it in with great gasps, even as Justin steered her around the building and into the passenger seat of her own car. "Sit here for a little while. I'll clean up."

Natalie caught his eye and tried not to look like she was surveying him as hard as she was. But there was an inflexibility in his voice that she'd never heard before. It wasn't demanding—rather, protective. It wasn't harsh, but it accepted no argument. He took charge and took care of Marie.

That's what a man is supposed to sound like.

The thought popped into her mind unbidden, and she jerked away. From the very idea. And from him.

A touch of pink seeped into Marie's lips, and she nodded slowly. "I'm not sure what—"

But there was no time for her to finish. She raced for the corner of the barn before becoming violently ill.

Maybe it wasn't the smell of the paint.

Natalie's stomach squirmed, but she took a few steps in the direction of Marie's hunched form.

"I'm fine. Just give me a minute."

No one had to tell her twice. Natalie ducked back into the barn, where Justin had already made his escape. He stood at the makeshift table, pounding lids back onto the paint containers and collecting the brushes.

She stooped to pick up his fallen tape measure, but he said, "Don't worry about it."

"It's fine."

"You're wrong, you know."

She almost dropped the tape measure but instead hugged it to her chest, lest she throw it at him. "About?"

He didn't look up from his work, but the line of his jaw worked like one of his prized heifers chewing her cud. The silence staggered on, and she was tempted to turn around and find Marie, but there was something inside her that had to know what he meant.

"What am I so wrong about?"

"Mama Kane." He looked up, one eye closed, the other open only enough for her to see the fire inside. "She'd like to go to your wedding."

"How do you know that?" She'd bet good money that he'd never had a sit-down conversation about her upcoming nuptials with his mom. Actually, she'd bet he'd never even thought about her at all when she wasn't around.

Except for that blasted song.

He'd thought about her at least long enough to write that song. And perform it enough to make it a town favorite.

"My mom couldn't have loved you any more if you were her own child. Of course she wants to be at your wedding. She wants to see you happy."

"If your mom loved me so much, she would have . . ."

Releasing her grip on the tape measure, she set it on the table in front of him.

The blue in his eyes like ice, he prodded her on. "She would have what? What did you want her to do?"

I wanted her to rescue me.

But she couldn't say that out loud. She couldn't admit that to anyone. Even if she was pretty sure that Justin had always known.

When it was clear that she wasn't going to go on, he gave her another nudge. "You wanted more than regular cheese sandwiches, her heart, and the run of our house?"

His push was about as gentle as a cattle prod.

"If she'd really loved me, it would have been my house too."

His jaw dropped, then closed, no sound escaping. But she could see him working out whatever he needed to say in the lines of his forehead. Finally he shook his head. "That's asking—" He stabbed his fingers through his hair, dislodging his ponytail.

"What?"

Before he could answer, Marie called from the entrance. "I'm ready whenever you are."

Natalie looked over her shoulder and nodded. "Be right there." While she spun back around, Justin scooped up the supplies and headed toward the exit. "Wait. What did you mean?"

"Nothing. Don't worry about it."

But it wasn't nothing. *Nothing* didn't gnaw on her stomach and make her heart work twice as hard. *Nothing* didn't whisper words in her ear that might have been lies.

Or worse. The truth.

Just before he reached the door, she stopped him cold with one quick sentence. "You're wrong too, you know."

He turned back, his hands steady, his eyes roving her face. "I did say good-bye."

He didn't bother to argue or try to pretend that he didn't understand her reference. His song hadn't been that well camouflaged. "I think I'd have remembered that."

With a tilt of her head, she asked, "Didn't you read it?"

"Read what?"

"I left you a good-bye. Just where I figured you'd find it. Right where you'd look."

His face screwed up like he couldn't believe her.

It wasn't possible. It couldn't be. He really thought she'd left without any word or warning. He thought she hadn't given him any indication of where she'd gone all those years before. He thought she'd meant their separation to be permanent.

There it was. The real reason he was so angry with her.

He didn't know that she'd asked him to come after her.

8

At his first opportunity that night, Justin ran inside, showered, and raced back toward his truck.

"Where are you going in such a hurry? Dinner will be ready in twenty minutes."

He skidded to a halt two feet from freedom. The weight of his mother's glare was nearly palpable, and he'd never been able to dodge it. No matter how sweet she seemed to everyone else in town, he knew she could see into his soul, and he couldn't get away with anything under her eye.

"I have an errand to run." He risked a glance over his shoulder before running his fingers through his still damp hair. It was mostly true. Actually, it was entirely true. He had something to do away from the house. By definition, an errand.

"Uh-huh."

Why didn't it sound like she believed him? And why did he suddenly feel guilty?

"What kind of trouble do you think I'm going to get my-self into?"

She crossed her arms over her brightly colored floral apron, her head cocked at a knowing angle, but she didn't say a word.

"What?"

"I didn't say anything."

He stared at the white cabinets, wondering not for the first time just how his life would be different if he'd left, or at least moved out of his childhood home. But it hadn't really been an option. Not after his dad's death. Not when Brooke and Doug had needed a stable fixture in their lives. Not with his mom trying so hard to be strong every day.

She had managed her grief and somehow pulled herself together. And if he'd asked her to, she would have found a way to care for her younger kids and fully run the dairy. Except he couldn't ask her to do that. He couldn't add to the weight of the grief she carried after the love of her life had been taken so suddenly. An aneurysm, the doctor had said. His father hadn't suffered.

But Justin would have counted himself half a man if he'd left his mom to suffer in his stead.

Besides, Brooke had just left for the University of PEI a few years ago. Doug, too, had needed to spread his wings with the knowledge that he could come back to the dairy if his pilot plans fell through.

Which left Justin to be scolded by his mother like a misbehaving fifteen-year-old for running out before dinner.

Adopting her stance, he folded his arms and met her gaze with as much steel as she displayed. "I'm thirty-two years old. And I'm going to pick something up."

"Uh-huh." Her flippant little singsong suggested she knew exactly what he was doing and where he was going.

"What?"

"Nothing at all." She walked across the spacious kitchen and scooped her mitts from the counter before opening the oven, which released a cloud of heavenly scents. The chicken and veggies of her potpie had mingled with the bready crust, all to make his mouth water. And she'd opened the oven just to remind him what he'd be missing if he left.

His stomach rumbled on cue, but he pressed a hand to it and shook off his hunger. Some things were more important than chicken potpie. Not many. But he could think of at least one.

Natalie had been adamant that she'd said good-bye. And he could think of only one place where she might have left her farewell.

"You didn't used to sneak out."

That made him laugh. "I'm not sneaking out. I'm a grown man, and I have an *errand*. I'll be back later."

She lifted an eyebrow. "Should I set a place for you at the table?"

"I'll probably pick up something at—" The thought snapped into place and rolled off his tongue faster than he could think about why it was there. "Why don't you invite Harrison over?"

Her other eyebrow followed her first, then she gave him a hard frown. "Why would I do that?"

"No reason exactly." He thumped the wall as he walked into the mudroom, calling behind him, "You've just been spending a lot of time with him lately."

"Yeah, well, you've been acting strange since Natalie came back."

He laughed. If that was the worst she could throw at him, he wasn't doing too bad. Besides, could she blame him? Natalie's arrival had thrown him for a loop. Moving her wedding reception to his barn had come out of left field too. Finding out her fiancé was an incredibly successful music producer had been the icing on a cake he had no desire to eat. But he'd managed to keep the dairy producing milk, his cows relatively happy, and his employees no more disgruntled than usual.

He cast a glance in the direction of the pasture as he reached his truck. Dillon Holt's pickup was still parked on the far side of the milking barn. Justin couldn't remember the last time Dillon had stayed late on his own. His mom said they were attached at the hip—he and Dillon. Maybe it was true. But where he was going tonight, Dillon couldn't join him. Some things had to be done solo.

Hoisting himself behind the wheel of his oversize four-wheel drive, Justin took a deep breath. The evening air had already begun to turn crisp, carrying the salt and sea past the shoreline. Perhaps it was because he'd grown up on this farm, but he didn't smell the cows anymore. Their aroma had become part of his every breath, and he was more likely to miss the odor when he was away than notice it when he was here.

It was the scent of his father's legacy. And his grandfather's before that.

He didn't have to go more than two minutes before he reached the turnoff for the lighthouse on Kane land. There was another lighthouse on the other side of North Rustico, past the inn, at the end of the boardwalk. That was the one the tourists visited. White with red trim, it included a small cabin built onto the back. From the water, it looked just as a lighthouse should.

But he'd always been partial to the little blue-and-white building on his family land. Right at the notch in a small inlet, the light at the top of the second story could reach clear to the red cliffs across the water on a cloudless day. And when the fog rolled in and the sky hung low, it pierced through them, a call to safety for the fishermen in the open waters.

Natalie had loved this lighthouse too. In fact, it was where they'd first met.

He pulled up to the old house, stopping in front of a stump that had never been removed. Whenever the big green pine trees had grown too thick and threatened to block the path of the light, his grandfather had come out and chopped them down. But the stumps remained. Just like the memories. An impotent reminder of the past.

Still, he pulled himself from the cab of his truck and walked over to the door. It was locked now. But it hadn't been almost thirty years ago. Inserting the key from his ring, he twisted the knob and pushed the door in. It squeaked like a lifetime had passed since anyone had opened it, although he knew his staff at the dairy took turns checking the light at regular intervals.

The first floor was so dark he couldn't see where to place his feet, so he took hesitant steps, afraid that someone had altered the room in his absence. But it hadn't changed. It still carried the strong smell of earth and rain and the wind that whipped off the sea in a storm. A small desk in the corner was a testament to a time when a man filled out a log and tracked all the events of this corner of the island. Now it sat empty.

Justin reached for the stair railing and angled his foot to find the first step. It wasn't much more than a ladder with its narrow rungs and steep grade, but it was so familiar he could almost hear the echoes of hours of laughter.

At the top of the flight, he pushed open a small hatch

and light flooded over him. Blinking against the brilliance, he pulled himself into the small room. Its ten sides were all made of glass, and he stared toward the ocean and away from the light on the console in the center. The sun had only just begun its evening descent, but somehow the light within was brighter than anything in the sky. The sweeping metal arm that rotated a partial cover around the bulb was his only reprieve.

Like he had so many times before, he closed the hatch and sank to the ground.

And looked into the far corner, half expecting to see Natalie.

The first time he'd seen her there, it had been their second day of kindergarten. Of course, he'd seen her in Sunday school and around the area. How could kids avoid at least a passing acquaintance in such a small town?

But that morning had been different. He'd forgotten that he'd left his favorite action figure in the lighthouse, and he'd wanted to take it for show-and-tell.

"Go get it," his mom had said. So he ran as fast as his little legs could carry him. Cutting through the pasture and wading through the tall grass, he emerged at his favorite hiding place.

Sure enough, his toy was right where he'd last played with it.

But he wasn't alone. A little girl's big blue eyes blinked at him from her low crouch in the far corner.

"What're you doin' here?"

"Hiding." There was no hesitancy in her voice, only the truth spelled out as plainly as a five-year-old could.

"What from? Ain't you goin' to school?"

"No."

"How come?"

111

"'Cause."

He didn't think her answer was good enough, so he walked around the light, which was so bright it made his eyes water. "'Cause why? Don't you like school?"

She shrugged, her shoulders so skinny that the bones nearly poked through the threadbare shirt she wore. He knew that wasn't right. It wasn't how it was supposed to be.

"Come on. Let's go. I've got a show-and-tell." He held up his toy.

She shook her head. Hard and certain. "Those girls at l-lunch. They said I w-was s-s-stupid."

He frowned. "Well, those girls are stupid. 'Sides, you can sit with me at lunch today." He held out his hand, and she stared at it for a long time before sliding her fingers into his. Her hand was cold—not even the heat of the lamp had warmed her.

Even in the winter months, when the snow was so high that his mom had warned him not to leave the yard, he had found warmth under that light. And always Natalie too.

They'd spent years meeting under this lamp, soothing broken hearts and broken dreams, failed auditions and failed relationships. But it wasn't all sad. There were inside jokes and shared books, celebrations and victories.

And enough memories to fill a hundred notebooks with lyrics. He'd come close. Scratching out his anger and pain line after rhyming line, song after song. He'd spent months here.

But he'd never thought to look for a message from Natalie.

Under the summer sky, the heat of the light made his skin tingle. Or maybe that was the anticipation rushing through his veins. Either way, he ignored the way his hands shook as he reached for a small metal latch on the center console.

The little door creaked open, and he squinted into the dim interior.

This had been their secret place, where they passed messages and left surprises. Once, when they were eight, she'd left her Christmas wish list. It was filled with things like a warm bed, new mittens, and a big dinner. He'd felt guilty about his list of video games, so he'd written out something else to leave for her. All these years later, he couldn't remember what he'd told her. But he still felt the guilt of that moment. Of realizing that he had so much and she had practically nothing.

Maybe it was that moment when he decided he wasn't going to let her face life alone.

Or maybe it hadn't been a conscious decision at all. He'd merely known they were a team. Two peas. One pod.

A small triangle of paper was lighter than the rest of the darkness of the hiding place, and he stuck his hand in to retrieve it. The edges had yellowed over time, the blue lines of the standard-issue notebook paper faded. The handwriting on the page trembled like a stiff breeze had seeped between the glass panes of the lighthouse's highest point as he held it up to the light. In her signature scrawl, Natalie had left him just what she'd said. A good-bye. And a map to find her.

When you're ready to follow your dreams, I'll be where the music is playing. Come find me.

Love, Natalie

Love. Had they really thrown that about so easily back then? He couldn't remember her ever saying it directly to him. He didn't recall if he'd ever said it to her.

It had just always been there. Understood.

But if she'd really loved him, how could she have left so easily? She'd strolled away without a backward glance. Except for this letter, this note.

It wasn't much. But it was something. A gentle nudge that maybe she hadn't been wholly heartless in her departure.

Still, had she really been so certain he'd follow his dreams that she'd headed straight for the one place he'd always talked about?

His gut gave a solid flip, and he sighed, leaning back against a metal support between two windows. She'd been so convinced he wouldn't give up his music that she'd gone to Nashville and waited for him to catch up.

He hadn't given it up. Exactly. But he'd settled for little shows within a stone's throw of the dairy. Because it had been his responsibility. His legacy.

He'd never found his way to Nashville. But Nashville had come to the island. And it was knocking on his door.

◆◆◆◆◆

"We could skip it, couldn't we?" Natalie gave Russell her most hopeful smile and a little squeeze of his hand.

"Skip it?" He shook his head. "Why would we do that? Come on. We're going to be late." He didn't release her hand, instead giving it a solid tug.

She offered only a grimace and a glance over her shoulder toward the candy-apple-red front door, which stood wide open to make way for a steady breeze off the bay. "We could go for a walk instead. It's lovely outside."

He frowned and followed her gaze through the screen, over the porch, and to the overcast sky beyond. "No it's not. It's about ready to rain, and the wind is starting to pick up."

"True. But you haven't really experienced the island until you've been for a long walk in the rain." Even to her own ears, the words sounded hollow, ridiculous. But she tried to make up for that with a smooth grin and an enticing wink. "It'll be fun."

"This will be too." He pulled her to him, tucking her into his side and wrapping an arm around her waist.

She felt like she fit there. Protected. Cherished. So why did he not understand?

Because you haven't told him.

The truth hit home with the force of a baseball bat. And when it connected with the ball in her chest, she could almost hear the crack.

Honesty. What a fresh idea. She could be honest with him.

Taking a steadying breath, she forced herself to make eye contact. "You know I'm a terrible cook."

He laughed. Not quite at her. But at the idea. "Honey, I don't care if you can't boil water."

"But I do." She dropped her arm from around his back and tried to pull away, but he held fast. "I'm not good at this kind of thing."

The humor in his deep brown eyes faded a fraction as his eyebrows met over the bridge of his nose. Parallel lines formed there, and the weight of his scrutiny was heavier than all the eyes at Grady's had ever been. He wasn't just curious. He wanted to know.

To know her. And her whys.

But she'd much rather keep them buried deep below the island's red clay.

"I'll be right there with you." He pulled her even closer to him and kissed her nose. Then her cheek. And when she tried to open her mouth to make another argument, he kissed her lips. "This will be fun," he vowed.

Because she was sure that if she pushed again, he'd only stare harder, dig deeper, she forced herself to smile and nod. "All right."

As they entered the kitchen, she tried to muster a smile that matched Caden's. But it wasn't easy. The executive chef bustled about the kitchen island with a toothy grin and a twinkle in her eyes. "I'm so glad you're here," she said to two other couples.

Natalie recognized the Butlers from breakfast that morning, and she'd seen the other pair but didn't know their names. Both of the women stood about half a step in front of their husbands, whose arms were crossed. Furrowed brows seemed to have been sold in bulk, and Natalie felt a sudden camaraderie with the men.

When Caden looked up from placing a large bowl of potatoes in the center of the island, she smiled right at Natalie. "Great! We're all here. And everyone has a partner, which you'll need to finish up on time. Today we're going to do a new take on a classic shepherd's pie, which has been a favorite on the island for over a hundred years. One of you will peel potatoes for the garlic mashed potato topping, and the other will be working on the beef and veggies for the bottom."

The announcement seemed to catch the attention of the men, and Russell gave a low mumble of appreciation. Meat and potatoes. That's apparently all it took to get his attention.

Apparently *she* should pay attention.

Suddenly his leg vibrated, and he pulled his phone out of his pocket. She gave it a quick glance as he read the text that had just come through, his jaw growing tighter with each pass of his gaze.

"Is everything okay?" she whispered.

He nodded. "Just a sec. There was a problem with one of the tracks Jodi laid down last week."

As he whipped out a two-thumbed response, Caden asked, "So who wants to peel and who wants to chop?"

The other couples looked at each other, pointing at themselves and mouthing their preferences, faces already beginning to brighten as they caught Caden's enthusiasm. Meanwhile Natalie stood around like a fool. While Russell was distracted with his work emergency, she stared at the floor, praying that no one would notice her. She reached for her pockets, which weren't there, and then dropped her hands to her sides. Russell kept up a steady stream of typing, and she cringed when the banter around the room stopped.

She knew the sound of silence. And what it meant.

Everyone had stopped what they were doing to stare at her. At the person who least wanted to be here.

Forcing her backbone straight, she lifted her chin high and swallowed against the desert that had become her mouth. Sure enough, five pairs of eyes stared in her direction. And one stared at a phone.

She lifted one shoulder and said, "I guess I'll peel." Maybe she would do less damage with a peeler than a knife.

Caden's eyes darted in Russell's direction, her questions clear but unspoken. Too bad Natalie couldn't say for sure if this was what they could expect from her fiancé this afternoon. It had been his idea, but when something came up at the studio, he would deal with it. He always did.

She shrugged again and said, "P-p—" Taking a gulp of air and forcing herself to slow down, she tried again. "Point me to my peeler."

Everyone chuckled and moved to their stations. Except Russell.

He was about five seconds behind, and when he looked up from his work, there was an arch to his eyebrow that said not everything had been handled.

"Where do you want me?" Natalie asked.

Caden waved her hand toward the counter. "You're over here with Ryan and Gina."

Natalie took her place around the square island and picked up the kitchen tool that looked more like a weapon. It felt strange in her hand. Maybe it was the first time she'd ever wielded one of these. Certainly the first time in her memory.

She grabbed a rich, brown potato and weighed it in her hand before setting it on the counter. Holding its end, she swiped down the middle of it. Suddenly the entire potato slipped from her grip. It flew over the kitchen island and smacked into Shannon Butler's chest before bouncing off the counter and landing with a thud by her sandal. Shannon's eyes grew wide as she let out a startled laugh. It was followed by another and another until the whole room had joined in.

Everyone except Natalie, who could only look between her potato and the peeler that had most certainly conspired against her.

Perfect. Just as she'd feared, she'd become the laughing-stock of Caden's cooking class. And probably in record time.

It had taken approximately eight seconds to go from doorway to class joke.

Each chuckle grated against her, knotting her nerves and making her hand shake. Dropping the peeler on the counter, she swallowed the memories that this moment conjured. Pointed fingers. Whispered words. Mocking giggles.

Her gaze jumped to Russell as she hoped for a rescue. But her hero was focused on his phone, his thumbs flying to send another text.

He probably didn't realize that she was the butt of the rousing guffaws. He didn't even realize they were laughing at all. Work didn't just call. It demanded. "There's no halfway in the music biz," he'd told her early on.

It was true. It made good sense. There were more than enough aspiring musicians and wannabe producers roaming Music City's narrow streets to fill every studio in town. A thousand times. Finding the next big thing, the next great voice, was only the first step. Launching that career wasn't for those willing to give 90 percent. Or even 99.

Music was everything. It had to be. Even if it meant leaving his fiancée standing like a fool in a ridiculous cooking class. That was the deal she'd made.

But she suddenly wondered if she was getting the short end of that bargain.

"Okay. It's no big deal. It happens to everyone." Caden couldn't quite keep the chuckle out of her voice as she stepped up to Natalie's side. The softness in her voice matched the kindness in her eyes as she picked up another spud. "Hold it like this." She wrapped her short fingers around the potato's waist, her grip firm as she demonstrated. "Then bring your peeler across the long way."

119

Natalie picked up another PEI potato and held it just like Caden suggested. But before she could take a swipe at it, Russell caught her eye. He waved his phone even as he drew it to his ear. "I've got to take this. It could be a little while."

She opened her mouth to tell him this had been his idea and he couldn't leave her on her own. But with a conciliatory smile to Caden, he slipped into the dining room, his footsteps quickly disappearing toward the front of the house. When the screen door slapped closed, she cringed. Every gaze that had followed his disappearance snapped back to her.

Wonderful.

Natalie attempted a smile, but her bottom lip quivered with something she couldn't control.

As she looked into Caden's eyes, she could hear the chef's words from earlier in the class. *Everyone has a partner, which you'll need. Everyone has a partner . . .*

"Umm . . ." Caden cleared her throat, her eyes roaming the room as though she was hunting for a previously invisible partner for Natalie.

The other two couples followed Caden's lead. Natalie could do nothing but stare down and press her hand to the knot in her stomach.

Suddenly another door slammed, this one much closer than the front of the house. And the voice that followed it tore the knot inside her apart.

"Hey, Caden, I brought you that cheese you asked—oh, sorry. I didn't know you were busy."

Natalie looked up, but only so far as Caden's face, which lit up like a cityscape at night. Her eyes brightened and the corners of her mouth flipped up.

No. This was not good. Not at all.

Natalie could read Caden's plan in her eyes, and she wanted to scream that this was a terrible idea. The worst. Ever.

But it was too late.

"Justin, I'm so glad you're here. Why don't you join us?"

9

Justin wasn't entirely sure what he'd walked in on. Caden looked straight at him like she'd hooked a marlin. A woman he didn't know—most likely a guest—stooped to pick up a potato at her toe. And Natalie looked like she was praying for a Jonah moment.

There never was a giant fish when he needed one.

He'd gladly suffer the same for a swift exit because there was no telling what Caden had gotten in her mind. But he'd recognized as soon as he'd stepped inside that he didn't want to know. Whatever it was, he didn't want any part of it. Except he'd never been able to say no to her.

"Come on in." Caden motioned for him to step up to the counter, and when he didn't move, she grabbed his arm. "Natalie needs a partner."

"Oh really? Where's that fancy fiancé of hers?"

As soon as the words popped out, he wished he could stuff them back in. Even more so when Natalie's neck turned the color of a beet, her eyes focused on her feet. The stiffness in her shoulders said she had no intention of looking up at him.

Especially not when Potato Woman let out a strained giggle.

Just great. He'd embarrassed her in front of a full room.

If he had to guess, he'd say her fiancé hadn't needed to be tossed overboard. He'd probably jumped ship all on his own from what could only be one of Caden's new cooking classes. He'd heard Dillon telling his mom about them. It was some sort of marketing ploy to help the inn gain more guests. And if the smiles on the faces of the knife-wielding guests at the counter were any indication, the ploy had worked.

Caden's smile had dimmed, and the tilt of her eyebrows broadcast a very clear message. *Be nice. Or else.*

He'd gotten that same glare from Caden more than once. "Be nice" seemed to be her motto. And something he'd forgotten how to do.

At least where Natalie was concerned.

His mother had often pinched his arm when he was misbehaving as a child, and Caden's response seemed to do the same to his heart.

"Um . . ." He shoved his free hand into his pocket, the other awkwardly holding the cheese round. "I'm sorry."

Natalie peeked up at him from under the fringe of her red hair, her gaze unblinking yet shrouded. He couldn't quite read whatever was going on behind her eyes, but Caden seemed to think his apology was enough.

"Good. Good. You'll join us then?"

It was definitely a question, one he needed to answer. Though it wasn't his question alone. It took two people to partner, and he wasn't about to force Natalie to work with him. But he still couldn't read her body language.

"Well, if . . ." He motioned to Natalie, hoping she would fill in the question. Knowing she wouldn't want him to ask it aloud. Praying she would turn him down.

"Uh, no. It's okay. I'm sure J-J-Justin needs to get back." Her entire body cringed under the weight of her stutter, and his gut clenched too. He'd thought she had kicked that particular habit back in early high school. But maybe not.

It transported him to another time when he'd risked a bloody nose and a stern lecture about fighting from his dad in order to protect Natalie from the mockery of their classmates.

He could chart a course from that point to this one, and it was in a canyon called bitterness.

If he was honest with himself, he was still there. He'd quit looking for a way out. He'd gotten used to wallowing in that gorge. Truth was, he kind of liked it. It was familiar. Comfortable.

Lonely.

Which was why he'd given that pretty brunette the brush-off after the concert. Because being alone was easier than letting someone else get too close and risking another broken heart.

He sought out Natalie's gaze and held it, even as she tried to look away. He swayed with her to keep their eyes locked and tried to read everything beyond the mask she wore for everyone else in the room.

Suddenly her stare darted to the door that led to the dining room. Maybe it was the glint of hope in her eyes or the wistful twitch of her lips, but somehow he knew she was looking for her fiancé, who still hadn't arrived.

Who still had the power to change his life in ways he'd only dreamed of.

There was no telling if it was Natalie's faltering smile or the hope that Russell Jacobs might be willing to put him in contact with a Nashville producer that made him take a small step forward and wave toward the counter. "Well, since I'm here . . ."

Natalie's head snapped toward him. Her mouth opened in what had to be an intended refusal, but her lips stopped moving and hung slack for several long ticks of the dining room clock. The whole room seemed to freeze, everyone watching her for her next move.

He could almost see her weighing her options, deciding which response would draw more attention—carrying on alone or sending him away.

Only she could answer that. And only she knew why it still mattered. But there was no mistaking the uncertainty in her gaze now, in the rigidness of her stance as she refused to look at anyone but him. It still mattered.

Her discomfort pinched at his chest again, and he brushed a hand across the spot as though he could dislodge it.

No such luck.

"Okay." Natalie's voice barely carried across the silent kitchen. "If you want to stay."

"Perfect!" Caden cut in, giving neither of them an opportunity to react to Natalie's response. Not that he wanted—or needed—to.

"Pick up a knife and start cutting those veggies." Caden turned him toward the counter, and he stumbled toward it, suddenly wishing he'd paid more attention when his mom had tried to teach him how to cook all those years ago. If he wasn't careful, he might end up making Potato Woman a Carrot Woman too.

He fell into place beside a tall man and a very short woman who looked like she might need a stool to reach the veggies on the counter, but she wielded her knife with a sure hand. In short order Justin fell into the rhythm of watching and mimicking her. He wasn't the only one. The other man, whose green eyes never stopped moving, seemed to be following her every step.

Still, Justin's carrots weren't nearly as even and clean as his neighbor's. But Caden gave him a kind smile as she looked around his arm and patted his shoulder. "Good work."

Before he could enjoy her compliment, a screech behind them turned everyone around. "Watch out!"

It was too late. It was only a potato peel, but it had the perfect distance and height. Before he could duck, it smacked into his cheek, wet and slimy as it slid down to the front of his plaid shirt. With the back of his hand, he wiped at the trail that had been left on his face, then picked up the offending sliver by its end, holding it at arm's length like Natalie had done with the worms every time they'd gone fishing.

Natalie's hands flew to her face, an attempt to cover the blush that had already made its way up her neck and across her cheeks. She shook her head and stared at him through unblinking eyes. Silence reigned for what felt like a full minute, everyone still and observant.

Hands still clapped to her face, Natalie said, "At least it wasn't the whole potato this time."

Suddenly the spud by Potato Woman's foot made sense, and he saw the entire scenario play out in his mind's eye, flying food and all.

Maybe it was the absurdity of the situation or the familiarity of Natalie's flushed skin or a sneaking memory of a burned birthday pie that he just couldn't bring himself to stomach, but he let out a laugh like he hadn't in years. It jiggled everything inside him until he had to bend over to gasp for air, and the sight of the potato peel pressed to his knee, where his hands held him up, made him laugh even harder.

"Oh, Natalie. You haven't changed a bit."

Amid the many other guffaws in the room, a low giggle stood out. He looked up from his hunched position to catch Natalie's shaking shoulders, her fingers still stretched across her mouth, but not in embarrassment. This was the laughter they'd shared for so many years. When things at home were too dark or the pressures of life and school too much, they'd hidden away in their lighthouse.

And they'd made each other laugh. They'd teased and prodded, poked and provoked until tears ran down their cheeks.

He swiped at the dampness below his eyes and realized she'd done it again. Without even trying. Without being anyone or anything but Natalie, she'd made him laugh so hard his belly ached and his eyes swam with tears.

Caden was the first to contain herself, herding the class back into order and helping Natalie spare herself another faux pas through the entire mashing process.

As they worked together to fill two little pans that looked like miniature pie plates with the meat, veggies, and mashed potatoes, Justin met Natalie's gaze. And every time a low glow inside promised that she clung to the same memories he did. The brief lift at the corner of her mouth hinted at the possibility that what they'd once shared might be restored.

No. That wasn't quite right. It could never be what they'd had before. But maybe—by some miracle—the animosity that had blossomed in the wake of their separation might be stifled. At least the anger might be released, the frustration freed.

As Natalie leaned in the oven to push the tray of their completed shepherd's pie onto the top rack, she glanced at him. "Thank you."

The meager volume wasn't equal to the weight of the words, which struck him dumb. He wanted to ask her what it was for, but he knew he'd come to her rescue. Saved her from having to take the class alone. And saved her from a truly embarrassing moment by simply enjoying the humor of it all.

He could have forced her to clarify, to point out what he'd done, but he didn't dare waste their first truly civil exchange. And he wouldn't use it up on common courtesies either. "You're welcome" wasn't what he wanted to say. Screwing up his face and his courage, he whispered what he most wanted her to know. "I finally got your last lighthouse letter."

Her eyes glistened beneath the kitchen bulbs, and he wondered if he'd caused the dampness there.

No. Surely not.

But he was a little less certain when she cleared her throat. "I . . ." She trailed off, clearly thinking better of what she'd planned to say. "I'm glad."

He wasn't sure if he was. It might have been easier to go on thinking she'd left without a word.

Actually, he was absolutely certain it would have been easier to go on as they had been. Shooting angry jabs at each other whenever they were alone. Letting the bitterness fester. Wallowing in a fair measure of self-pity and buckets of self-indulgence.

He frowned, and she immediately matched his expression,

adding a suggestion of uncertainty. This was far too much introspection for a man who spent his days with four-legged milk machines.

Coughing behind his hand, he nodded. "Good, I guess."

With a false start Natalie began to speak but was immediately cut off as Caden raised her voice. "We'll take a thirty-minute break while our pies bake. Dinner will be served at five thirty in the dining room."

"Dinner?" Justin swung toward the microwave and the clock there. The blue lights had shone all afternoon. He'd just ignored them for the last hour, which had flown by. Which had surely found Dillon grumbling as he did the dairy's evening chores all by himself. "I've got to go."

Natalie's shoulders drooped. The movement wasn't much, but it tugged at a spot deep in his heart as she asked, "Do you?"

Forget a tug. Her soft words made him feel like he was being dragged behind his truck. They were so gentle, but there was a power in them. A clear hope that he wouldn't leave her on her own.

She doesn't want you. *She just doesn't want to be left on her own.*

Right. She wanted her fiancé by her side. But in a pinch Justin would do. That was the truth.

And apparently this particular truth was hornet sharp.

He stepped away, battling the urge to turn his back on the expectation in her eyes. He didn't need to rescue her any longer. That wasn't his job. She'd made that decision for him.

With a firm shake of his head, he met her eyes. "It's late. I have an appointment with some dairy cows."

Her swallow was clear and audible, even over the low hum of conversation from the couples leaving the class. "If you—"

"What'd I miss?"

Justin turned toward Russell, whose smile was practiced but didn't quite wrinkle the corners of his eyes. His gaze settled on Natalie, and she plastered an equally experienced but no more true grin into place.

"Nothing, honey." She turned her face up and received a quick peck on the lips. It was about as romantic as Justin's egg layers going after their morning kernels.

Justin tried not to stare. Or sneer. Or gag. In fact, he tried to steel his features against any indication that he'd even noticed their stiff greeting, but something about their inter-action picked at him. It was everything polite and well-bred.

And it lacked anything remotely related to honesty.

Shouldn't she want to throw a punch—at least a verbal one—in Russell's direction? After all, the man had left her alone in a class that couldn't have been her idea. Justin sure would have if he'd been in her shoes. And she'd never backed down from telling Justin exactly what she thought of him when he ticked her off.

So why this facade? Why hold the reins so tight with the man she was going to spend the rest of her life with?

Or maybe it wasn't that bad. Maybe she wasn't holding back all of her true self. Perhaps that's what he wanted to see, so that's what he saw.

"How was your call?" she asked.

Russell shook his head, the carefully played tilt of his lips flickering under the weight of what was certainly something unpleasant. "Jodi's recordings are almost completely gone."

"What about backups?"

"They've been corrupted."

Her smile flickered too.

He should turn and go, but Justin could read on Russell's face that there was something else. And both men knew that Natalie wasn't going to like it.

By the tone of her voice, Natalie knew as well. "What are you going to do?"

"I have to go back to Nashville." He frowned. "It's going to take more than a few days. Maybe several weeks."

Her eyebrows rose to full mast as her gaze shot around the room to confirm that they were the only ones left. Her eyes landed on Justin for a long second, and he wondered if she'd dismiss him, but then she turned back to Russell. "Can't it wait until after the wedding? There's so much left to do to get ready. The wedding's in five weeks."

"Five weeks and three days."

Based on her narrowed eyes, Russell's correction was not well received, and Justin couldn't help the surge through his veins, anticipating her retaliation.

Before she could say a word, Russell continued on. "We'll figure it out." With those dismissive words, he patted her shoulder, as though all was well and resolved.

Those blue eyes flashed as he'd seen them do so many times, and she worked her bottom lip like it was her job. Her nostrils flared, and her shoulders rose in a rapid staccato.

There it was. This was what her fiery hair promised—enough temper to put a man in his place and save some left-overs for anyone else in the vicinity. She wasn't the pushover she appeared to be in Russell's presence. And Justin liked her all the more for it.

He leaned in. He might be in the blast zone, but better there than with a limp version of the woman who had always known how to stir up his ire with a dose of her own.

Then, faster than the fire had started, Natalie let out a quick sigh. The color high in her cheeks disappeared, and the limpid grin returned to her face. "Sure."

Sure? That's what she was going with now? *Sure?*

The man had just announced his intention to cut their—what had Marie called it?—pre-honeymoon short.

No. Worse. He was leaving, but Natalie had to stay. It was almost like Russell didn't understand that Natalie didn't want to be on the island. That she *wouldn't* want to be on the island.

He sucked in a sharp breath and nearly choked on it, their interaction riveting yet wholly confusing. But this wasn't his scene to watch. It wasn't his story to butt into. Justin took a deliberate step back. Then another. He didn't need to know if they were simply playing the part of a loving couple, or if there were secrets Natalie had never told the man she was about to promise the rest of her life to.

Moreover, he didn't want to know. He didn't. Really.

"I knew you'd understand." Russell planted another kiss on top of her head, and he had to miss the uncertainty and anger warring across her face.

All the better angels screamed at Justin to keep his mouth shut. Every experience he'd ever had with this couple promised he'd do better to keep quiet. But one small voice in his head prompted him to goad them.

He picked the wrong prodding.

"What about everything you have left to get done for the wedding?"

◆◆◆◆◆

Natalie fought the urge to stomp on Justin's toe, instead keeping her focus on maintaining the smile that she needed

132

Russell to see. The one he expected. But she had a few choice words for her class partner.

What on earth had he been thinking? Was he trying to make Russell feel guilty?

She wanted Russell to feel guilty for bailing on their plans.

But this wasn't Justin's battle, and he seemed to know it. With a flushed face, he scooped up a stack of plates that Caden had set on the counter for dinner and hurried toward the door.

It was hard to tell from across the room, but she thought she saw him mouth "I'm sorry" in her direction.

With a squeeze of her elbow, Russell drew her attention back. "Oh, honey. I'm sorry I'm going to miss out. But there has to be someone here who can help. What about Marie?"

Natalie shook her head. "She's already doing everything she can, but she's also responsible for the inn."

"How about that woman, Aretha Franklin?" He chuckled, as though her musical name was an inside joke he'd just discovered and not one Aretha herself made with every introduction. "You said you were friends."

Eyes burning and heart picking up speed, she licked her lips, searching for an answer. Yes, Aretha was kind. She'd been the first to truly welcome Natalie back to the island. And she'd always seemed to keep a watchful eye on Natalie. But she wasn't sure that was enough. Aretha had other things to do. "No. She's already busy enough."

Besides, what she really wanted was for her fiancé to be here. To plan by her side. So why couldn't she tell him that?

A brick fell all the way to the bottom of her stomach. She knew it wasn't right. She knew it wasn't how she wanted this relationship to be. Only it was too late to be honest with him.

Wasn't it?

Questions about Aretha danced across Russell's face, and Natalie brushed her hand through the air. "She has other things to worry about. Her store. A husband. It's not a good time to ask her."

From his spot at the swinging kitchen door, Justin didn't look convinced. But Russell nodded and moved on. "What about the woman we met at the cheese store? Mama . . . Kane?"

Her heart skipped a beat, and she couldn't keep her gaze off of Justin, who'd said that his mom wanted Natalie to be happy. He'd said she would want to come to the wedding. If that was true, maybe she'd want to help plan it too. Except . . .

She had an excuse for every person in town. Because she hadn't just abandoned Justin. She'd walked out on everyone.

But for every Stella Burke, who couldn't see her shadow disappear soon enough, there was a Mama Cheese Sandwich and an Aretha Franklin. Maybe they'd missed her half as much as she'd missed them.

That brick gave another flip with a hard landing, and she pressed her hand to her mouth, pushing her breath through her fingers.

"Mama Kane would—"

Before Justin could complete whatever he was going to say, Russell turned on him like he'd forgotten there was a third person in the room. "What about him? It's at his barn." He spoke as a man used to money solving his problems. "I'll pay you for your time. Whatever it costs."

"Me?" Justin's voice cracked on the single syllable, his eyes narrowing with uncertainty.

"Sure. You're going to be on the property anyway. You're fixing up the barn for Marie, right?"

"Well, sure, but . . ."

He shook his head frantically, and Natalie clung to a thread of hope. He had to refuse. He had to.

"I have a dairy to run."

She let out a silent sigh, but it was premature at best.

"Of course. But this stuff won't take too much extra. Natalie was going to take care of most of it anyway, and Marie will be around. Besides, you know the local shops and vendors. You could probably be more help than I could anyway. You'll have a man's opinion, which is about all I was going to offer to the whole process."

"No." She grabbed Russell's arm, tugging on his wrist, doing her best to ignore the weight of Justin's gaze. "I want *your* opinion. Not just any man's."

But it wasn't enough.

Justin stepped forward to balance the stack of dishes on the corner of the island counter and said, "I don't think I could be of much use to Natalie on the wedding front."

"Of course you can. Right, honey?" Russell glanced at her but failed to really see her.

"Um . . ." Natalie fought for the power of speech or some approximation of it, but words were slipping away.

"I don't know anything about weddings," Justin said. "If it's not cows, milk, or a by-product of the two, I'm not going to be of any help."

Yes. That. Justin was right. He wouldn't be any help. Russell had to see it.

When his face softened and the certainty there drained away, she managed a full breath.

Lifting one hand to cup her elbow, he caught her gaze. "I understand. I get it. But music is my life. I have to save this album." Russell turned to Justin. "You understand, right?"

She cringed. Justin flinched. She couldn't tear her gaze away from her former best friend. Fifteen years hadn't been enough to forget how to read his face. The emotions flowed like the bay, rippling in and out again—understanding and concern, worry and hope.

His pinched features seemed to weigh the options. But what options were there? Only "no" and "absolutely not."

They couldn't work together. They'd kill each other. They'd fight and yell. And maybe get all the hurt out on the table.

And then what?

Her stomach lurched. There was no telling what would happen. But it wasn't safe, and it sure wasn't part of her plan. Which was to marry Russell. Live happily ever after. Never return to the island.

A sudden spark in Justin's eyes caught her attention, and she wanted to wave him off, beg him to think about what he was considering.

Clinging to one man who loved music, she stared at another who wanted what her fiancé would provide. The whole thing. The album. The tour. The elusive dream.

The brick in her stomach shattered, shards piercing her insides. He wanted what Russell could give him. And it was reason enough to agree to this wedding-planning farce.

If Justin did this favor for Russell, then maybe Russell would help him launch a career he'd been dreaming about since he played her his first song under the spotlight of the bulb in the lighthouse.

"All right. I'll help."

10

"Why did you do that?"

Natalie charged into Justin's barn and slammed her hands on her hips while the marching of her feet echoed into the cavernous ceiling.

"Do what?" Justin spoke with a drawl slower than any native Nashvillian. And every dragged-out, extra syllable grated at her, as surely as she'd attacked the potato in Caden's kitchen two days before. He knew exactly what he'd done or he'd have bothered to look up from the gallon of wood stain that Marie had selected for the barn's interior.

He didn't. Look up, that is. He just kept the paintbrush going in long, smooth strokes. Up and down. From the top of his reach to his waist. Then back up. Filling in the narrow confines of the corner. His chin—and presumably his bright blue eyes—followed the motion. Decidedly unperturbed.

She knew why he had agreed to work with her, and she was going to get him to admit it. Even if he didn't realize he was supposed to be upset too. She had no intention of being the only person distraught that he'd weaseled his way into helping her plan the wedding. Irked that they'd have to spend the next few weeks in too close proximity.

Okay, maybe Russell had talked him into it. But that wasn't the point.

He was supposed to be upset. That was the point.

"You know what you did. You—you—you saddled me with *you* for the next month."

"Whoa there, lady." He kept his shoulder to her, never bothering to peek in her direction.

"Lady? Lady?" Fists clenched so hard her arms shook, she nearly stomped her foot. "You know my name. You know who I am. And you know perfectly well why this is a terrible idea."

"First of all, of course I know your name. Doesn't mean I'm inclined to use it when you're yelling at me."

First of all? Oh dear. Clearly this list could go on for a while.

Lips pursed and eyes narrowed, she tried to glare him into the cement floor. But he remained upright, his brush moving up and down. From one board to the next. The painting stopped only long enough for him to wipe a rag down the boards he'd just covered. It resumed again without a hint that he'd noticed her displeasure.

"Second, if you're going to be here, you might as well put in some of that elbow grease I was promised when I kindly offered you the use of my barn." Finally deigning to look in her direction, he nodded at the sawhorse table behind him. "There's a roller and a cloth."

Natalie looked down at her black ankle pants and cream-colored sweater set. She could feel Justin's assessment following the same path. It was almost as tangible as the frown that he settled on her. But she ignored it, painting on that fake smile she used with hotel guests who insisted on being difficult. Sweeping her hand over her outfit, she said, "I'm not exactly dressed for it."

Before she could say anything more, he began tearing at the buttons of his oversize cotton shirt. His fingers moved with a smooth efficiency, revealing first his neck and then more.

For some reason, she couldn't look away from the patch of deeply tanned skin at his throat, where his Adam's apple bobbed twice.

Maybe his mouth had gone dry. Hers certainly had. Swallowing quickly, she took a quick step back. And then another to her side, jamming her hip into the corner of the table. When she let out an involuntary cry, Justin looked up from where his nimble fingers were still undoing his buttons.

He didn't stop.

Something like a rubber band around her chest snapped into place, and she gasped.

Oh dear. Not good. The worst, actually.

Finally she waved her arms and found her tongue. "What are you doing?"

But she was too late. The shirt skimmed over his broad shoulders and down his brawny arms. Thank goodness for white undershirts.

But this particular T-shirt didn't do much to hide the changes that she'd known had taken place. She'd been aware that he'd grown up. But now she was *aware*.

Once spindly arms had been filled out by manual labor and were covered with an easy smattering of dark hair. His neck looked twice as thick as it had been. And his wide chest tapered to a narrower waist. But even at his slimmest point, he was solid. Sturdy. Unyielding.

And utterly mesmerizing.

No. No. No.

She jerked her head down as he held out the shirt. She had no business thinking about how he had changed. Especially physically. That was bound to lead to bad news.

She'd never . . . Well, she knew how it ended up when eyes strayed.

Her dad's drinking hadn't been the only thing that made the O'Ryans a hot topic of conversation. Her mom had suffered the worst kind of broken heart. Again and again.

Russell deserved better than that.

So she stared at her sandals and prayed that he'd put the shirt back on—even if he was technically covered.

He did not. He simply shook it beneath her nose. "Put it on over your clothes."

"Why would I do that?" Despite the way his direct order rankled her, she kept her head bowed and her voice subdued.

"So you don't ruin those fancy pants."

Her head whipped up at the snarkiness in his tone, her gaze locking with his, her lips already forming her defense.

But the left corner of his mouth rose a notch. Then another. And then his eyes flamed with mirth.

"You . . ." There were no words, so she settled for shoving his shoulder, which should not have moved. But he gave an exaggerated sway as though she'd thrown him completely off balance, complete with a feigned stumble.

When he was back on stable footing, he smiled. "Just wear the shirt. It'll protect your clothes."

"All right." She snatched it away from him and, after shrugging out of her own sweater, whipped the shirt around her shoulders. Shoving her hands down the sleeves proved futile when her fingers didn't pass the cuffs, so she raised her hands over her head until the light fabric pooled at her shoulders, her hands reappearing.

"Need some help with that?"

"No."

He nodded. But his smirk said he was just waiting for her to fail.

Well, he'd be waiting awhile. Rolling the cuff on the left and then the right sleeve, she raised her eyebrows at him. As she pushed the buttons through their holes, he nodded his conceit.

That's right. She didn't need to be rescued.

It was an odd thing to be proud of, dressing herself in a shirt that nearly reached her knees. But at the moment, she'd take it.

Nothing else in her life was going quite right—what with Russell's departure the day before and a call from a local decorator that she was unavailable to help with staging the event. Covered and capable was the best Natalie could do, so she'd do it.

With an approving nod, Justin turned back to his patch of wall. "Where were we?"

She ignored the question and picked up the roller.

The wind carried a burst of ocean scent through the barn door, and the waves below the red cliffs sounded their time-honored cadence.

Natalie leaned her head back to relish the familiar aroma. This close to the red cliffs, with her nose in the sea air, the memories were closer. Brighter.

It was the difference between vinyl and digital. Black and white and Technicolor. But she didn't particularly want to watch either version.

Screwing up her face, she cleared her throat and set to work under Justin's watchful eye. Giving him a hard stare, which she hoped said she could handle this, she tried to ignore the pinpricks that danced down her spine.

"So, tell me how this works."

One eyebrow shot into a tight arch. "You've never used a roller before?"

She pursed her lips to the side as she loaded the stain onto the roller. "Of course I have." Once or twice. "But what are you doing with that rag?"

"Wiping off any extra, smoothing out the drips. Like this." He demonstrated again, and she followed his movements, mimicking them across the wide-open wall.

After a few solid stripes, she stood back to admire her work.

Suddenly he said, "Watch my shirt."

"What?" She jumped, jerking her hand away from her waist, where she'd nearly added a cherry-brown stripe.

"Just because I lent it to you doesn't mean I want it ruined. It's still a good shirt."

He looks better without it.

She clamped her mouth closed to keep from saying that out loud, hating as the words rang in her head. With forced nonchalance she managed, "Okay."

"So . . . third . . ."

Third? Was he still on that silly list of grumbles?

"I think this is more your fault than mine."

Apparently so.

"Ha!" The burst of laughter had begun derisively, but as it made its way to the open air, it changed shape and sound, turning lighter than air and floating toward the exposed beams above.

This he noticed. This was enough to draw the tangible weight of his gaze.

Forcing herself to keep her roller moving, covering wide swaths of the wooden slats of the wall and following side to side with the crunchy cloth, she reined in her giggle and tried for a more serious follow-up. "How exactly did you come to such a very wrong conclusion?"

That earned her a full smirk and a shake of his head until his ponytail flopped. "I think you're the one with wrong conclusions. With the grain of the wood."

"Huh?" How had they jumped from his mistaken understanding of this terrible ordeal to lumber?

He waved his darkening rag. "When you wipe the extra stain off, go *with* the grain."

"Oh. Sure. Of course. I knew that." Actually, not so much. But what was one little white lie between former friends?

"Fourth—"

"Wait just a second. We haven't cleared up your misunderstanding of point three. This is not my fault. I did *not* ask you to step in as pseudo wedding planner."

"Uh-uh." He shook his head hard, sending that stupid ponytail dancing again. "Not a wedding planner. I'm more . . . more like a pseudo gr—" He stopped with a wince like he'd chomped on his tongue.

She nearly bit into her own. Anything to keep from picturing Justin at the end of the aisle. At the end of *her* aisle. Anything to keep from dwelling on why that was such a problem.

This wedding was already hard enough. No need to add never-going-to-happen scenarios to the pot.

"You didn't have to agree, you know. You could have—no, you should have—turned Russell down."

"The guy needed a favor."

"The guy? You make it sound like you go way back."

He shrugged beneath that flimsy little T-shirt, which was growing a bit damp and a little sticky while he labored in his corner. "Adam's a friend of mine."

He treated it like the end of his case, but she knew. "So the fact that Russell could connect you with the right people in Nashville has nothing to do with this?"

The broad expanse of his shoulders suddenly went stiff, and his arms stilled. She'd hit the nail on the head.

She just wasn't so sure how she felt about it. The spark of knowing she was right should have burned warm in her chest. Instead she could nearly feel the wind whip through her.

He sucked on his front tooth for a long moment, his squinting gaze sending shivers down to the tips of her fingers. "We both had dreams. If yours is coming true, why shouldn't mine?"

That was fair.

"Besides, I couldn't give up the pleasure of your extended company, now could I?"

The laugh poured out of her before she had a chance to measure it. Even she could see the ridiculousness of continuing the volley of barbs if they were stuck together for the next month.

"I suppose not."

"Well, we were friends once. Closer than friends."

A toad settled into her throat, and something burned at the back of her eyes. Her only response was a gentle nod.

"And even though we haven't been in a long time . . ."

He didn't have to finish it.

He'd always been the quicker one to lay down a grudge. Maybe she wanted to carry hers for a little longer. The pain had become like a security blanket, and each resentment provided a certain amount of warmth on cool Nashville nights. She could tuck the fact that he'd let her leave without him under an arm and pull it out when she really needed it.

He cocked his head to the side, following the motion of his paintbrush once again. "Besides, if I stick around, maybe I'll be there to see you throw a whole potato."

"Ha! You should be so lucky."

"I know. That's what I'm saying."

The bristles of his paintbrush scratching at the lumber was the only sound for a long moment as she worked up what she needed to say. She could come up with barely two words.

"Thank you."

"For?"

"For saving me at Caden's cooking class. It could have . . . It would have been awful. Without you there."

For half a second they froze, eyes locked. Her breath bottled somewhere in the region of her sternum, and she prayed he'd say what he had as a child. *Always.* It had been their promise and their guarantee. Always they'd stand side by side against whatever the world could throw at them. *Always.*

But when he opened his mouth, he offered two very different syllables.

"Okay."

◆ ◆ ◆ ◆ ◆

Natalie was still chewing on her strange exchange with Justin three days later as she stepped into Grady's. Marie said that Harrison had called the inn and asked about catering the reception. Natalie just couldn't refuse him.

She also didn't have any other local choices.

The smells of his fried cooking had baked into the walls over the years and hung thick in the air, leaving a fine coat of fish and chips on her as she squeezed between the full tables of the dining room.

From the near corner Stella Burke and her cronies shot Natalie hard stares. They made the hairs on her arms stand up and salute. But she refused to give in to the urge to search for her pockets or roll her shoulders against the battery.

Instead she marched forward, ignoring their icy appraisal and trying for all she was worth to forget the last thing Stella Burke had said to her before she left the island.

She couldn't forget.

In fact, every time Natalie glimpsed the bottle-blonde bob, she heard the same words ringing in her ears, and not even the chatter bubbling up at the four occupied tables in the middle of the afternoon could block out that memory . . . those words.

You're going to become just like your mother.

Just like your mother.

Your mother.

No. No. No.

She'd left to ensure she never did. She'd fled this town, this province, and even the whole country to make sure she never—ever—became like Connie O'Ryan.

146

But that didn't shut off the taunting torrents every time she was in a room with Mrs. Burke.

Don't look in her direction. Just don't.

Maybe she couldn't help herself. Maybe she missed the punishment.

Most likely she had to know if they were whispering about her. After all, she was old enough and capable enough to defend herself now. Maybe she hadn't been at seventeen. Definitely she hadn't been then. She'd been scared and embarrassed and too long the topic of town gossip.

Not anymore. She held an important—and visible—role at her work. She was respected and trusted. And she was about to marry a very successful, very handsome music producer.

A bead of pride rolled around her insides, easing her load.

She was no longer a child weighed down under the shame of her parents' name. But what good did that do if she attempted to ignore the snide remarks and sideways glances?

Smoothing down the legs of her cuffed jeans and straightening her blouse, she breezed across the dining room. Before they could ignore her, Natalie flashed a winning grin at each of the ladies at the table, beginning with Mrs. Burke. "Stella, Dorothea, Lois." With a condescending nod to each of them, she held their gazes as she drawled their names. She lingered on the last, praying that Lois was no longer the area's only florist but certain that when she checked with Marie, she'd find no such thing. "Such a pleasure to see y'all today." Perhaps she laid the Southern charm on a little thick. The accent wasn't really hers. She'd just heard variations on the slow twang a hundred times a day, every day.

But what could it hurt to commandeer a sugar-sweet line or two? Besides, she hadn't dropped a "bless your heart" yet.

Even if that was the only reasonable response to someone like Stella Burke.

"Natalie." Whether she'd been voted their leader or hadn't bothered to pass around ballots, Stella clearly spoke for the table. "We didn't think you'd stick around this long."

Two weeks? They thought they could push her out of town in two measly weeks? "Oh, bless your heart!" She laughed, not even pretending it was anything but fake. "I'm here until I say, 'I do.' So we'll be bumping into each other plenty, I'm sure." With a flippant wave, she marched away. Her only farewell was a quick "I look forward to it" tossed over her shoulder.

There. Let them talk about that.

She was going to get married here. And she was going to show them all that Rick and Connie O'Ryan didn't define their daughter.

It wasn't until she reached the pickup counter that she heard the slow, quiet clapping.

Harrison's eye glowed as his hands came together. "Well done, Miss O'Ryan."

She rolled her eyes. Even when she actively tried to stay out of the spotlight in this town, she failed. "Hi, Harrison. Marie said you had some things you wanted me to try."

"Yes, ma'am." He motioned her toward the door behind the front counter, which led into the kitchen. "You're going to love this."

He wasn't wrong.

Between whipping up meals for the incoming orders, he'd laid a spread out on a metal counter. Each plate was perfectly presented, the mashed potatoes shaped into a perfect flower and adorned with a sprig of basil, the julienned carrots a pristine pile beside a roasted Cornish game hen.

And that was just one plate.

"Did you go to culinary school while I've been away?"

Harrison's belly shook with the force of his laugh. "Oh no. But a friend of mine taught me a few tricks."

"A friend, huh?" With an elbow to his arm, she gave him a conspiratorial smile. She wouldn't have thought that the big man's ruddy, windswept cheeks could go any redder, but even under day-old whiskers, his face burned brighter than the lighthouse.

"Oh, it's nothing like that." His eye never straying from the plates in front of him, he said, "She's just a friend." But there was a light in his only eye that she'd never noticed before. Just like she had as a child, she wondered what had become of the other eye, and why the patch rather than a glass replacement.

But she knew not to ask. Unless it was a need-to-know question, she kept it to herself.

"Then you do have a special lady!" She tried—and mostly succeeded—to keep the surprise from her voice. She'd only been teasing. Harrison O'Grady had been the town's most famous bachelor. Older than her dad, he'd never even dated, at least as far as Natalie knew. Then again, things could have changed.

Some *had* changed.

But Harrison . . . she'd counted on the man who had snuck her a plate of food when she'd only ordered a glass of water. And somehow, this was still him. And maybe more. Definitely different.

"I thought since . . . well, you don't live in the Crick anymore, so I figured you'd want something more . . ."

She watched as he struggled to find his words, hands clasped in front of him and head bowed. His voice wasn't much more than a whisper. It never had been booming, but there was a hesitancy in it just now that tugged at her heart, had her leaning into him.

It was a fear of rejection, fear of being turned down.

She knew it well.

Resting her hand on his forearm, she said, "Why don't you tell me what you've made?"

He went down the row of plates, listing each entrée and their sides. Game hens and steak. Tuna and lobster rolls. "Because it's not an island wedding without lobster."

She laughed. Marie had suggested lobster traps as decorations for the wedding. Certainly PEI thrived on the fishing industry. She just wasn't sure it belonged at a wedding.

"But won't the lobsters get expensive?" Her practical side reared its head, surely looking for an excuse to keep the whole ordeal from becoming too "island." After all, the location hadn't been her choice. But she could do a thing or two to keep it from being a full-on celebration of red cliffs and lighthouses and lobsters.

"Oh, Captain Mark said he'd sell them to me for a better-than-fair price. Give it a taste."

She did, savoring the sweet meat soaked in melted butter inside a soft bun. Its flavor exploded on her tongue, somehow well-known and brand-new.

This was why everyone wanted to have lobster at their wedding. It was divine.

Then again, so were the tuna and steak and game hen. All of it was perfection. How was she supposed to choose? This was what Russell was supposed to be here for. He was the foodie, the wannabe chef. He'd take a bite of each of these, close his eyes, and moan with pleasure as he experienced every intricate flavor. And then he'd make a decision.

But he wasn't here, and she was alone. Because no one was going to persuade her to call in Justin for help with something as simple as choosing the menu for the reception.

"I guess . . . the . . . Well, what do you do think?"

Harrison looked like no one had ever asked his opinion on anything before. "What do you mean?"

"Which one do you like? Which is your favorite?"

His eyebrows formed a deep ravine as they pulled together, the patch over his eye bunching as his face shifted. "They're all my favorites. That's why I chose them for you."

Such a simple phrase, but it struck her like a softball to the chest. Suddenly the air in the kitchen vanished, and she wheezed, leaning against the cool metal counter for support.

Confusion remained on Harrison's face, but she guessed that he had no idea what he'd just said. Or what it meant. *That's why I chose them for you.*

He'd picked his favorites. Not the easiest. Not the biggest crowd pleasers. Not the cheapest or the most famous. He'd picked what he loved. And he'd done it for her.

She'd walked away from this town, but he hadn't given up on her.

Harrison. Mama Kane. Aretha. Even Justin. Maybe she had more friends here than she remembered.

That realization was enough to squeeze whatever air was left in her lungs all the way out. She gasped and stumbled, but his firm grip on her arm kept her upright. The squint of his eye never wavered from her.

"You okay, Natalie?"

Yes. No.

There were too many memories, the ones she'd hung on to and the ones she'd forgotten.

"Can I get back to you?" She just managed to squeak out the question, but Harrison quickly nodded.

"Sure. Anytime. And if you want to go with someone else to cater, no hard feelings."

She waved and rushed for the door, not even stopping to see if Stella was still holding court at her table. Her gaze zeroed in on the restaurant's glass door, and she charged toward it, bumping into a chair that hadn't been tucked into place. She apologized to the piece of furniture but didn't slow down.

Until she came to a hard stop.

It wasn't the jingling bell or the sudden breeze that accompanied the open door that drew her up short. Neither was it the low whistle that could only have come from Harrison himself.

She came up temporarily lame because of the figure standing in the entryway. He held on to the metal handle, and his posture was relaxed, at ease.

Strangely enough, his nonchalance had the opposite effect on her as every muscle from her toes to her neck pulled tight. But his eyes were bright, lucid, maybe for the first time since she'd been born.

"Hello, Natalie Joy. I heard you were back in town and hoped I'd find you."

His voice hadn't changed much. Still gravelly and deep enough to rattle the windows. But there was a softness to it now. A quiet calm that had always been missing during her childhood.

He held her gaze but kept his distance, like a hunter eye-

152

ing a deer. And she was just as skittish as a newborn fawn. But he blocked her only escape route, so she waited. And she watched.

When the silence had hung in the air for what felt like hours, he finally said, "It's good to see you."

She couldn't say the same, so she settled for an old standard. "Hello, D-D-Dad."

11

Justin couldn't look away from the path of the beacon. As the sun sank toward the horizon in the west, the lighthouse's beam stretched across the dark waters to the east. Each wave shone as it rippled toward the shoreline. The light reached and pulled, calling all ships and vessels to find a safe harbor, because beyond where the light reached, a storm brewed. Its dark clouds unfurled in the wind, their long fingers reaching for the land.

But it wasn't the way the tops of the trees bent beneath the power of the wind that kept him so riveted. It was the way the light illuminated one cove where the land seemed to reach into the sea. The cliffs were gentler there, the sea closer to the land. All around it was only darkness.

And then the light swept over it, illuminating a magical moment.

For an instant he imagined that he could see the glowing twin eyes of a lonely fox. But then the light moved on, and he was left to only his meandering mind, which had a terrible habit of dwelling in the past lately.

As though she was sitting right next to him at the top of

the lighthouse, he could hear Natalie's tale of pirates and fairies. They had been about twelve and reading *Treasure Island* in school. As he did most nights, he found her in the lighthouse, a book covering her face and giggles escaping past the pages.

"Don't you think there might be pirates out there?"

As always, he'd stepped on the squeaky stair on his way up, and she didn't bother to look up at him before she began her story.

"What if Mr. Grady is one of them? What if he escaped but there are fairies out there looking for him? They live in the trees right there." She pointed at the cove just as the light reached it. "And they only come out at night. They wait for us to see them."

Justin nodded, because what was he supposed to say to something so ridiculous? But she didn't really need him. Her eyes glazed over, and she set the book down, staring through the windowpane and into the night, seeing things no one else saw.

"Maybe they want us to help them bring him in. Maybe they hide until we're here, and then they're calling to us to come out there."

"Why would they want our help?"

She looked at him like he had lost his mind, the freckles on her nose disappearing amid the wrinkles there. "Because the pirates are after the gold, of course."

"Of course." Except there hadn't been pirates near the island for a hundred years or more. At least he thought that's what their teacher had said. He might have been thinking about a melody he couldn't get out of his head while Mrs. Abbott was talking.

Natalie rambled on about the pirates and the treasure the fairies guarded and how Harrison Grady fit into the whole thing. It was well past midnight when they took off for their own homes. But the next day Natalie wasn't at the lighthouse or at school. For a minute he wondered if she'd run off to find the fairies.

The next Monday she was back in class and back at the light.

It wasn't until later—many years later—that he learned her mother had locked her in her room for three days that weekend. When Natalie had finally told him the truth, she'd blamed her late-night lighthouse excursions for her mother's anger.

But if the town gossips were to be believed, her mom's anger had a whole lot more to do with Mr. O'Ryan's extra-curricular escapades.

Justin couldn't imagine the pain of a spouse's betrayal like that. He prayed he'd never know it. He thanked God, too, that despite the relative short length of their marriage, his parents had remained true.

But the timeline was never quite clear to him. Maybe Mrs. O'Ryan had lost touch with reality, and then her husband turned his back on his vows. Or maybe she'd snapped *because* he began openly seeing other women.

From what Justin could tell, Mrs. O'Ryan had been a deeply disturbed woman, haunted by voices no one else could hear and battling wars no one else could see.

It didn't mean the whole situation hadn't made him so angry he could punch a wall. So angry he actually had put his fist through drywall. But knowing even a fraction of the poor woman's struggles helped now. If he couldn't ever truly understand, at least he could find some compassion for a family in shreds and a little girl in agony.

Whatever the true reason for that three-day hole, nothing her mother did could keep Natalie away from the lighthouse. Sometimes she'd disappear for a day or two, but she always found her way back. Like perhaps the lighthouse called to her as much as it did to any boat at sea.

One thing he knew for sure. It still called to him.

Half the lyrics in his notebook had been scribbled beneath this light. He'd written the song that he'd been goaded into playing at his last kitchen party right here. This was the place his memories were strongest, which was probably why all of his songs were about Natalie.

As he squinted one more time at the fairies' cove, the old house gave out a loud moan. Probably the wind. Except it was followed quickly by the telltale squeak of the step that had never been fixed.

He jumped to his feet, his notebook falling facedown on the floor. And while his heart suddenly pounded in his throat, he wasn't really surprised to see a head of red hair ascend the steps. In fact, he wondered if he'd conjured her just by dwelling on the past.

But the yelp of surprise she let out when her gaze met his was entirely real.

"Justin! Oh, I'm sorry I didn't mean to bother you I didn't know you were here I'll go."

Natalie's words came out so fast that they were practically a single sentence. But they made him smile, so much like his own when they'd first met here.

"No. It's okay. You can stay." Those weren't exactly the words he'd planned. But when he spoke them, her shoulders drooped, and she heaved a great sigh. He felt like a knight who'd rescued the maiden.

"Thanks. I just needed a . . . quiet space."

"All right." He motioned to the floor, only then stooping to pick up his lyric book. "Welcome to my humble abode. You might find the floor is a little less comfortable than it used to be."

She winced when her hip made contact with the metal. "When did this get so hard?"

"About the time we turned thirty."

A giggle bubbled out of her, low and easy like the inlets that trickled their way into the island. "It has been a while, hasn't it?"

He nodded. Because he didn't have anything to say, he remained silent. The cover on the light spun once. Twice. A third time. She didn't say anything either. Maybe they were afraid to break the spell. Or maybe she didn't have anything on her mind.

Except he knew that wasn't true.

She fiddled with the hem of her pants where her ankles were crossed beneath her. Then she straightened her legs, which lasted for about three seconds. Then they were bent and tucked beneath her chin. All the while, her eyes never strayed from the cove, especially under its blanket of darkness.

There were no fairylike eyes out there tonight. The howling wind and chilly air kept all of the island's animals confined to their homes. But strangely enough, he had no desire to go to his own.

"What're you looking for out there?"

She shrugged, and the valley above her nose deepened. "I'm not sure. Maybe there's a fairy out tonight."

A sudden crack of thunder seemed to signify the collision of their memories, and he reached out a hand to steady her when she jumped. They weren't more than three feet apart, but as far as they could be in the tight circle. It seemed to take an hour for him to reach her arm. When he finally got there, her skin was cool like the night.

Again she refused to look at him, but he could feel something flowing off of her in waves. It was relentless and made her tremble.

Something inside him swore he needed to stay right where he was. So he waited silently.

At the exact moment the clouds released their stores from above, Natalie opened up a storm of her own. "I saw my dad tonight."

He choked on his own tongue, coughing and sputtering and trying for all he was worth to make sense of her words. They couldn't be true. Her dad had been gone for years. He disappeared not too long after she did. Her mom had sort of given up after that.

Maybe he'd misunderstood her. After all, the steady ping of rain against the lighthouse was distracting at best. Maybe she'd seen an old friend or received a call from Russell.

Except there was nothing else she could have said that would make the lines of her neck so tight and her lips narrow beyond recognition. There was no misunderstanding.

Her dad was back in town.

His fist shook where it rested against his bent knee, a knot in his gut pulling tighter and tighter. Rick O'Ryan had no right to come back to the Crick. Not after the way he'd neglected his only daughter. He'd left a trail of broken hearts and broken marriages in his wake, and no one had been sad to see him go.

Least of all Justin, who would have gladly spit at the man, save for the island values his mother had hammered into him in his youth. He'd watched time and again from afar as Rick let his only daughter suffer at the hands of her mother, every scene a painful reminder of his own impotence.

Why hadn't he been able to save her? Why couldn't he step in and rescue her? Why had he been confined to the sidelines, forced to watch his best friend bear such agony?

He'd only ever been able to be there after the fact, to hug her and hold her and make promises he couldn't keep.

And it wasn't enough. It had never been enough.

A flash of lightning severed the sky, a mirror of the anger building in his chest. There was no release for his ire, though, so he clasped his hands in front of him, bowed his head, and prayed for brilliance. There had to be something he could say.

Only there wasn't. So he squeezed her arm again and nodded, hoping to encourage her to continue.

After another boom shook the lighthouse, the rain stopped pelting the windows. Now it came like tears, rolling down each pane with a great and solemn sadness, mimicking every tear they'd shared in this place.

"I was at Grady's, sampling some food for the reception menu. When I went to leave, there he was. Just standing in the doorway. Blocking me in." She fiddled with her watch for a silent second before her eyes lifted to meet his gaze. "I just froze. I didn't have a clue what to do."

"Sure. I mean, no one would have expected him to come back. But we didn't—" He pulled the reins tight before the dig could escape. No one had expected her to come back either. That didn't mean he needed to rub it in.

Apparently he didn't need to spell it out for her, if the

lines around her mouth were any indication. "I know. You never thought you'd see me again, did you?"

He shook his head. "After a year, I gave up hoping. And after that . . . well, I suppose I quit looking for you."

"You were looking for me?"

He bobbed his head and ran his hand over his hair before tugging on his ponytail. "It wasn't like I was sending out a search party or anything. I just had my eyes open. I was paying attention, wondering if you'd show up somewhere, hoping you'd call the house."

She shook her head and bowed it low. "I was mad. I was seventeen and stupid, and I was hurt. I felt like my best friend had abandoned all of our plans."

How was he supposed to respond to that? He could remind her of his dad and the dairy, but she already knew. It didn't seem fair to throw it at her again. And he didn't need to.

Waves of wrinkles crossed her forehead as she lifted her head to look at him. "I felt so guilty for leaving you when you were hurting so badly. But things were getting . . . worse. I had to go, but I wanted you to find me. It's why I left the note."

"I know. Now." He steepled his fingers beneath his chin and watched the sweeping arm of light for several long moments. "Back then I just thought you'd given up on me. On us. But I don't know what I would have done if I'd found your letter." He shrugged. "I like to think I'd have gone looking for you."

A tiny smile crept across her face and then slowly morphed into a frown. "My dad said he'd been looking for me too."

He clenched his fist again, the urge to punch the other man sizzling through his veins. "What did you say?"

Like an owl pulled from a deep sleep, she blinked slowly. "Nothing. I said hi and then got out of there as fast as I could." A strangely satisfied smile replaced her frown, and it was followed by an easy chuckle. "Stella Burke was there, and I think she had apoplexy when she recognized Dad."

He laughed too, a sweet reminder that they'd always known how to find joy in the midst of a storm. As long as they were together, they'd survived.

"When Stella swooned, everyone looked at her, but I ran out the door. I nearly pushed Dad flat on his back to get past him."

"Seems to me that he deserved that. Or more."

She patted his arm. "I'm not going to lie. It felt pretty good not to be cowed in his presence. I mean, I froze up for a second, but I wasn't afraid of him. And I wasn't bullied by him."

A surge of pride swept over him like he hadn't felt since he wrote his first song. "Good for you."

"And you know what the weird thing is?"

"Hmm?" He didn't dare speak too much and risk her shutting down.

"I was really happy to be alone."

"Why's that?"

She pursed her lips to the side, the light shimmering on their gloss. "I'd told myself I could face whatever happened here as long as Russell was by my side."

He tried to keep that particular gut punch from showing on his face, so he steeled his features and gave her a noncommittal grunt.

"But I was really thankful he wasn't here today. As long as he's gone, they can't meet."

"Why don't you want your fiancé to meet your dad?"

Her look said some questions were stupid, and he'd just asked one. "Come on, Kane. You know why."

Of course he knew. But he wasn't entirely clear if she did.

She could tiptoe around the truth all she wanted, claiming that no one should have to meet her dad. He wouldn't blame her one bit for being embarrassed of the philandering drunk.

But he had a sneaking and sure suspicion that Natalie's desire to keep her fiancé and her dad a continent apart had very little to do with keeping Russell from knowing her dad and a whole lot more to do with keeping Russell from knowing *her*.

She was working hard to present a certain version of herself to Russell. He'd seen it when Russell said he was going back to Nashville and at the kitchen party. She'd put on a good front when Russell was by her side. But the minute he stepped away, she'd lit into Justin like he'd set her house on fire.

Which, of course, had only happened that one time. And it had been entirely an accident. *And* he'd put it out with a bag of flour, which they'd cleaned up. So really, the little scar on the wood floor of the kitchen was probably still there, but no one had noticed it as far as he knew.

Natalie probably hadn't told Russell about that experience either.

What else hadn't she told her future husband?

As a tear leaked down her face, he knew her father's return had affected her much more than she wanted to show even him. This wasn't the moment to force the issue. She wasn't ready for him to push.

That raised even more important questions. Would she ever be? And if she wasn't, should he pursue it anyway? Was any of this his concern?

The collective weight of the questions made his brain hurt, so he did the only thing he knew to do. He made a joke. "So, really, the moral of this story is you never know who you're going to run into, so you should never go taste testing without me."

Her hiccuped sob ended on a laugh, and she shook her head. "Of course you're worried about missing out on the food."

"Well, I'm just saying that I have priorities, and you should too. And they should involve making sure I get invited to things like food tastings."

Her mouth hitched in an almost smile. It was more than enough to loosen the knot that had built inside him.

"Speaking of, when do we taste the cake?"

"Um . . . Caden is going to make it. But she's busy with a project for her other job right now."

"The after-school program for teens in Toronto?"

Her head tipped to the side. "How do you know about that?"

He chuckled and shook his head. "You forget that I work with Caden's brother every day. He's pretty proud of his little sister's accomplishments, what with her partnership with Jerome Gale. I could probably tell you every newspaper that's covered their program, every dish she's prepared with her students, and which students show promise."

"That's a small-town hazard, I guess." One pointy shoulder lifted beneath her knit shirt. "Maybe I forgot that everyone here knows everyone and everything going on."

He doubted that she'd forgotten. If anyone would remember that certainty of North Rustico, it was Natalie O'Ryan.

"So, what are you going to do?"

"Wait for Caden to have some spare time, I suppose."

"No, I mean about your dad."

She didn't even flinch. She'd known what he meant, but she was still deft at avoiding that confrontation. With such a direct question, she couldn't dance around it quite as easily. "The only thing I can do." When her eyes met his, they were sure and defiant. "I'm going to avoid him at all costs."

12

"Do you want to meet the florist with me?"

What on earth had compelled her to ask Justin Kane to go to a florist? Worse than that, she'd purposefully tracked him down to ask.

Justin's forehead wrinkled as his eyes squinted. "I think I was pretty clear the other night. I want to be involved with the food tastings."

"Yes, well . . ." Natalie waved him off as her cheeks burned under his scrutiny. And Mama Cheese Sandwich's too. Mama's eyes were bright and her smile all too knowing from her place behind the counter in the little shop attached to the dairy barn.

"There will be more of those. But for now, I have to pick out centerpieces and bouquets and boutonnieres and something for the end of the pews at the church. And I haven't even been in the church since I was fifteen. This is where you come in handy."

He shot a dark gaze at his mother before saying, "You're assuming that I still attend First Church."

Her mouth dropped open, and she couldn't stop blinking. "You're kidding me, right?"

He shrugged. "I'm just saying, you're assuming a lot here."

"I'm sorry. I didn't mean to, I just figured . . ."

Well, she'd figured that his family had had a designated pew at First Church of North Rustico for as long as she could remember. She'd even sat in it with them. And it wasn't just the family legacy. He'd always had a childlike faith, an easy, firm belief that God was with them and had a plan for them. She couldn't remember how old they were when Jeremiah 29:11 was their memory verse for the week, but Justin had marched around the Sunday school room chanting those words until she'd dreamed about them. "For I know the plans I have for you."

Natalie had sometimes wondered if the God who made plans had forgotten to make a plan for her. If he'd known what she faced, why didn't he care?

But Justin had always cared. And he'd believed. And somehow his belief had been hers. When she was lost, he always knew the way back to faith.

She couldn't reconcile the idea of that faith-filled child with a man who no longer attended services, who had given up on God. Even she, amid her deepest questions, hadn't turned her back on the God of the Bible.

"You didn't really stop?" She dropped her voice to a whisper as she prayed he hadn't. "Did you?"

The three lines between his dark eyebrows vanished like they'd never been there. "Of course not. But you shouldn't assume that things are just the same."

She screwed up her face, made a fist, and playfully slugged him in the shoulder. "Don't do that to me."

Some change was to be expected. Other changes could throw off the axis of her entire world. Her father had already returned. Justin couldn't go anywhere.

He laughed and rubbed his arm. "I see your jab hasn't changed much. Or improved at all."

A chuckle from Mama Kane said she was enjoying their interchange, perhaps almost as much as Natalie. But playful banter wasn't why she'd walked down the boardwalk from the inn to the dairy.

She was here to call on Justin for his promised assistance. And if having him with her when she went to see Lois Bernard—who was still the only florist within an hour's drive—meant she might have an easier conversation, then that was an added perk.

Natalie didn't *need* him to accompany her. She'd faced down Stella Burke already. And she was plenty capable of handling whatever gossip grenades Lois might toss in her direction. Back when Rick O'Ryan had found every way he could to make his family the scandal of the community, Lois had been merely an apprentice to Stella's master.

Maybe that hadn't changed either.

But just in case, it wouldn't hurt to have some backup. And if Justin was her only choice, well, so be it. He'd proved he cared enough to let her join him at their lighthouse. He'd even listened while she talked—or didn't—about her dad. If nothing else, their evening in the lighthouse was a reminder that they'd been friends once. And they might be able to be again.

"So, what do you say? Want to look at some flowers?"

He narrowed one eye and rubbed at his chin. His fingernails caught on his whiskers, the gentle raking barely making it past the low bawl of the cattle next door.

"Promise to take me next time you're checking out anything to do with food?"

She snickered. "I suppose."

"Good enough." With a tip of his head toward the door that led to the barn, he said, "Let me finish up my chores and let Dillon know I'm going to be gone. I'll be back in fifteen minutes."

After Justin disappeared, Mama Kane's gaze fell on Natalie so heavy that she tried to shrug it off. But the older woman said nothing. In fact, she barely moved. Only the slow rise and fall of her eyebrows indicated she had something on her mind. And if it was on her mind, it was soon to be on her tongue.

But strangely, she remained silent. Which only made the weight of her inspection that much heavier.

Natalie squirmed in the silence, sidling over to a display of pungent cheese rounds, some nearly strong enough to knock her on her backside.

Still Mama Kane's eyes followed her. The paperwork spread across the counter lay forgotten, her elbows propped on the wooden slab and her chin on folded hands. Her eyes narrowed, her general survey turning pointed and intentional.

Shooting a glance out of the corner of her eye, Natalie waited for Mama Kane to look away.

She didn't so much as blink.

The silence felt like it had been lingering for nearly an hour, but when she glanced at her watch, Justin had been gone exactly ninety seconds. She couldn't handle this for another thirteen minutes, so she finally faced her surrogate mother.

"What?"

Mama Kane shook her head as a smile crawled across her

pale pink lips. She adjusted the black ponytail that matched her son's and said, "It's just so nice to see you back here. It's like a piece of our life has been missing. And now you're back."

Natalie wheezed on an uneven breath, suddenly finding the air too thin. Who said stuff like that? She wasn't a missing piece. She was just Natalie. And certainly no one had been lost without her. They'd all gone on with their lives. They hadn't needed her.

Just like she hadn't needed this island or this town.

"Oh, not really. I'm sure you've all been better than good. I mean, look at the farm. It's thriving." She wasn't entirely sure that was true, but when Mama Kane's sapphire eyes lit up, she knew she'd been right.

"Justin is doing a wonderful job. We're growing and have increased production and sales by nearly 50 percent in the last year." She ran her fingers across the spreadsheets on the counter. "He's so talented. But . . ."

The way she drew out the word felt like a hand around Natalie's throat. As her mind filled in the blank, the fingers tightened.

But this farm was never quite enough for him.

But his music will always be his first love.

But he's met someone else. Someone special. And she hates the farm and will take him far away.

At the last, Natalie clawed at her throat, trying to release the pressure there. Trying to snag a thimble of air. What if there was another woman in his life? Someone he hadn't bothered to mention. Someone she didn't have a right to know.

"But it doesn't mean that there hasn't been something missing." As Mama Kane looked toward the door where her son had disappeared, her smile faltered. "He's laughed more in the last three days than in the three years before that."

"That can't be true." She ended on a strangled laugh, desperate to hear Mama Kane confirm it. Equally eager to hear her deny it.

Mama Kane's eyes zeroed in on hers until she couldn't break away. She was pinned, frozen in place, and even her heart seemed to slow down as she waited for whatever bomb was about to drop.

"Just because someone keeps moving forward doesn't mean he's moved on."

Moved on? From what? From her?

She had so many questions but no time to ask them as Justin barreled into the room. His expression was as sour as if he'd gotten a whiff of rotting cheese.

"Stupid cow," he mumbled.

"All right, dear?" The intensity in Mama Kane's voice from three seconds before disappeared.

He nodded. "That mom in the pasture is refusing to feed her calf. Even after I walked through that slop to bottle-feed it at four in the morning. And then she gave me an angry head to the stomach for my trouble. If she does that again"—he flailed an arm in the general direction of the recalcitrant cow and her hungry offspring—"then . . ."

His eye caught Natalie's, her gaze wide and disbelieving.

"Well, never mind. Let's go buy some flowers."

She wasn't quite sure she wanted this version of Justin to run the errand with her. She wasn't sure she could survive spending a few minutes with him, let alone a few hours.

He scowled as he wiped the muddy bottom of his shoe onto a metal rug.

Then again, scowly Justin might be just the version she needed to face Lois Bernard.

◆◆◆◆◆

Lois had set up her "flower shoppe" in a structure that was little more than a potting shed, most likely built sometime before either Natalie or Justin was born and situated directly beside her old farmhouse. She'd been a Kane Dairy neighbor for as far back as anyone could remember.

The midmorning sun danced behind passing clouds, which seemed to be caught in a riptide that pulled them toward the deep ocean, but the sky hadn't ever been quite so blue. It nearly hurt her eyes, so Natalie kept her gaze on the lush grass that grew right along where the road met the dirt. Between green blades, she could just make out the red earth below. With each gust of wind, the dirt seemed to wink below the moving grass.

Before she even realized why, she began to smile. It couldn't be from something as simple as red dirt or towering pines that swayed to a song she couldn't hear.

But maybe it was.

"So why didn't Marie make this grand trip with you? I thought she was your wedding planner."

Natalie sucked on her tooth for a long second. "I'm not really sure what's going on with her. But I don't think she's feeling very well."

He made a face, and she knew he remembered the last time they'd all been together at his barn. Natalie could only ever remember one of her friends having the flu for several weeks. But that hadn't ended up being the flu at all. It had been so much worse.

Something was definitely going on with Marie, but Natalie wasn't sure it was her place to ask. And she wasn't going to say a word about her suspicions to anyone else. That's how rumors got started and feelings got hurt.

"I think she'd rather stay near the house, so I promised her that I had all the help I needed." She flashed him the cheesiest smile she could muster, showing off all her teeth. "See? Help."

His mouth scowled, but it didn't reach his eyes, which were lit by something akin to humor. "And what exactly is it you want me to do?"

"Be there. Offer sage advice. Suggest floral arrangements. Identify every plant by its Latin name." She tried to keep a straight face but broke on her last instruction, giggles bubbling free.

"So it's going to be like this?"

Swallowing a chuckle, she tried to remain serious. "Like what?"

"You just wanting to waste my time."

"Not at all." She shook her head hard as they turned down the long gravel lane. A towering elm cast shadows over their every step, and the breeze sent shivers down her arms. "I'm just trying to help you get the most out of helping a friend. I wouldn't want Adam to ask what you've been doing for Russell lately and you to have nothing to report."

He didn't even try to scowl this time, and his laughter matched hers. "Fair enough, O'Ryan. At least you're honest about it."

Honest. Sure. Because this invitation, this trip, had nothing to do with a niggling feeling deep in her stomach that kept reminding her that when her dad was around, Justin had always been her safe place.

At least not much.

The two-story house had long since lost the green paint off its ocean-facing side, the wind and salt spray taking care of that. And the gingerbread details along the top of the porch had become lost beneath layers of cobwebs.

She'd read the story of Hansel and Gretel as a child and immediately thought of Lois Bernard and her home. There was a sweetness to the house that had always appealed to the children of the town. But Mrs. Bernard wasn't quite as appealing as the old woman in the story.

So Natalie had avoided the house for most of her childhood, lest she end up with a fate worse than Hansel and his sister.

When they reached the shed, Justin put his hand on the door handle and raised his eyebrows. The question was clear. *Are you ready?*

Of course not. And not just because of silly childhood imaginings. But she didn't have another option. This was entirely about flowers for her wedding. So she forced a tight smile and nodded.

With a sweep of his arm, he opened the door and ushered her into the dimly lit room, his hand light on the small of her back, his fingers shooting sparks up and down her spine.

There was no time to consider why her body insisted on reacting like they'd never touched before, as they were immediately confronted by the short woman standing at a work-table that took up most of the room.

"What do you need?" Her words were curt and sour, and Natalie had to wonder, if she treated all of her customers this way, how had she ever managed to keep a business going for so many years? Perhaps it had more to do with a dearth of options than excellent customer service.

"Do you have an appointment?"

Yep, definitely that lack of options thing.

As much as she wanted to give Lois what she deserved, a little voice in the back of her mind reminded her that she was back in the spotlight and back in front of a gossip ring that must have loved having her family down the street. So she swallowed whatever retort was begging for release and cleared her throat. But before she could speak, Justin cut her off.

"Mrs. Bernard, of course we have an appointment. For the Jacobs-O'Ryan wedding. It's bound to be the biggest event of the summer."

The baggy skin around Lois's eyes drooped a little less, her hunched shoulders perking up just a bit. "The biggest event?" she mumbled.

"Absolutely. Nearly a hundred and fifty *out-of-town* guests, who are just dying to see the beauty of the island." He motioned to the arrangement on her table, its rich purples and blues a testament to the island's extravagant flora. Stems of lavender complemented bulbs of ivory tucked into rich greenery as deep as the pine trees that towered over the coast like sentinels. "Your flowers could be the thing that makes all of those guests fall in love with the island."

Lois gave a little pat to her white curls and curved her painted lips. With a narrowed gaze, she stared at Justin, purposefully ignoring Natalie. "You're Kathleen's boy, aren't you?" She asked it like she hadn't seen him nearly every day of his life and been in the ladies' auxiliary with Mama Kane for a hundred years, and it made Natalie want to roll her eyes at whatever game Lois was playing.

If Justin had the same impulse, he didn't act on it. When he spoke, there wasn't even a hint of sarcasm. "Yes, ma'am."

She pursed those wrinkled lips, her lipstick seeping into the cracks as she pinched her stem trimmer with knobby fingers. The little tool clicked together, echoing without a blossom to snip.

"I suppose that girl at the inn called me about someone stopping by."

That was certainly Marie. Natalie was sure Lois knew it.

They didn't have to put up with this. She'd go pick some wildflowers for the wedding if this kept up.

But just when she was about to tell Lois that, Justin put his hand on her back. It was still and infinitely calming, and she heaved a sigh, releasing every choice word she had for Lois.

This wasn't exactly the scowling Justin Natalie had expected, but she was grateful for him in any form at the moment.

"Do you have some pictures or something we could look at?"

Through a narrowed gaze, Lois eyed them like she worried they couldn't be trusted with her samples. Finally she nodded and turned to pick up an enormous photo album before dumping it on the worktable across from the half-filled vase at her elbow. "You can look through that. I can do any of those."

She went back to work without another word, leaving Natalie and Justin to shrug at each other and begin flipping through the thick pages.

Natalie wasn't sure if she'd expected pictures cut out from bridal magazines or printed off the internet, but with each page her jaw dropped.

Every corner of every sheet was filled with stunning images of bright bouquets and boutonnieres. First Church was recognizable but dressed in its finest ferns and white lilies.

The gazebo along the boardwalk had been adorned in floral garlands twisting around each pole, and a bride and groom kissed unashamedly, framed by Lois's stunning work.

For a split second Natalie thought someone else must have crafted such lovely and creative arrangements.

And then there was Lois, unmistakable in a floral tea-length skirt and bright pink blouse, with an arm around a bride who looked an awful lot like little Laura Masser.

She did a triple take before jerking back. "Is that Laura Masser?" she whispered.

Justin tugged on the end of his ponytail and nodded.

"But she's eight."

"More like twenty-two. And it's Hughes now."

She couldn't explain why that felt like such a punch in the gut. She'd barely known the little girl who lived three houses down. Natalie was almost done with school by the time Laura started, and they'd never had much reason to nod at each other in the street. But . . . married? It was like this town insisted on reminding her what she'd have had to look forward to if she'd stayed.

A wedding at twenty. To a man like her father. Only to end up like her mother.

She cringed at the very idea, her stomach suddenly feeling as steady as a buoy in a hurricane.

"Laura picked the traditional red roses." Lois didn't bother to look up at them.

Right. Focus on the flowers. For her wedding. To a man completely unlike her father. Who would take her back to a place far away from here.

"I like the purple ones."

"Orchids." Again, Lois couldn't be bothered to look up

from her steady snip-snipping. But she was right. "Fragile but pretty. Bouquet and centerpieces?"

"And something for the end of the pews in the church."

This caught Lois's eyebrows like a fishhook, which seemed to ask, *They're letting you have the wedding at the church?* But she said only, "Where's the reception?"

"The old barn at Kane Dairy."

Knowing eyes traveled to Justin and assessed him. "Rustic?"

"With soft accents like the flowers."

"I'll show you what I'm going to do in a couple weeks. Come back on the Thursday after next." Lois pointed to the door, effectively dismissing them before tucking long stems into her vase.

"Um . . ." Natalie took an awkward step toward the door.

"We'll see you then," Justin said, escorting her out the door and into the fresh air, which was sweeter than land to a drowning man. Compared to the dimness indoors, the sun burned her eyes, and she hobbled along as she rubbed her face to dispel the spots that had been seared into her corneas.

When they reached the end of the drive, Justin chuckled. "She's something else."

Natalie nodded. "That's an understatement. Why is she so . . . hostile?" Despite the laugh that carried her words, another question leapt to Natalie's mind. *Why am I so hostile?*

That wasn't fair. She had a right to be angry in this town. Hadn't she suffered here? No one knew how bad it had gotten. Not even Justin.

She'd never told him about the rumors whispered in the girls' locker room just loud enough for her to hear. Or the guys who had thought she'd inherited her dad's wayward morals.

If she'd ever told Justin about those, he'd have ended up kicked out of school. There weren't enough detention slips for him to defend her honor, which he'd have insisted on doing.

And certainly she'd never told him what Stella Burke had said when she'd so eloquently invited Natalie to leave town.

She'd given herself permission to carry that bitterness around. She'd told her therapist that she'd dealt with it. And in Nashville, maybe she had. On PE Island, not so much.

But, God help her, she did *not* want to end up like Lois Bernard.

13

The only bad thing about Caden's breakfasts was that Natalie could barely move after indulging. This particular morning, she hadn't been able to stop halfway through her two fluffy blueberry pancakes covered in sweet berry compote and topped with a dollop of light-as-air fresh whipped cream.

A double helping of perfectly crisp smoked bacon hadn't helped. But it sure had tasted good.

When the little curly-haired boy at the table next to hers had eyed her lone spice muffin, she'd jokingly picked it up and pretended to take a bite. Except there was no pretending when she got a whiff of it. The rich scents had caught her attention and held on. One bite was never going to be enough.

By the time she pressed the pad of her finger to the crumbs on her plate and popped them in her mouth, she couldn't meet the little boy's gaze. Or breathe. She needed to loosen her belt.

As she pushed back her chair, Marie sidled up to the table, her hands full of empty dishes. Apparently Natalie wasn't the only one who'd cleaned her plate this morning.

"Good morning." Marie's face was tight, her eyes narrow,

hollow. Dark purple circles marred the area below each eye. And the color that had once been in her cheeks had disappeared. Even her lips were white.

Natalie shot to her feet and passed over the traditional greetings in favor of grabbing for the pile in Marie's arms that seemed in imminent danger of tumbling to the floor. "Are you all right?"

Marie perked up. At least she seemed to try. But her smile fell flat, and her eyes glistened with unshed tears.

"Bless your heart." Natalie pulled her chair farther out and tried to guide Marie into it. "What's wrong? Should I get Caden? Or Seth?"

A small shake of Marie's head silenced her. "Seth's gone this week. He's—he's in Boston delivering a . . . Well, it doesn't matter. I just don't sleep so well when he's not here. I'll be fine."

Fine seemed an awfully relative term for someone who looked like she'd fall over under the weight of a sneeze.

Marie didn't give her room to argue as she waved toward the kitchen. "I need to talk with you about a few wedding things. Do you have time now? Let me just drop these off and I'll be right back."

"Of course." Stretchy yoga pants and a place to lie down would have to wait until after their discussion.

When Marie arrived back at the table, Natalie couldn't help but ask, "Are you sure you're okay? We can do this later. I'm free. I'm just . . . well, I was thinking about going to do some more work at the barn. It's coming along. Nearly the whole interior is painted, and Justin is bringing in the tables next week. Surely this can wait until you're feeling better."

"I'm all right. Really." Marie slid into the seat across from Natalie.

She leaned forward as Marie flipped a notebook open.

Pen in hand, Marie pointed to three lines. "Caden is working on the cake options."

Oh dear. Not more food. Her stomach churned, and she had to physically bite back another moan.

And yet, somehow her mouth was watering already at the very idea of Caden's light, decadent sweets. Fluffy cake that literally melted with each bite. Creamy frosting so rich that it zinged at the back of her throat and made her feel a little light-headed. A tangy fruit filling between layers.

Oh dear, indeed. This was the stuff of dreams.

And stomachaches.

Marie circled something on her paper. "She'll have them ready next Thursday. Will Russell be back by then?"

The question was completely innocent, but it still felt like a slap to the face. She swung a hand up to cover the stinging on her cheek, even if it wasn't real.

Forcing her hand back to her lap, she said, "I don't think so. His last call said they have to rerecord half the album. And he's the producer. He has to be there. He also has to get the album out on time or risk the distribution deal he made with a bigger label."

Marie nodded like she actually understood, but Natalie wasn't even sure she'd gotten the language right. Russell hadn't exactly invited her into his work world. Everything she'd learned about music had come from picking up snippets in his conversation. And from listening to Justin talk about his dreams for years.

"I'm so sorry to hear that. I'm sure he'll be back in plenty of time for the wedding."

Natalie wasn't quite so confident, but she pushed down

the doom that rose in her throat. Her and Russell's definitions of "plenty of time" were at least three weeks off. In her book, he should be here. Now. This was his idea, after all.

In his mind, he could pop in the day before the ceremony, don his tux, stand at the front of the church, and call it good.

But that wasn't Marie's fault. She was only trying to be encouraging.

So Natalie quickly agreed and forced the conversation into other—although she realized too late, perhaps not safer—waters. "Justin will be here to help me choose the cake."

"Justin?" Marie's tone took on a decidedly teasing note, the corner of her mouth ticking up two notches. "Aretha said you two were 'thick as thieves' when you were kids. Is that true?"

Staring at the ceiling, she debated if there was any use in denying the truth. But it was irrefutable. No matter who Marie talked to, everyone in this town would testify to the friendship that had kept them both afloat all those years.

"Yes. We were friends. The very best."

The bags below Marie's eyes seemed to twitch with sadness. "But not now?"

Her mouth went dry, and nothing could make it easier to swallow. When she finally managed to get a response out, it sounded like it had been run through sand. "Not now. We . . . we lost touch." What a lame explanation. What a weak confession.

They hadn't lost touch. They'd lost each other. She'd given up on him. She'd stopped waiting for him, and she'd refused to come back for him.

It was a smack to her other cheek, this one coming with regret that billowed around her.

Wiping her nose with the back of her hand, Natalie suddenly shoved her chair out. "Excuse me. I need to go. Can we talk about the rest of this later?"

"I'm sorry if I asked too many questions."

Not too many. Just the wrong ones.

Natalie nearly ran to her room, where she flung off her too tight belt, shucked her restricting jeans, and tugged on a pair of black stretch pants that had seen her through hours and hours on the treadmill in her living room. These weren't going-out pants, not even for the gym. As much as the harbor boardwalk and its tangy air tangling her hair called to her, what she wanted and needed most right now was a moment alone. And maybe a good cry.

And definitely not thinking about how Justin might have had every right to be angry with her for leaving.

Maybe she shouldn't have left without telling him good-bye in person.

But she'd been afraid. Afraid that he'd beg her to stay. Afraid she'd have been unable to refuse. Afraid that she'd end up like Connie O'Ryan—married to a man who didn't love her and raising a child who only served to remind her of that fact.

Except she still should have seen him . . .

Her mind played out the scene as it could have been, as it should have been. Held so tenderly in his arms, hearing the sadness in his voice. But the hope. The promise.

It didn't have to be the end.

The moment replayed time and again as she curled into a ball on her bed, her eyes closed to focus on what might have been. On the moment she'd robbed herself of.

Why had she let Stella Burke rob her of that good-bye?

◆◆◆◆◆

Hours later Natalie woke to a soft knock on the door, and her rumbling stomach responded loudly. She'd wondered if she'd ever be hungry again, but the breads and pastries hadn't lingered, their effects wearing off too quickly. The clock said it was well after two in the afternoon.

Her eyes felt like sandpaper against her eyelids, but the tears had dried, the fog lifted.

She stumbled from the bed, which was still fully made, and bumped into the door.

"Housekeeping," came the call from the other side.

"Oh, I'm fine." Her voice sounded more Rip van Winkle than short-term napper, so she cleared her throat and tried again. "Thank you, though."

A soft set of footsteps disappeared down the hall, and Natalie leaned against the wall, a hand to her empty stomach.

Caden always put snacks on the buffet in the afternoons. Maybe she'd set them out early today. Ignoring her hair and her outfit, which probably looked as wrinkled as her voice sounded, she cracked open the door, peeked out to make sure the housekeeper had left, and tiptoed toward the back staircase. It emptied out to the hallway near the kitchen, which led straight into the dining room.

Perfect. She could avoid running into nearly everyone, except maybe Caden, who wouldn't give her any grief for not looking her best.

The house was cool, the walls smooth as she ran her fingers along them. The steps were nearly silent until she reached the third-to-last one, which gave a low groan. She froze, her heart skipping a beat.

But it drew no notice, and she kept going. The dining room was empty, even its tables stripped bare. She heard nothing coming from the kitchen. Apparently Caden wasn't teaching a class today.

Surely that meant she'd gotten the treats out early.

Stealing across the room, Natalie held her breath. Please let there be something to tide her over. A cookie. A cupcake. Hope burst inside her. Maybe even a brownie.

But when she reached the antique credenza, the glass cake stand that usually housed the goodies was empty.

Rats.

She let out a stiff breath through her nose and crossed her arms. She was either going to have to—

A sudden crash made her jump. Instantly she ran for the kitchen, where the banging originated. Shoving the swinging door open, she plowed into the room, which at first glance appeared to be empty.

Then a low groan came from the far side of the kitchen island. From the floor.

Natalie burst around the edge of the counter and fell to her knees beside the crumpled form leaning against the island's cabinet doors, careful to dodge the chocolate cupcakes scattered across the tile.

Brushing the curls out of Marie's face, Natalie pressed her hands to the other woman's cheeks. "Marie? Marie? Can you hear me?"

Her eyelids didn't even flicker, but her lips parted on a moan.

Everything inside Natalie knotted up, her eyes burning and ears ringing.

Do something. Do something.

She had to do something.

"Caden! Caden!" She held her breath, waiting, praying. *God, please let Caden be here.* But there was no response. No running footfalls that correlated to the urgency in Natalie's voice.

The housekeeper! But what was her name?

Her brain bounced and twirled and reached for any memory of actually meeting the woman face-to-face. She had nothing.

Gasping for as much as air as she could, she closed her eyes and yelled what she hoped would reach every part of the house. "Help! Please! We're in the kitchen! Help us!"

She wrapped her arm around Marie's frail shoulders and pulled Marie against her chest. The angle was awkward, but it was the best she could do on her knees beside a silver tray that must have caused the clatter.

She waited. She prayed and waited and cried for help. But the house was empty. Seth had gone to Boston, Marie had said. And Caden and the housekeeper had clearly left. It was just her and Marie.

And a fear like she'd never known before.

Marie's shoulders rose and fell in odd, uneven patterns, her lips still open and eyes unmoving.

She was breathing. But for how much longer? Icy fingers slashed down Natalie's back, and she jumped into action.

After resting Marie on the floor, she dashed for the stairs, taking them two at a time despite her short legs. Her side ached like she'd run a marathon when she made it to the top, her breathing gasps at best.

Still, she didn't slow down, her feet eating up the hardwood flooring as she slid past her room, caught herself on the jamb, and yanked herself inside. Scrambling for her phone, she wrenched it off the dresser and dashed back down the stairs.

"Oh, Lord." It was the only prayer she could manage, and it seemed so inadequate as she pressed the button on her phone that would connect her to local emergency services. The operator picked up just as she slid back onto her knees by Marie's head.

"What is your emergency?"

The man on the other end of the line sounded so calm and collected. While she knew he was trained to do just that, she wanted to yell that he wouldn't be so cool if he was on this side of the phone. "A woman fainted."

"Okay, where is she now?"

Natalie froze. She had no idea what the address of the inn was. Her eyes scoured the kitchen for something that might tell her. Or she could run to the front of the house and check. But there was no time for that. "We're at Rose's Red Door Inn in North Rustico. Right on the harbor. Along the boardwalk. Big blue house. Red door."

The sound of his keyboard on the other end matched the tempo of her nerves tightening. Each tap making her want to jump out of her own skin.

"Hurry. Please. I think . . ." She couldn't say it. She wasn't sure if it was true. But if it was . . . They just had to get here.

"All right. We have someone on their way. Have you tried to revive her? Call her name?"

"Of course." How stupid did he think she was?

"Did she hit her head?"

"I don't know." She ran her hand over Marie's head, her fingers reaching past the hairline to the side of her skull.

There. What was that? Gently she pressed her hand to a distinct bump. "I think maybe she did. I'm not really sure."

"Is she bleeding?" He was still so ridiculously calm, she wanted to scream.

Just hurry. Didn't he understand? Marie was in trouble.

"No. I don't see any blood." That was a good sign, right? There was always blood in the worst scenarios, at least in the movies. But there was nothing here. The floor was clear, save for the cupcakes she'd given up watching out for, which were now mashed against the hardwood.

"All right. Stay on the line with me. It's going to be okay." Suddenly the last thing in the world she wanted to hear was this too calm man making promises that he couldn't possibly guarantee. "No, I need to call—I need to call Justin."

It was out before she even realized what she was saying, but it was exactly what she needed.

"I need you to stay on the phone with me."

"Just send help. We'll be here." And she hung up on the emergency services operator. It was like being freed from a chain she didn't even know she'd been wearing.

Then she was calling Justin, her fingers flying over numbers that weren't saved in her phone but had been stored in her mind for decades. It was his home number, and she prayed he'd be there. *Please let him answer.* It rang once, and her stomach flipped. Then again. Her lungs stopped. A third time, and she squeezed her eyes closed. On the fourth she let out a sigh. He wasn't there.

"Hello?" His tone was clipped. He was out of breath. But it was unmistakably Justin on the other end of the line.

"It's me. It's Natalie."

"Natalie? What's—"

"Marie. She fainted. Something's wrong. She won't wake up. I called 9-1-1. They're on the way, but I-I just . . ."

"Are you at the inn?"

She nodded and then remembered that he couldn't see her. "Yes."

"I'll be right there." The call ended, and she stayed right where she was, cradling Marie's head in her lap and whispering a prayer she didn't even know the words to. At some point, someone had told her that it was okay not to know what to pray. God knew what was on her heart. So as she whispered, "Please, please, please," she trusted that heaven knew her real cry.

Suddenly the back door slammed, feet pounded, and Justin appeared. His shoulders nearly spanned the entry, but he barely paused to take in the scene before him.

From her place on the ground, Natalie watched him with eyes that suddenly rushed with tears. She wasn't alone any longer. And it somehow gave her permission to let go of whatever had been holding her together.

He dropped to her side, his fingers immediately at Marie's throat. "Where's Seth?"

"She said he went out of town."

"When did she say that? Did you talk to her right before she collapsed?"

"No." Her hair shook in her frantic refusal. "This morning she told me. I was coming downstairs to get something to eat a few minutes ago, and I heard a crash in here. She was already passed out."

"Her pulse is weak but there. And her skin is kind of clammy, but her lips aren't turning blue. She's getting enough oxygen."

He stabbed his fingers through his hair, which hung loose and damp at his shoulders.

Only then did she realize that he had the freshly scrubbed glow of a recent shower about him. He smelled of man's soap, clean and crisp as island air. Had she called him out of the shower?

She didn't have the guts to ask. She had no reason to. But the question prodded at the back of her skull anyway.

"You called for the ambulance?"

"They're on their way. I just didn't want to . . ." It wasn't easy to tell him that she couldn't handle this alone.

Because she could handle it. She just didn't want to.

"It's okay. I'm here. I'll stay with you."

She nodded her thanks, then shook her head. "Shouldn't we call someone?"

"I told Dillon where I was going. He'll track his sister down, and she'll find us."

"Caden. Goo-d." A tiny sob escaped on the tail of a hiccup, and he slipped his arm around her shoulders. It was big and strong and so different from what it had been fifteen years before. His embrace was warm and soothing, yet it launched a riot inside her that she couldn't—wouldn't—name.

Something inside her demanded to lean against him, while something else fought the urge like her life depended on it.

In the end, the sirens saved her. As they wailed through town, echoing across the harbor, Justin scooped up Marie and hurried through the house toward the red door. Natalie flung it open for him, and they met the paramedics at the front of the walkway.

She glanced down the street, suddenly aware of just how public this was going to be. But if there were peeping eyes investigating the flashing lights, they remained indoors. *Thank you, Lord*.

"Is she still unconscious?" A man in a blue uniform rushed toward them.

Justin frowned, looking about as pleased with the stupid question as she had been with the too-calm operator. Adjusting the limp form in his arms, he said, "It would appear that way."

"Right." The man disappeared with his partner to get the gurney from the back of the truck and then reappeared, rolling it up the paving stones of the front walk. "Does she have any conditions we should know about?"

Justin set Marie down with a soft, "I don't think so," and the EMTs immediately began checking her vitals. With fingers below her jaw and a flashlight dilating her eyes, they worked efficiently and quietly until the silence was nearly enough to make Natalie scream.

Mostly it made her want to tell them what she suspected. Justin had been so decisive. He would know better than she would, right?

If she revealed her guess and it was wrong, she'd be the start of a whirlwind of rumors.

Or worse—what if she was right, but Marie didn't want anyone to know?

Say something. Say something.

The EMTs didn't.

She didn't.

As they began strapping Marie in place with bright yellow restraints, the tension in the air was palpable. Or maybe that was just her. She reached for anything to hold, anything to stabilize the emotions swirling inside her chest.

The nearest option was Justin's hand. So she grabbed it and held on until her fingers trembled. But even then she didn't let go.

All of a sudden they were wheeling her down the walk, and Natalie burst. "Where are you taking her?"

"Queen Elizabeth."

The hospital in Charlottetown. Of course. They were just over an hour away. Faster for the ambulance.

"Are either of you relatives?" The shorter one eyed them with suspicion.

"No. Just friends."

"Then you can't ride with us."

Right. Sure. That made sense. But then who would be with her? And what if something happened and they gave her something that could hurt her?

Just as the short one slammed the bay door, she sucked in a deep breath and let it out as fast as she could before she could talk herself out of it. "I think she might be pregnant!"

14

The hospital was as cold and sterile as any one building could be, its hallways starkly white. Even the doctors in their lab coats seemed to blend into the background and disappear against the whitewashed walls.

Natalie, on the other hand, stood out like a hippo in an ant farm.

Her hair flashed beneath the fluorescent lights, and her eyes slashed back and forth as she cornered a poor nurse for some information.

Justin found that he much preferred to stay out of her way and wait for the nurse to succumb to Hurricane Natalie.

"Where's my friend? Marie Sloane. They just brought her by ambulance."

The nurse shook her head—for the fifth time since they'd arrived ten minutes ago. They'd been on the heels of the ambulance every kilometer of the drive, but when they reached the hospital, they'd had to find a spot in the parking lot while the big white beast pulled up to the sliding emergency doors. He hadn't even turned his truck off before Natalie was out the door and sailing toward the main entrance.

She hadn't slowed down since.

"I don't know where your friend is. If they just brought her in, they could still be processing her."

"She's all alone, but I don't want her to be alone." Natalie wrung her hands against the midlevel counter, but her face remained set. "I need to see her."

The nurse rolled her eyes as though Natalie couldn't understand a word she said. "If she just came in, they're probably treating her."

"When can I see her?"

Okay, maybe the nurse wasn't far off. Natalie ignored everything the petite brunette said, forcing her way into more information with each exchange.

The nurse huffed a loud sigh. "I'm sorry. I can't let you see her. *I* don't even know where she is."

"Can you find her then?" The skin at her jaw tightened, and she whispered, "Please."

"I will." The crisp retorts from behind the desk softened, and the nurse, probably five years younger than Natalie, reached out and patted her arm like she was someone's grandmother. "It's going to take a little time, though. And she may not be able to see anyone right away."

The motion was a kick in the chest for Justin. Some stranger should not be comforting Natalie right now.

He should be.

Sliding to her side, he slipped his arm around her. With a smile at the nurse, he said, "We'll be in the waiting area. Let us know as soon as we can see Marie."

Natalie opened her mouth like she was going to fight him, but when he squeezed her waist, she sagged into him, her fight failing, fear sapping her strength. He half-walked, half-carried her to the little waiting room. It was filled with blue padded chairs, their wooden arms lined up in perfect order. Letting her sink into one, he stood over her to make sure she was stable.

Her eyes were rimmed in red, and her hair had gone flat under the pressure of her combing fingers. But she looked up at him with so much gratitude that he nearly floated right out of the hospital.

Dropping into the seat next to her, he squinted at her, trying to figure out what she was thinking. But she was a vault, a mask holding everything in.

"What's going on in that head of yours?"

She wrinkled her pretty little nose, those freckles that had always fascinated him disappearing into little valleys. And he had a sudden urge to lean forward and kiss it.

To kiss her.

The bottom dropped out of his stomach. Like a roller coaster he'd never agreed to ride, his insides swooped and flipped and spun, leaving him breathless. And more than a little bit angry.

He was not attracted to Natalie O'Ryan. Not anymore. Besides, she was getting married.

Married. Married. Married.

He'd repeat it to himself as many times as he needed to. Because he was not that man. He was not her father.

She'd made her choice. And she'd live with it. She might even be happy with it.

Even if she wasn't, it wasn't his concern. He'd help her out with the wedding stuff. He'd make sure the barn was perfect. And he'd pray that Russell Jacobs took notice before he took off.

Scrubbing a hand down his face, he turned toward the far wall. It'd be much easier to talk with her if he wasn't looking at her. "You're pretty upset. I didn't know you and Marie were so close."

He felt more than saw her shrug.

"We're not *great* friends or anything. It's just . . ."

He didn't want to interrupt her, but he prompted her when she stopped. "Mm-hmm?" But she didn't continue. "Well, you knew she was pregnant. That's something."

"No. Sh." She pressed a finger to her rosy lips as her gaze darted around the nearly empty room. "I don't know that for sure."

His gaze narrowed, and he shook his head. "Then why'd you say that to the EMTs?"

Chewing her lip, she stared at the ceiling as though waiting for a divine answer. Apparently it didn't come because she shook her head and sighed. "It's just a guess. A friend of mine in Nashville, she had some"—her voice dropped even further—"morning sickness like that."

Justin scratched his forehead. "Morning sickness? I thought she had the flu."

"I've never seen the flu last for three weeks."

"Good point." But that didn't explain why she'd waited to tell him and the paramedics. "Why not say something sooner?"

Her eyes grew round, and he could read the truth as plainly as a newspaper.

"Right. You don't like to talk about people."

Another shrug. "Can you blame me?"

No. In fact, it was one of the things he liked best about her. When other girls he knew were busy chirping about so-and-so's terrible haircut or why what's-her-name got fired, Natalie had always walked away. She didn't listen and she didn't share. Probably because she'd been on the other side of gossip for so long.

How much had it cost her to say something about Marie? Especially when she didn't know if it was true.

The sadness in her eyes was easier to recognize now. She'd been caught off guard. She'd been terrified. She'd been forced to speak when she'd felt she shouldn't.

The steel he'd put in place to keep from thinking about how cute her nose was began to soften. He wasn't going to kiss her or anything. Ever. But he could give her some comfort. Slipping an arm across the back of her seat, he let her lean against his shoulder, the chair arms firmly between them.

She hesitated for a fraction of a second. And then she let out a breath and eased against him.

Her shoulder fit into his embrace like it always had, like it had been made for that.

He pushed that thought aside. Maybe he could just think about what needed to be done at the dairy. Yes, feeding schedules and repairs were much safer territories.

They sat together in silence for a long time, watching other waiting friends and family come in and then leave. But still there was no word about Marie. He had to physically hold himself back from voicing the troublesome thoughts that popped up.

Marie would have to be conscious to give them permission to see her. The nurse wouldn't give out her room number without someone giving permission. And if they didn't hear anything, they could end up waiting for the rest of the day and into the night.

Suddenly his phone rang, and he yanked it out of his pocket, jostling Natalie and earning a stern scowl from the nurse. "Sorry," he mouthed in the direction of the desk as he looked at the screen. Caden. Finally.

"Where is she? What's going on?"

"We're at Queen Elizabeth. But we don't have any information."

"I'll call Seth, and then I'll be right there."

"All right."

He expected her to hang up on him, but she sucked in a quick breath before adding quickly, "The hospital needs to know that she's pregnant. Fourteen weeks."

And that was the end of their conversation. Caden hung up without any good-bye, and he stared at his phone for a second, his mind racing to catch up with everything that had just happened. Natalie had been right. And maybe, by doing the thing she'd always abhorred, she'd saved two lives today.

"What'd she say?" He was still a bit dumbstruck when Natalie began badgering him for information. "Is she on her way?"

"Yes." He stared into Natalie's expectant eyes. The crinkles at the corners grew deep with concern and twitched when she tried to hold herself together. And then it struck him. Why this was all so personal for her. Why she didn't want to face this alone. "What happened to your friend who had morning sickness so bad?"

She wiggled away from his shoulder, catching his hair and pulling it. He winced, and she latched on to that movement.

"You should cut your hair." She pinched the end of a strand, picked it up, and let it drop. "It never used to be long."

"I like it this way." At least, he liked that it made a statement. Even if it happened to be a juvenile one. Natalie had never liked guys with long hair. She'd said so at least half a dozen times in their youth. And growing his hair out had been a subtle reminder to himself that he didn't care what she thought.

"No you don't." She sat forward and leaned her elbows on her knees. Her narrowed gaze said she was looking for a fight, looking for a distraction.

He wasn't going to play into her hand. "Your friend, you said she got sick a lot. What happened?"

Natalie pulled away, crossing her arms over her chest. Her eyes closed, and the lines around her mouth grew distinct. Finally her forehead wrinkled the space between her eyebrows. "I don't want to—"

"I'm not asking you to talk about someone else. Tell me how it affected you."

The tension in her face released by fractions, but always the lines at her mouth remained. "Melody was my first friend in Nashville. She was a little bit older. More established." Her gaze lifted to the ceiling as her voice trailed off.

"How did you meet?"

"She was the night manager at the hotel." Her crossed arms made a subtle shift, and she began hugging herself, preparing for whatever was to come. "She was so kind to me. She would bring in these pecan caramel brownies that she made every weekend. Her husband couldn't get enough of them, but she'd always steal a few away for me and the other front desk staff. And then she got pregnant."

In his experience that was a statement usually followed by squeals of glee between women, but Natalie looked on the verge of tears. Just as he was about to cut her off, to tell her that it was all right to end the story there, she let the rest loose.

"She was so sick. Always sick. I'd thought it was supposed to just come in the morning, but if she was awake, she was sick. She started missing work, and then they brought in a temporary replacement. She'd be back after maternity leave, they said. She just needed bed rest. But I went to visit her. And her eyes . . . they were . . . hollow. Her skin sagged. She was this wonderfully curvy woman who lit up a room. Before."

She swallowed, and it was audible. Maybe because he couldn't focus on anything else. Or maybe because he could see the movement at her slender throat, unable to look away.

"She was really ill, but the last time I saw her, she said the baby was fine, and she'd be okay too. But she wasn't."

Natalie didn't move—not even to swipe at a lone tear that had found its way down her cheek. He had to reach for her, to somehow comfort her in the midst of this painful memory. He'd pushed for it. And now it was tearing him apart to hear her voice crack. Squeezing her hand, he tried to tell her that she wasn't alone even though no words could do it justice.

"They admitted her into the hospital on a Tuesday night. It was my first day of work that week, and I remember thinking that I'd go visit her when I had a day off." She licked her lips, closed her eyes, and didn't seem to care about the stream of tears running down her cheeks. "She died on Wednesday morning. Her and the baby. She was my only friend."

That realization stabbed at him. Natalie had left everything for the promise of a better home. And the first friend she'd made had died.

And now Marie seemed to be in danger of the same fate. Gut wrenched, heart torn, he tugged on her wrist and pulled her into his lap. She didn't fight it as he wrapped his arms around her. Laying her head on his shoulder, she let out a shaky sigh and melted into him.

His hand made a slow figure eight on her back, his chin on top of her hair.

They sat like that for what felt like hours, only the strangled sound of her breathing breaking the silence. If the occasional scrape of another chair or random footsteps tried to break into their bubble, he needed only to hold on tighter to remember that it was truly just the two of them in that moment.

Friends who had lost friends.

He knew her feelings. They'd been his when he realized he'd never see her again.

And just now that pain reared again. No matter how often he thought he'd overcome it, it returned. It waited in the wings until he thought he was healed. Then it returned, center stage beneath the spotlight.

Of course, holding her this close couldn't help. But he also couldn't leave her to grieve on her own.

Besides, she would never see Melody again. But he could twine his arms around the one he'd lost. And she'd called him when she needed someone to face this day and that memory.

Suddenly, a voice penetrated their little world. It was vaguely familiar and terribly persistent.

"For Marie Sloane. Friends of Marie Sloane."

When the words registered, he eased his arms from around Natalie and looked up to meet the nurse's gaze. "Can we see her?"

"She's asking for you."

Natalie's limbs flailed like a newborn colt. Nothing seemed

quite stable, but she pushed herself, scurrying after the nurse, Justin hot on her heels.

Marie shared the room with another patient, but a thick curtain hung between the beds to give some semblance of privacy. Her eyes were closed as she reclined against two pillows, and her face looked peaceful. The IV bag hanging at her side dripped into the port in the back of her hand and was likely responsible for the touch of color that had returned to her cheeks.

Natalie let out a soft peep, and Marie's eyes fluttered open. She reached out her hand with an exhausted smile. "Natalie." It was barely a whisper, a little gravelly, but he couldn't deny how sweet it sounded.

Natalie rushed forward and caught her hand, squeezing it between both of hers. "Are you all right? How do you feel?"

"I feel like an idiot. I haven't been able to keep much down lately." She pressed her free hand against the bland brown blanket tucked in around her stomach. "And the doctor said I was terribly dehydrated."

Natalie nodded. "I'm so sorry."

Marie's smile, still tired, turned thoughtful. "You knew, didn't you? You're the one who told them."

With a small nod, she confirmed Marie's suspicion. "Is the baby . . ."

"He or she is just fine. Thanks to you, we're both going to be fine."

Natalie looked over her shoulder, her face glowing like she might never have reason to cry again.

And Justin felt like he'd been struck by lightning.

◆◆◆◆◆

Natalie could barely keep her eyes open as Justin drove them back to the inn later that night. Her legs twitched sporadically, even when she tried to keep herself perfectly still. As she watched the passing pine trees silhouetted by the young moon, her chin dipped. She fought the desire to succumb to it but had no strength to carry the conversation.

Justin seemed to be lost somewhere in the recesses of his mind, his gaze trained on the farthest reaches of the beams in front of them.

She didn't have the energy to ask him what he was thinking about, even though she'd earned it. She'd opened up to him, told him about Melody and about the baby. Explained why she'd nearly frozen when she'd seen Marie sprawled on the floor.

But the baby was all right. Marie was too. Dehydrated, in need of some fluids and plenty of bed rest, but okay.

She let out a slow breath and the tension in her shoulders with it.

Thank you, God. Thank you for protecting Marie. She shot a glance at the square outline of Justin's jaw. *Thank you that I didn't have to face this day alone. Thank you that Russell didn't see me like this.*

Something inside her twisted tighter than the threads of a rope. She knew she shouldn't feel that way. She wasn't supposed to hide the hard parts of life from the man she was going to spend the rest of her life with.

But it was true. She didn't want him to see it.

If he did, he might change his mind about her. If he saw the real her, he might see what her mother and father and so many others in this town had seen.

Justin pulled up to the inn and parked the truck in front,

cutting off her train of thought before it could get to even more dangerous ground.

Relief flooded through her as she popped open the door, but when she turned to thank Justin, he was gone. She whipped around as far as the bucket seat would allow, finally realizing he was already at her side.

With a hand out, he said, "Need help?"

"I'm okay." But suddenly the twitching in her legs had turned to shaking in her knees, and she wasn't sure she'd be able to reach the ground without falling into a heap. Maybe he intuitively understood what the day had cost her. Maybe he could read it on her face. Either way, he reached for her waist with both hands and lifted her to the grass at the curb.

An unbidden sigh escaped. It came from somewhere low in her throat and hummed with a contentment she hadn't known she could find on this island.

Cheeks burning and heart racing, she shot him a glance to see if he'd heard her. If she was lucky, the hum of the boat in the harbor had drowned her out. Or maybe he'd thought it was just the sound of the waves clapping their gentle applause.

Nope. No such break. When he arched a brow in her direction, it spoke more than a thousand questions. But a smile crept across his lips, despite the tug and pull at the corners that said he was trying to keep just that from happening.

And that grin, no matter how hard he fought it, reminded her why he had always been a safe place.

Her hand found its way to his arm, solid and unmoving beneath her fingers. "Thank you for today."

He dipped his head in humility—faux or true, she couldn't tell. "I didn't do much."

"I think you did. You were barely out of the shower—" Her head cocked as she realized what she'd said. "Why were you taking a shower at two o'clock in the afternoon?"

Looking like he might spit, he grunted. "Stupid cow. She's still refusing to let her calf eat, so when I took it a bottle, she thought I was a danger. She butted me right into a mud puddle."

Her giggle couldn't be contained, despite the sharp flicker in his eyes. "I'm sorry. I didn't mean to bring up sour memories."

He shrugged. "Not the first time I've been tossed to the ground."

There was a light of humor in his tone, but there was something deeper too. Something that suggested that maybe she'd done the tossing. It made her chest ache. Why had she thought leaving was her only option?

She stared hard into his eyes, trying to convey her regrets. All of them. "I'm sorry you ended up—"

"Natalie? Natalie Joy?"

The low voice skittered across her skin, stole her breath, and sent a shiver rushing through her despite the warm summer air.

She turned slowly, praying she was mistaken. Praying he hadn't sought her out again.

But there was her father, standing between her and Justin and the inn's red door, blocking her escape yet again.

"Could we talk? Just for a minute." He held his hands against his front as though holding a hat, which wasn't there. And his chin stayed low to his chest. But his eyes never left her. His gaze wasn't aggressive or unhappy. Somehow it felt like he was drinking her in, like he couldn't get enough of the sight of her.

Probably he couldn't believe that the kid who had left the island was the same woman who had returned.

Only she wasn't the same. She wouldn't be controlled by his bad choices. And choosing to ambush her after a day like this was definitely a bad choice.

With a haggard breath, she put her hands up between them. Maybe she could push him away even with twenty feet between them. "I don't have anything to say to you."

The streetlight cast a strange shadow over his face, but the illuminated portion held firm and tense. He'd always been loose and relaxed when she was younger. Or maybe that had been the alcohol.

But there was a set to his chin now that said he intended to speak whatever was on his mind. Whatever had made him track her down. Twice.

She steeled herself for his rant, for his anger, although he had no good reason to be angry. She'd been a good daughter. He was the one who'd torn their family apart. He was the one who'd ignored everything going on under his roof. Maybe that had been the alcohol too.

But it had still been his choice.

Instead of marching toward her, he put his hands into his pockets and hung his head, his red hair so much like her own, his posture so similar to the one she always sought out amid uncertainty.

Maybe she'd learned it from him. Maybe it was an inherited trait.

That stung. She didn't want to think about being like her father. Or worse—like her mother.

It rushed over her, a cloak too heavy to carry. Suddenly it was all too much. Flashes of Marie on the kitchen floor.

The hospital. The baby. Memories of Melody too sweet and bitter to stomach.

Her hands began to tremble, and her shoulders shook. Her heart had already taken a beating, and facing her father was too much for this day.

She glanced up at Justin, whose hand still rested on her back, and his gaze was heavy on her dad. "I need to go."

He didn't look down at her. "All right. Good night."

"Thank you." She wasn't entirely sure what she'd meant that whispered farewell to include, but it covered the entirety of the day and maybe all their years of friendship. Mostly it covered that she didn't have to explain why she might crack under one more conversation. He understood.

She could feel his gaze on her as she walked toward the inn, holding her breath and giving her dad's still figure a wide berth.

Her dad said nothing else until she closed the door behind her. Only when she leaned against the solid wood did she hear the low murmurs of their deep voices carrying across the lawn. The words were too garbled to distinguish, and she heaved a tired sigh as she wiped an errant tear from her cheek.

Good. Let them talk. For now she'd skirted having to face him.

But the reprieve wouldn't last forever. At some point, she'd have to face her father.

And if she wasn't careful, Russell would be by her side instead of Justin.

15

Four days later Justin still had trouble falling asleep. Of course his mom had picked up on a problem after his first sleepless night.

"Are you all right? You have dark circles under your eyes," she had said. Just what every man wanted to hear over the breakfast table.

He'd brushed her comment off. The sleeplessness too.

Yet every night when he closed his eyes, his conversation with Rick O'Ryan flashed in front of him.

"You have to help me," Rick had said. He looked like a boxer leaving the ring after a losing fight, his shoulders slumped in defeat and his shadowed face drawn tight in pain.

Justin crossed his arms, the fabric of his cotton work shirt suddenly too snug across his shoulders. He flexed them anyway. "Why on earth would I help you?"

"You're her best friend, right?"

"Wrong." While there was plenty of pleasure in cutting Rick off, the truth of what he said was about as fun as hitting his thumb with a hammer.

"You're not?" Rick scratched his cheek and took a step closer. "But you're always together. She spent more time at your house than at our own."

Justin dodged the question by spitting out one of his own. "And why do you think that is?"

It was hard to tell in the yellow light over the street, but the man's fair skin might have turned pink. His hands went back into his pockets, his shoulders tucking under his ears. Rick's chin fell to his chest, his defeat soundly in the record books. "Justin, I was a terrible father."

He snorted at the vast understatement.

"I know. I *know*." Looking back up, he squinted until his left eye nearly disappeared beneath his eyebrow. His forehead a sea of wrinkles, he sighed loudly. "I wasn't fit to be a dad. No one should have let me take anyone so special home with me."

"At least we agree on one thing."

Rick's eyebrows jumped, and a flicker of hope crossed his face.

That was not what Justin had been aiming for. He shot the older man his hardest scowl and clenched his jaw as he leaned forward. "You don't have any right to ask for Natalie's time."

"I understand that. I'm just . . . I'm asking for grace."

The word slapped him across the face. *Grace*. It was a word he expected to hear from Father Chuck standing behind the pulpit at First Church. It was a word he expected to hear when his mom watched that dancing show. It applied to the wind in the trees and specific hockey plays.

But nothing could have prepared him to hear it from Natalie's deadbeat, alcoholic father.

"What's that supposed to mean?"

Rick's eyes closed as peace settled over his features, the tense wrinkles easing away. "I don't deserve her forgiveness, but she deserves my apology."

Justin stood, his mouth hanging open, for a long moment. He wasn't sure he could believe Rick. Was this a ploy to get close to Natalie only to hurt her again? Or had there really been a change in his life?

Rick tugged at the back of his neck. "I'm not asking for myself. I know I'm out of chances. But I heard she's getting married." He cocked his head to the side, one eyebrow arched. "I thought it was to you."

"Not to me."

"Well . . ." He shrugged like the groom didn't matter. Although if he cared about Natalie, shouldn't he care about who she married? "I just figured maybe it was the right time to tell her the truth."

Justin hated himself for it, yet he couldn't help but ask. "The truth?"

"You don't know?"

Let it go, Kane. Let it go. Don't fall into his trap.

But he didn't listen to himself. "Know what?"

Rick mumbled words that might have been intended for himself but still reached Justin. "Thought your mom or Aretha would have said *something* by now."

Bringing his mom into this was a low blow. "What about my mom?" He was in too deep to let go, so he took several steps across the grass to be sure he didn't miss anything else Rick might mutter.

"Oh, um . . . Nothing."

"This is not nothing. If you want my help with Natalie, you'll fill me in."

A stricken look crossed Rick's features, and he shifted his weight from one foot to the other. But he didn't speak.

Justin fought it, fought the urge to fill the emptiness between them, but when he closed his eyes to muster his strength, all he could see were Natalie's eyes. So big. So blue. So filled with sadness that he wanted nothing more than to protect her.

He should still be angry with her. He should let that cold shoulder he'd perfected fall back into place.

But he wasn't angry anymore. All he wanted to do was keep this man from hurting her any further.

Rick rubbed the top of his head, his short hair thinning and lighter than Justin remembered it. But he still didn't speak. Only the rolling waves and chirping bugs filled the night air.

And Justin's tense breathing, which picked up speed with every passing moment, coming out in short bursts.

Finally the moment exploded. "If you can't tell me what's going on, then you don't deserve to talk to her."

Rick held his gaze, sadness etched in his features. But there was no shame in his eyes. "If that's how you feel, I understand." Stuffing his hands back into his pockets, he strolled toward the street and disappeared between pools of yellow light.

Justin hadn't been able to stop thinking about what it was that Rick wouldn't say. What it was that Justin's mom had never told him.

What secrets had this little town been saving for at least fifteen years?

Justin had thought about asking his mom, but there were some things a son just couldn't ask his mother. Like what exactly was the nature of her connection with Rick O'Ryan?

Every loose-lipped biddy in the county could probably come to a single conclusion. There was a reason Rick had been a favorite in the rumor mills. He'd earned his reputation. And Justin wasn't about to even hint at a connection with his mother. No way.

Besides, Aretha was somehow connected to this whole thing. What did it have to do with Natalie and what Rick wanted to tell her?

His stomach ached and his head pounded. He just needed to get some sleep.

Instead he stared at the ceiling, watching the shifting shadows of the moon dancing across his room.

The last time he'd felt like this, he'd written "Good-bye, Girl."

He rolled out of bed, his bare feet landing hard on the second-story floor. Cringing, he prayed his mom hadn't been bothered by that. She didn't take kindly to his late-night meanderings right above her bedroom.

Yet another reason to move out.

Except as much as she groused at him, she understood that he needed to be close to the dairy. Besides, she'd be awfully lonely without him. And vice versa.

He strode across his room, then back. Then again. He tried to keep his feet light, his steps careful in the relative darkness. But he wasn't quite careful enough. His pinky toe caught the leg of his bed, and he stifled a cry as he hopped on one foot to the wall. Falling against the faded paint that had more than earned a fresh coat, he leaned his shoulder into the window frame. From this angle, he could see the lighthouse, its beam sweeping across the water, into the trees, and over the pastures where his herd grazed.

And suddenly he needed to be there.

Shrugging into a T-shirt, he grabbed the notebook on his nightstand and swiped his keys from their hook by the door. He tiptoed down the stairs, skipping the last step. He was out the door, into his truck, and rolling toward the lighthouse before he could think better of it.

With the windows rolled down, the air caressed his face with all of its warmth and serenity. Stars sparkled and disappeared behind dancing clouds, their gray outlines shifting and swirling. And always, the ocean beckoned, its call gentle yet insistent.

As he raced up the ladder in the lighthouse, words had already begun tumbling through him—the cry of the island, the same cry of his heart.

> When the storm is rolling o'er the sea
> And the light can't even reach the trees,
> You can find a peace with me
> Somewhere on this shore.

As he scribbled the words into his notebook, he ignored what they meant. He did his best to wipe her picture from his mind. But the memory of her glistening eyes and the tremble of her bottom lip tore him open.

He'd always been Natalie's protector, and those instincts were hard to turn off.

Sure. That's what he was going to go with. That's the story he'd tell himself.

A niggling voice in his mind asked him if the stories he told himself were any better than the story Natalie had been telling her fiancé.

But that was a question he didn't want to answer. And Russell Jacobs wasn't someone he wanted to think about. Not tonight. Not when he could still smell Natalie's citrusy perfume.

He might need Russell's help. But tonight wasn't about producing a record or making the music he loved.

Tonight was about excising feelings that had no business showing up.

He watched the beacon for hours as it swept over the rolling bay. By the time the sun rose, he'd filled a page with notes, scratching out line after line and refilling them with better words. With the right words. Words he couldn't say, but words that needed a place to live. This notebook had always been a safe place for that.

And always in the back of his mind, the question of Rick O'Ryan.

As the orange glow in the east became more insistent, he closed the pages and crawled down the ladder and into his truck.

There were cows to be fed and milked, but first he needed to talk to his mom.

She was right where she'd been every morning of his life, in front of the stove making something that smelled of cheese and heaven—not that those two things were mutually exclusive. In his estimation, heaven would have an excellent dairy section of cheeses from around the world. And the marriage supper of the Lamb would probably be topped off with a cheesecake made by Caden. That sounded just about perfect to him.

"Morning, hon. You were out early." She glanced over her shoulder in his direction, and he took a quick survey of what she must see.

A wrinkled T-shirt that smelled like it hadn't been washed in this century, sleeping shorts that had a hole along the seam at the outside of his thigh. A quick run of his hand through his hair reminded him that he hadn't bothered to comb it at any point during the night.

She raised both eyebrows. "Or out late, I suppose."

He shrugged, tapping his notebook against his flat palm. "Little of both."

"Uh-huh." Her tone was serious, but the corner of her mouth crinkled in the way it always did when she was amused. "Got something on your mind?"

"Actually, yes."

She spun around then, leaving the eggs she'd been stirring to fend for themselves for a few minutes. "Well, it's about time. You've been walking around like a zombie for days. Is this about Natalie?"

"No. Yes. Not really. Wait, why would it be about her?"

All innocence, his mom put a hand to her mouth. "Oh, I just assumed. You haven't been yourself lately, and it all started about the time Natalie got back to town."

"What's that supposed to mean?" He was definitely himself. He hadn't changed. And if he had, it certainly wasn't a result of Natalie's arrival.

"Oh, you know." She waved the plastic spoon that carried a few remnants of the eggs. "Running off to the lighthouse in the middle of the night."

"I do that all the time."

Her eyebrows arched higher. "After stomping around your room in the middle of the night?"

That was a fair point. Hard work meant hard sleep, but lately sleep had been more acquaintance than friend.

She turned back to the pan on the stove, and as she ran her spoon along the edge, a puff of steam escaped, carrying with it the scent of spicy bacon and Monterey Jack mixed into breakfast. "And you've been sociable."

His brow furrowed of its own accord. "You think it's unusual that I'm spending time with people? What's that supposed to mean? I spend time with people. I hang out with Dillon every day."

"No, you work with Dillon. That's different. Set the table."

She said her words like they were all one thought, and he had to shake himself out of the argument he was already preparing in his mind. The table. Right. He pulled two plates from the cabinet as he opened his mouth to reject her premise.

But her command wasn't the end of her argument. "Dillon has been a staple in your life since Natalie left. And he's wonderful."

Well, that might be taking it a little too far. *Wonderful* wasn't the word Justin would use. Dillon talked way too much, had a bad habit of pulling practical jokes, and had no qualms about leaving the least fun chores for the boss. But he was still a hard worker and a reliable friend, and the two had formed an easy camaraderie.

"But since Natalie's been back, you've been spending time with her and Marie and Caden—"

"I spend time with Caden."

She gave him a patronizing smile as she dished the eggs onto the plates. "Of course you do. I'm just saying your circle has widened. I mean, you've been to see Pete at the hardware store in Cavendish three times this week."

He rolled his eyes before pulling out a chair and plopping into it. "Because Seth was gone, and I needed supplies to fix up Natalie's barn. It's not like we're going out to dinner and a movie."

"But you're still getting off the farm and seeing people."

Without any preamble, she bowed her head, and he did the same. "Father, thank you for this food and your good provision to us. Thank you for your mercy and forgiveness. In your Son's name, amen."

As though she hadn't even stopped to pray, she continued with her case. "Even Lois Bernard said you'd been by her shop. Of course, I heard that as she was telling Biddy Oatway that she was sure you and Natalie were up to no good and probably sneaking around town like Natalie's old man had done."

Suddenly his chest seized, and air ceased to exist. "She said what?" He managed barely a wheeze.

"Oh, don't you worry. I set Lois and Biddy straight."

But they'd been talking about Natalie. They'd been gossiping about her. Probably because of him.

He gave himself a quick reality check. Okay, it wasn't *because* of him. They were going to talk about Natalie's return no matter what. But they certainly wouldn't be talking about her in such rude terms if he wasn't showing up with her wherever she went.

"And Harrison said that you only came in for lunch once this week."

"We were working on the barn. Wait. Now you and Harrison are talking about me? That man doesn't talk to anyone."

She popped a forkful of fluffy eggs into her mouth and pretended she couldn't possibly answer.

First his mom and Harrison had been sitting together at the kitchen party. And now they were having private conversations. What was she up to?

Acid flowing in the wrong direction, his stomach sizzled. He grabbed his glass of water and guzzled it, but it did nothing to stem the burn.

Too many. There were too many things going on right now. He was happy to handle them one at a time, but all of them woven together made him want to go back to the lighthouse and sit there until Natalie left, Rick's secrets were revealed, and his mom went back to normal.

He swallowed his water and eyed his mother.

One at a time. One at a time. He just had to get to the heart of one thing. Then he'd tackle the next.

"Mom, Natalie's dad is back in town."

She nodded. "I heard that. Have you seen him?"

"Yeah, the other night when I dropped off Natalie. The day that Marie went into the hospital." He pushed the food around on his plate, his usual appetite washed away. "He wants my help to talk to her about something. He said she should know before she got married." He lifted his gaze, staring hard at his mom, guarding himself against whatever she might reveal. "He made it sound like you and Aretha knew about it."

Suddenly her chin quivered, and everything that he'd eaten threatened to make a swift and violent return.

This was going to be much worse than he'd feared.

But all she said was, "He should tell her." Her voice was soft, and her shoulders slumped under a sadness that he couldn't identify.

"What? What is he going to tell her?"

She shook her head. "It was a long time ago."

His heart stopped, and he couldn't move. "Mom, there are too many secrets and half-truths running around this town.

Tell me the whole truth." As soon as he said it, her eyes turned glassy, and he suddenly wasn't so sure he actually wanted to know. But as long as he didn't, he'd never get any sleep.

She heaved a soft sigh, and she reached for him, squeezing his arm with a sad smile. "You know that I always loved Natalie like she was one of my own."

He nodded. Natalie had been a fixture at their dinner table for more years than he could remember. And when he was in high school, his mom had taken special shopping trips to Charlottetown just before the start of the school year, coming home with enormous bags of new clothes, all in Natalie's size.

"But there wasn't anything we could do for her. We tried."

"We?"

"Aretha, your father, and I." She stared off into the space above his head, and Justin released the breath he'd been holding. This wasn't about Rick at all. At least not in the way the gossips would suggest.

"What happened?"

"It was before you even became friends—although I was so happy when you did. It gave me an excuse to provide for her. To protect her." She cleared her throat and pushed her plate away, leaving her jelly toast completely untouched. "We all saw it. The whole town."

He hated to pull his mom from her memories, but this was too important to leave any ambiguity. "It?"

"The neglect. The abuse." She sniffed and pressed a finger to the corner of her eye. "She was so skinny, and when we saw her around town, she tried to fade into the background. Her dad could have single-handedly kept the liquor store in business, so we all assumed it was him. When we saw bruises, we assumed he was . . . we assumed they were from him. And that maybe Natalie wasn't his only victim. But when I asked Connie if everything was all right at home, she brushed me off and avoided me for years."

Natalie had rarely talked about her life at home. Even in the lighthouse, she preferred to dream about the outside world, about a place far from North Rustico. But he'd assumed too. It had always been her father she avoided talking about. Her father who caused such embarrassment.

But a sinking feeling inside had him questioning everything he'd ever thought about her childhood. And it hurt like it had been his own.

"It was Aretha who saw it first, the way Natalie always flinched away from the women. The other girls would run up and hug Aretha at church. Natalie put as much space as she could between them. But she didn't mind hugging your Sunday school teacher or Father Chuck."

A lump formed in his throat, and he had to force the words past it. "Because it was her mom?"

"Yes. So we went to Rick."

"And it didn't go well." It wasn't even a question. He could fill in the blanks for himself now. Each one made him sick to his stomach. But one gaping hole remained. "What about child welfare? Why not call the authorities?"

She hung her head as though this was her greatest shame. "We did. But they couldn't prove any abuse, and Natalie wouldn't tell them anything."

Justin pushed back from the table, his chair rocking back at the force. "Because she was scared, Mom. Couldn't you do something? Why didn't you tell Natalie? Or me?"

"Tell you what? That we wanted to save her but couldn't?"

She reached again for his arm, but he jerked it away. "You were just kids, and you hardly knew her at that point."

His eyes burned, and he pressed the heels of his hands against them. Somehow it was so much worse realizing that Natalie had had an escape but hadn't known it. If he'd known, he would have snuck her out of her house, gotten her to safety.

He wasn't sure what he'd expected his mom to say, but this wasn't it. This was so much worse than what he'd imagined, because his best friend had been in a pit and he'd been unable to save her.

Maybe you can save her from a new pit now.

The voice in his head came out of nowhere, but he knew instantly what it meant.

She had constructed a very careful facade for her fiancé. She was about to marry a man who had no idea of the passionate, fiery woman she really was. It was bound to be a disaster that neither could see coming.

Perhaps he could save her from that. But if he did, he'd also ruin any hope of signing with Russell Jacobs.

16

I t's cake-tasting day. Are you coming over?"

Natalie didn't know why the invitation felt so intimate. It was just food. What she'd promised Justin from the beginning.

This wasn't even her house. It was the inn. But she had a sneaking suspicion that any hesitancy about the invitation had very little to do with the location and a whole lot more to do with who she was inviting.

She hadn't seen him in over a week. Not since the trip to the hospital, actually. Not since her dad had nearly ambushed her.

While Marie had returned home—Seth too from his trip to Boston—Justin hadn't come around the inn even once. If he'd checked in about the progress of the barn, it hadn't been with her. But she'd stopped by and checked three times this week. The barn was coming along nicely, but he was nowhere to be found.

Little Natalie would have worried that he was avoiding her. Adult Natalie knew he was.

In response to her invitation, Justin hemmed for a moment. Didn't he want to see her?

That didn't matter. It didn't. He was only helping her out with reception preparations.

So what if he didn't want to see her? She hadn't wanted to see him when she arrived in town. She didn't need his attention or help. She didn't need him hanging around the barn, making her laugh, making her feel free to be herself.

But . . . maybe she wanted it anyway.

Something had reminded her of all that she'd lost when she'd walked away from him, and now her stomach was in knots as she awaited his rejection.

It didn't matter. It didn't matter.

It didn't matter how many times she told herself that. Nothing could make a lie the truth.

"What time were you thinking?" His voice sounded like it had been dragged through gravel.

"Are you feeling okay?"

"Sure. The calves and their mamas are just being stubborn."

Whatever uncertainty she'd had a moment before disappeared, and the words popped out unbidden. "Sounds like something you'd know a thing or two about."

He grunted in good humor. "Fair enough." But he didn't go on, and he didn't respond to her invitation.

"The barn's looking good."

Another grunt. This one less committed.

"I mean, the inside's almost done, and they'll be delivering tables soon, so we can figure out the arrangement."

"Still have to get the outside painted. I guess I should probably work on that."

"I could help you."

What was with her mouth today? For all the weird places

her mind was going, her tongue seemed completely uncon-cerned. She shouldn't want to be spending time with him. But she did. He was safe. He wasn't easy, but he required no explanation of her story. And somehow he always knew what to say to get a rise out of her.

She'd never felt quite so alive.

Even if he didn't want to see her.

Doubts and desires warred within her, but that was of little concern to her flapping tongue. "If you'll help me choose the cake, I'll help you paint."

Even from the other end of the phone, a low hum from his throat made her stomach flip. She pressed her hand to it, forcing it down. Nope. This wasn't happening. They were just friends. Barely friends.

She just liked that she didn't have to play a part or try to remember how she'd phrased her past with him.

Right. Yes. She'd go with that.

And pray that it was true. *God, please let it be true.*

"Sounds like I'll be getting the better end of that deal."

"Maybe."

And three hours later, as they sat at one of the tables in the dining room, she was sure he had. When Caden set a large platter of cake slices in front of them, her mouth watered instantly. Their table had been set with only two forks, but somehow the platter made it feel like it was ready for the queen. Six thick slices of cake made a full circle, nearly filling the platter. Yellow and chocolate and white, the frosting was bright and creamy and so rich it made her head spin before she even took a bite.

"This one is a lemon cake with raspberry filling and lemon buttercream frosting."

Justin let out a low moan and shifted like he might need to adjust his pants for this. Making people eat too much seemed to be a habit of Caden's.

When he met Natalie's gaze, his was a little hesitant, and she wondered again if he'd rather be anywhere else in the world. But when his eyes devoured the array of sweets, pure joy swept across his features.

He was here for the cake, and it would do her well to remember that.

On several levels.

Caden pointed to another slice, a wicked gleam in her eye. "This is devil's food cake—and it lives up to its name—with chocolate ganache."

Now it was Natalie's turn to sigh at the decadent dessert options. But she tried to keep it soft.

Justin shot her a sly smile filled with mocking, and she knew she hadn't succeeded in staying silent. So she picked up her fork and stabbed it in his direction—a silent threat. Without a sound, he whipped his fork up like he was going to parry her attack.

Caden was either ignoring their childish antics or enamored with her baking. Either way, she kept the descriptions going. Red velvet with cream cheese frosting. Carrot cake with walnuts. Strawberry cake with strawberry cream filling and whipped lemon frosting. And, of course, traditional wedding cake, white with white frosting. When she was done pointing out her masterpieces, she put her hands on her hips and swayed, almost a little dance of joy.

Natalie lowered her fork and watched the pleasure on Caden's face. Had she been so spunky back in high school? She'd been a few years younger, so they hadn't shared a lot of classes or run in the same circles. But Natalie remembered Caden as being shy, something of a loner.

But as she proudly displayed the rose petal designs and intricate frosting scallops along the white cake, she wasn't the same girl she'd been. What Natalie didn't know was if the change had occurred naturally or if it was the result of one of the Jacobs brothers.

She waited for the reminder of Russell to bring with it a swarm of butterflies. After all, he'd been gone for a few weeks already, and she missed him. Or she would have, if she wasn't quite so busy getting ready for the wedding.

But instead of the warmth she expected, the thought of him brought a swarm of bees, which made her stomach ache.

Not what she needed before gorging herself on sweets.

"Any questions?" Caden asked.

"Got any milk?" Justin said.

She chuckled. "I should have known." Despite the shake of her head and the faux annoyance in her tone, Caden sashayed into the kitchen and returned with two glasses brimming with creamy milk that had surely come from Justin's farm. "I'll leave you to it."

"So, how are we going to tackle this?" Justin asked after Caden left.

"Well, I know it's a new concept for you, but you see, you use your fork to scoop up a bite, then carry it to your mouth and—"

"Don't try getting smart with me," he said. "It doesn't suit you." But he couldn't even finish his thought before laughter spilled out. It was low and throaty and bubbled from somewhere deep in his chest.

"All right, wise guy." She was laughing too, and she couldn't cover it up. "Let's try the same piece and then compare notes. Start with the devil's food?"

He suddenly turned serious, his fork held at the ready. "Nope. That's too rich. Let's start with the lighter ones. Lemon or white."

"Thought about this quite a bit, have you?"

"Been planning it since I sat down."

"Of course you have." But he was right. The overly rich chocolate could spoil their appreciation of the lighter fare, so she spun the platter to the yellow cake. They each poked a bite free—hers about a third of the size of his. As she brought it to her lips, she closed her eyes, breathed in, and let the scent prepare her. Except nothing could have prepared her for the explosion of flavor. Some cakes were so sweet that all she could taste was sugar. But this one—this lemon-raspberry wonder—was refreshing like a cold glass of lemonade. The tartness of the fresh raspberry filling balanced the rich frosting, which tingled at the back of her throat.

"You like it, huh?"

"What?" She jerked her eyes open to find another chunk of the slice gone.

Justin licked the corner of his lips, and a speck of frosting disappeared. "I figured that moan was a good sign."

"I did not."

Now it was his turn to jab his fork at her. "Don't even try denying it, young lady."

"Oh, so we're back to *lady*?"

"If the shoe fits and all that." He stabbed for another bite of her precious slice, but she parried with her own fork. "Hey! Do you want my help or not?"

"You've already had three bites. Aren't you going to save room for the others?"

With a huff at her apparently absurd question, he waved his hand over the platter. "I could eat this whole plate."

"And then what?"

"Then you'd have to drive me to the hospital in Charlottetown. But I could eat it."

Tears of mirth flooded her eyes, and she had to wipe them away. "You are ridiculous, Justin Kane."

"Yes, I am. But it never bothered you before."

"I didn't say it bothered me *now*." There went her completely unhinged tongue again. But it wasn't wrong. She'd always enjoyed his laughter and silliness. And right up until this moment, she hadn't realized how much she'd missed it in her life.

The blue in his eyes sparked. "So this is an option then?"

It took her a second to follow the tines of his fork to the cake remnants and realize what he was talking about, because her stupid brain was trying to twist his words to mean something else. What exactly, she wasn't sure. But she was sure it wasn't good. "Umm. Yes. The cake. I liked it. Did you?"

He forked another scoop and popped it in his mouth. Then he tried to talk around it. "I'd ask for seconds."

"Okay. Good." Time to get back on track. Yes. More cake. That's exactly what she needed.

Right.

She kept her mouth stuffed through three more flavors. The red velvet wasn't as moist. The carrot cake was delicious but too heavy. Plus she didn't want to risk sending one of her wedding guests to the emergency room with an allergic reaction to nuts. Best keep to the basics.

The white-on-white was as basic—and as delicious—as it came. She couldn't hold back another moan as she eased the fork past her lips, catching every last shred of frosting. It rushed through her like lightning in her veins, popping as it reached her fingers and toes. So sweet and utterly simple. And wonderfully perfect.

"So, the white?" Justin asked, again speaking around a mouthful. It made him look like a boy, shoveling cheese sandwiches into his cheeks, afraid he'd never eat again.

"Yes. Definitely the white."

"With the lemon. That's good."

She shook her head. "No, the red velvet."

He frowned. He didn't have to ask the question.

"It's Russell's favorite."

His eyes turned stormy.

But he's not here.

It was written on every line of Justin's face. Along the angles of his darkened jaw. Down his slightly crooked nose. Along the furrows of his forehead.

He's not here.

It matched the tempo of her heart. *Not here. Not here.* Blood was pounding in her ears. Surely it was the sugar making her dizzy. That and the stress of planning a wedding while her wedding planner was on bed rest.

But she couldn't look away from Justin, who had an argument at the ready. She could see it in his eyes. The red velvet was her least favorite. It was good, but certainly not the best of Caden's options. No one liked red velvet. No one would miss it.

Except Russell. And this was his wedding too.

She managed a deep breath and held it for a long second.

Until her head righted itself. Until the buzzing inside her calmed. Until she could remember that she missed Russell.

Because there was definitely something going on that she couldn't name. Something that wouldn't let her forget she was her father's daughter.

With a startled jerk, she shoved her chair back and found her feet. "I have to go see Lois." No prelude. No explanation. Just an excuse to bail on their previously made plans.

"All right." He nodded but didn't stand. "Do you want me to go with you?"

No. Absolutely not.

"Yes."

◆◆◆◆◆

If Justin hadn't been so wholly wound up in his own battle of *should he or shouldn't he*—tell her about her dad, that is—he might have been able to study Natalie enough to figure out what was going on behind those shifty eyes.

Of course, the cake hadn't helped. You can't just put cake in front of a man and expect him to concentrate on anything else.

Buzzing on enough sugar to knock out a Guernsey, he'd decided it was a good idea to accompany her back to the florist.

Because he was brilliant. Just the smartest.

Halfway between the inn and Lois's shed, the jitters were starting to fade and his mind was beginning to clear. And he was stuck spending the rest of the afternoon with Natalie.

Which would have been fine on any ordinary day. Or at least tolerable.

Sure. He'd stick with that story because the other ones—

the ones where he had any right to press his finger to the corner of her mouth to free the frosting flake stuck there— were not okay.

Not okay, Kane.

But under the influence of high levels of giddy laughter and a pound of cake, he wasn't sure he could be so circumspect.

He'd been holding on to his mother's secret for five days. All he'd wanted to do every day was call Natalie and tell her. She'd been loved. People had cared. People had tried to help her.

But that particular news ought to come from her father.

At least that's what his mom had said. Maybe she was right. Probably she was. Usually she was.

But this was something Natalie had a right to know. If she refused to talk to her father, she'd never hear the truth. And that was not okay.

Natalie swayed a little as she strolled down the boardwalk, then caught herself with an awkward crossover step.

He grabbed for her elbow. "All right there, Bambi?"

As she looked up at him, she closed one eye against the sun. Then again, maybe she was nursing a pounding headache. He had one of those starting behind his left eye.

"Is it possible to be drunk on sweets? I can't seem to get my legs to work."

The resemblance to her dad no longer stopped with her hair, as her legs buckled and she tumbled. Right into him.

Every inch of him burned where she grabbed on to him, hanging off his shoulder, leaning against his arm. This was different than when he'd held her at the hospital. That had been about comfort.

This was . . . well, he had no idea what *this* was, even as his arm slipped around her waist. Even as he pulled her closer to him. Even as he closed his eyes and drank in the scent of oranges that clung to her.

She was sweeter than the cake, her hair as soft as a kitten. Pressing his nose into the top of her hair, he let himself inhale all of her. She fit in his arms like she'd never left, like he'd sometimes let himself imagine she would. But those had been dreams. Reality was infinitely more satisfying.

When he opened his eyes, she was staring up at him with the strangest expression. Confusion and clarity mixed together. Wonder and shock battled for dominance, pulling her face to the side, her lips pursed and her pert little nose wrinkled.

His heart gave a little flutter and then slammed against his breastbone. He hunted for anything to say, but the quip he sought had found a good hiding place. So he stood like a fool with his mouth open and his arms holding her against his chest.

Because, despite everything he knew to be right, he couldn't talk himself into letting her go. Not quite yet.

In the end, it was Natalie who regained her senses first. Natalie who pulled away.

As confusion won out in her eyes, he could only apologize. "Sorry. I'm not sure—"

She yanked her hand back from where it still rested on his shoulder. "It was my fault. I'm not very steady on my feet, I guess." Heavy lids covered her eyes, long lashes sweeping over her cheeks. "I'll be more careful."

"I'll be careful too." But it wasn't unstable legs he had to worry about.

Falling into an easy stroll in the direction of the florist, they didn't say anything else until they reached the little shed.

Silence was good for Justin. It gave him plenty of time to chastise himself. And then to make a list of all the reasons he could never—*never*—get so close to Natalie again. But he only had one item on the list.

She was engaged to another man.

It was that simple. That hard.

And Lord help him, he wished she were free. The seasick feeling in his stomach was evidence of that.

But she's not. Get that through your thick skull.

Although a large Closed sign hung on the outside of the green door to the shop, Justin pulled it open and held out his hand to usher her in. But he jerked away when he realized how close he'd come to touching the small of her back. That was off-limits too.

All of her. Off-limits.

He was so busy reminding himself not to look at her or touch her or smell her that he walked right into Lois's work-table.

The older woman frowned at him as she righted the flowers he'd knocked off-kilter. "You're here about the samples, I suppose."

Natalie managed a polite smile. "You did call and tell me to come see them today."

She harrumphed, and her hair shook under the weight of her displeasure. How on earth had a woman like this ever kept her shop open for a hundred years without driving away everyone in town?

"I went with simple for the centerpieces. The barn will have plenty going on, and you don't want the flowers to be distracting. Also, you mentioned adding an antique, so these are small enough to add to." Lois pulled a squat, square vase of white roses from the refrigerator on the far wall and set it on the edge of the table.

Natalie let out a disappointed groan but clamped her lips between her teeth.

Fine. She didn't want to speak up. He would. "We talked about purple orchids, right?"

As he spoke, Lois turned back to the fridge and produced a stunning arrangement. Even a guy like him, who hadn't been sure what an orchid was, could recognize the simple elegance in the way the greenery embraced the colorful flowers. It wasn't too tall—something his sister had complained about at her best friend's wedding. And it was just rustic enough not to feel out of place under the wooden arches of the barn.

"It's perfect," Natalie whispered.

"Good. I take cash or check. I usually ask for half now and half two weeks before the ceremony, but we're only two weeks out, so we'd best settle it now."

Natalie nodded and pulled her wallet out of her little purse, an array of colorful bills cascading on the table as she counted out Lois's price.

As the woman pocketed the bills, the sagging skin above her eyes drooped even further. "So, your father's back in town, eh?"

Natalie's sudden stiffness nearly made Justin choke. Or it could have been Lois's gall. She had no business bringing up Natalie's parents. The little smirk on her face said she knew as much.

Natalie forced a strained smile, the edges of her lips pinching together. "I suppose so."

"I thought he'd have a glass of wine with me, but he said he doesn't drink anymore."

Natalie's face twitched, and Justin could guess how she wanted to respond. But instead of letting loose with a smart retort, her lips twisted into something akin to panic. The angle of her eyebrows matched the sinking in his stomach.

Lois either didn't notice or didn't care that this topic was clearly distasteful. "He going to be at the wedding? Is that why he's back in town?"

"Umm . . ." Natalie tried for an answer but instead did a decent impression of a fish, her mouth opening and closing without much noise.

His hands itched to pull her close, to wipe that fear away. But that wasn't part of his plan. That was clearly the opposite of his plan. So he made two fists and forced them to his sides. Except that made him want to punch something.

"He's aged well. He always was so handsome." Lois gave a wink that made bile rise at the back of his throat.

Nope. They didn't need to stick around a minute longer.

Breaking his promise to himself, he grabbed Natalie's trembling shoulders and pushed her toward the door. "We'll see you on the day of the wedding. But we don't need to see or hear from you before then."

As the door snicked closed, he heard Lois's appalled gasp. He was pretty sure his mom would hear about what a rude son she'd raised.

Well, so be it. He wasn't about to subject Natalie to another minute of that tactless woman. Maybe she was simply clueless. That was the best he could say about her. But if not, she was careless and callous.

If anyone in this town deserved at least a modicum of civility, it was Natalie. Who was still shaking beneath his hands.

"I'm sorry," she whispered. "I don't know what got into me. I just couldn't say anything."

"It's all right. You don't have to apologize."

She swallowed, and the sound echoed below the branches of the big elm tree in Lois's lawn. "Thank you."

He had slid his hands down to her elbows and back up before he realized he was still touching her. Quickly pulling back, he nodded. "Always."

The sudden pink in her cheeks was his first clue that he'd misspoken. That he'd brought them back to a time when he'd had *always* to promise her.

But now she was about to promise her *always* to someone else. Someone who would take her away from this town and spare her the gossip of the idle. Someone who didn't come home smelling like ornery cows. Someone who would provide her with everything she'd ever been denied as a child.

She deserved someone like Russell.

A voice in his head began a slow chant. *Now. Do it now. Tell her now.*

Great. Now he was the one shaking, his hands trembling so violently that he shoved them in the pockets of his jeans. Forcing himself to stand still, he stared at the ground. This wasn't the right time or place.

But there would never be a *right* time or place. There were only moments he did what he knew he should. What he knew was best for Natalie.

If Natalie noticed the tick in his jaw or the way he couldn't make eye contact, she kindly left it unmentioned. Instead she gave a low, humorless snort. "I don't know why everyone is so eager to talk about my dad."

Do it. Tell her.

"He's been gone a long time."

"I know. But why would I want to hear about him?" She tugged on her ponytail, the fire in her curls refusing to be subdued in the shade of the tree. Every trickle of light through the leaves caught a strand and made it glow warm and rich.

Do it. Tell her.

Sucking in a quick breath, he steeled himself for her response. Whatever it was, he was going to hate it. "I think you should talk to him."

Her long hair whipped over her shoulder like he'd struck her. "Who? My dad? Why would I do that?"

"Because he came home to see you."

"I have *nothing* to say to him." Her voice rose, and he wondered if Lois was pressed to the shed window watching, listening. If so, she was about to have a story to tell. "I can never forgive him. He did nothing while she made my life miserable."

He bowed his head and tugged at the back of his neck. "I know it's hard. I'm not saying it's easy. But . . . well, you forgave me, right?"

He looked up just in time to see a flash in her eyes that made him wonder if she was going to disagree with him. He'd thought she'd forgiven him. Things had certainly changed between them. They didn't yell at each other or accuse the other of purposeful heartbreak.

He'd figured that somewhere between that first tour of the barn and Marie's trip to the ER, she'd found a way to let go of the past.

He had.

After a long pause, she nodded. "But it's different with you. We both had a hand in all that. And you weren't trying to hurt me. You needed to be here for your mom."

"True. But forgiveness is forgiveness, right?"

"Wrong." Her words were like iron. "What you did, you did for someone else. What my dad did, he did out of self-ishness."

"I know." He tried to keep his tone gentle, his words soft. She was as skittish as a newborn calf, but it was too late to back down now. "Maybe he has something you should hear."

"Why would I want to hear anything he has to say?" Her snap was sharper than the crack of a whip, and she scrunched her face and balled her fists in front of her, a defense against the tears already leaking out of the pinched corners of her eyes. "He doesn't deserve my time."

"I didn't say he did. But I think maybe you need to hear him out as much as he needs to talk to you."

When she opened her eyes, their blue turned liquid. With a trembling lip, she took several small steps away from him. "I thought you understood. B-b-but you d-d-don't know me at all."

Her words knocked the breath out of him, leaving him stunned and alone.

17

o to the antique store,' she said. 'It'll be an adventure,' she said." Natalie traipsed down yet another aisle of useless knickknacks. "'Find something for the cake table,' she said. 'It'll be easy,' she said."

"Can I help you find something, honey?"

Natalie jumped, her cheeks instantly flaming as she wondered how much of her grumbling Aretha had heard, but the older woman said nothing more. She simply stood with her hands clasped in front of her, swaying to the sound of the bells on the closing door.

"Oh, um . . . hi, Aretha."

"Did Marie send you? She told me she was going to try to stop by, but I haven't seen her this week."

Natalie nodded. "She was going to come with me, but she just doesn't have the stamina right now. Seth suggested a nap, and she looked like he'd given her a million dollars." She managed a half smile, thankful that at least one of them was enjoying a peaceful afternoon.

Natalie, on the other hand, had been wandering the store for twenty minutes, unable to focus on anything except the repeat that had been playing in her mind for three days. *Maybe you need to hear him out as much as he needs to talk to you.*

Over and over Justin's words wandered through her, only pausing when she managed to snatch a moment of sleep. Not that she'd gotten much of that.

She didn't want to think about her dad, much less talk with him. So what if he'd sought her out? That didn't mean she was obligated. No matter what Justin said, she did not need to hear whatever he had to say. She owed him exactly what he'd given her. Neglect and absence.

Justin should know that. He of all the people in her life should understand.

Yes, she'd forgiven Justin. That had been unexpected but natural. Because he cared. But if he did, why would he push her to make nice with her dad? That was just another performance, and he was all about authenticity, right?

As she pictured his face and felt the urgency in his words once again, she balled her fists and jabbed them onto her hips. She wasn't going to be talked into anything she didn't want.

And what she wanted right now was to marry Russell and leave this island without giving Lois or Stella or any of the other old gossips one more thing to talk about.

Suddenly Natalie realized that the silence had been dragging on between her and Aretha for an awkwardly long moment, and she turned so she could look Aretha directly in the eyes. "I need the perfect wedding. Can you help me?"

Aretha's faded eyes danced as she patted her curls into place. "Well, let's see what we can do. How much of PE Island do you want?"

"Just enough."

Aretha nodded firmly, waved her hand over her shoulder, and led the way down a side row. Big wooden bookcases lined the path, their shelves stacked high with leather-bound books and navigational tools and toys from centuries gone by. An old spinning wheel stuck into the lane, but Aretha marched around it without glancing down. They passed a secretary desk with a rolltop and a row of ships in glass bottles.

When they finally stopped, Aretha pointed to a lantern, its glass panels colored by time, its iron framework sturdy and free of rust.

"The island is all about lights and gentle shores."

Images of her childhood spent playing in Justin's lighthouse, skipping across the sandy beach, and running into the rolling waves flashed through her mind. "I guess you're right."

"'Course I'm right." With a Cheshire grin, she picked up the lantern and plopped it into Natalie's arms. It was surprisingly heavy, and Natalie nearly dropped it, bobbling it for a second before Aretha gave her a firm look that seemed to say she'd have to buy whatever she broke. "I've lived here my whole life, and we won't talk about just how long that might be."

Natalie giggled. "Yes, ma'am."

"I think every table ought to have some sort of light." She picked up a kerosene lamp. Its wick was tattered and the base was in need of a dose of silver polish, but the glass chimney rested in place, clear and beautiful. "If the lamps don't work, we'll put a candle in each."

"It's . . . perfect. How did you ever come up with such an idea?"

"Oh, I wish I could take all the credit, but that sweet Marie has been teaching me a thing or two. You know she decorated the entire inn by herself."

Actually, no, she hadn't known that. But it made sense. The way Marie chose the color of the stain for the barn and talked about patterns for the tablecloths, the thought that she put into each table setting at the inn—she loved those little details that made the inn a home away from home. Natalie's home back home.

"But what about the shore? We have light but no shore."

"Well, I had an idea about that. The tables will be full. Lights and orchids, I hear."

A sudden ache behind her right eye made her squint. "Where'd you hear about the orchids?"

Aretha's cheeks turned pink, rivaling the bright shade of her lipstick. As always, people inevitably let it slip that they'd been talking about her and showed appropriate embarrassment. "I'm sorry. I shouldn't have . . . That wasn't very thoughtful of me."

Here she was, the topic of town gossip again. Maybe she should expect it. After all, her wedding guests had booked all the rooms in town and would probably fill Grady's and every other eating establishment within a ten-mile radius for a few days. The wedding was big business in this small town.

But it wasn't easy to let go of half a lifetime of hearing her family's name bandied about.

At least she was close to being free. She just had to get to the wedding. Get it done. Then she could leave. And then no one would talk about her.

No one in Nashville even noticed her. Among the uber talented and stunningly beautiful, she blended easily into the background. Exactly where she wanted to be.

But not here. Never here.

"Was Lois talking about me?"

"No. It wasn't Lois." Aretha set two more antique lamps on the counter beside the cash register before meeting Natalie's gaze. Her shoulders drooped, and the grin she so often wore had disappeared. "I was talking with Kathleen. She told me that you and Justin have been spending a lot of time together."

She half expected a teasing lilt to Aretha's island accent, but no matter how hard she listened, it wasn't there. There was no innuendo woven into the words or knowing wink to accompany them. There was only the fact. They had been spending a lot of time together. And then avoiding each other. And then spending more time together.

"Kathleen was worried when Justin came home upset the other day."

A little voice in her head told her to run. This wasn't information she needed or should even be privy to. She didn't listen to fabricated stories. She didn't care what Mama Kane had said. But still she asked, "Oh?"

"She was worried that you'd had an argument."

It took everything inside her to keep her face impassive, unresponsive.

"He said that Lois had been terrible to you."

Her breath came out at once, her mind playing fill-in-the-blank. What else had Justin had said? Had he told his mom how terrible she'd been? How she'd lashed out when he pushed about her dad?

Aretha pulled the lantern from her arms, set it on the counter, and grabbed both of her hands. "I understand he was pretty upset."

That shouldn't make her feel better. But it warmed her chest like one of these kerosene lamps being turned all the way up.

Aretha squeezed her fingers, her skin silky but thin. "He told his mom he'd start a boycott of Lois's shop after the way she spoke to you."

"That's ridiculous." She huffed something that sounded like a laugh but felt more like a sob. "She's the only florist in town. And she's good."

"Honey, I know it wasn't easy for you." Aretha's gaze grew more intense, the pressure of her grip increasing. "I know you heard the rumors and all the talk. But it's not ridiculous that someone would stand up for you and defend you. Justin's only saying what so many of us feel—have always felt."

Then why hadn't they done something?

The question bounced against the pressure behind her eye, its ache drawing tears she hadn't expected or wanted.

All she really wanted was to be done with this place. Done with the memories. Done with the pain. But as long as she remained on the island, they were hungry hounds.

Her limbs twitched, her stomach rolling. She ripped her hands free and rushed for the door, nearly running into a couple on their way in.

"I'll send someone for the lamps." She threw it over her shoulder, hoping that Aretha would save them, but not able to stay if she didn't. "All of them." She ducked outside.

The midday sun was too bright. It shone like a spotlight, highlighting all of her faults and fears, and she spun, searching for a safe place to hide.

Instead, she stumbled into a steady body, and two hands rested on her shoulders.

"Whoa there. Are you all right?"

Oh, she knew that voice. As she jerked away from her

father's grasp, she wanted to wipe that smug look off his face, so she lashed out with her only weapon. "You don't care one way or the other. And you never did." With that, she spun and marched down the street toward the diner. Maybe Harrison could give her a safe haven.

But the footsteps behind her followed. "Natalie. Please. Won't you talk to me?"

"No. I'm not interested in anything you have to say."

But Justin's words rang through her again. Maybe, just maybe, if she did talk with her dad—and that was a big *if*—it could help her. Maybe she could close that chapter in her life for good.

If she didn't, he might shadow her forever.

She slowed as she reached the big glass panes of Grady's, and a glance inside told her that the ladies' auxiliary was enjoying a midday meal, with Stella at the head of the table.

Perfect. There would be no sanctuary there today.

As she moved to stride across the street, her dad grabbed her elbow, his grip firm but not painful. "I owe you an apology, Natalie Joy."

"Don't." She wasn't entirely sure if she was responding to his use of her middle name or the fact that he was attempting to smooth over his sins. Which were too many to enumerate and far too many to sweep under the rug.

"Please." He tugged on his earlobe, which hung lower than she remembered. Not that she'd spent a lot of time thinking about what he looked like. In fact, she'd spent a whole lot of time purposefully not thinking about him at all.

"I don't want to do this. Not here. Not with the entire population of the Crick trying to get a look at us through Grady's window. And definitely not so close to my wedding."

She crossed her arms. Then uncrossed them. Then searched for her pockets.

But the pockets were still absent from her tailored jeans. She settled her hands on her hips as her dad grabbed the back of his neck and stared at the ground. Good. He shouldn't be able to make eye contact with her. Not after everything he'd done. Or worse, what he hadn't done.

"That's why I need to talk to you. You should know—before you get married—that you deserve the very best, and I should have done better by you. You deserved better than a lousy father who liked to drink a little too much."

"A little too much?" The words tasted like lemons, and she spat them out.

Why did he do that? Why did he downplay his sins? He made it seem like his affinity for alcohol was merely a preference for a cool beverage and not the thing that had landed him in jail on more than a few nights. Like it wasn't the reason his family had combusted.

Well, that and his other preferences, which she had no desire to unearth on a public street. Or any street, for that matter.

It was better to walk away, forget that she'd ever seen him again, and avoid whatever scene was sure to follow. She turned, but her dad caught her arm again, holding her in place despite the glare she shot over her shoulder.

"I made a lot of mistakes."

She snorted. Understatement of the century.

"I deserve that. Worse, really." His gaze traveled up to meet hers, and in it was a lifetime of heartache. Enough to chip at something frozen in her chest. It was relentless and infinitely uncomfortable. She needed to end this charade. Now.

"Just say whatever you need to and go."

He flinched, but he didn't back away. Instead he stepped closer and dropped his voice. "I regret so many things. The way I hurt your mother. The way I dragged our family's name through the mud. The way I ruined other marriages."

She let out a slow breath through her nose and jerked her arm free. But she stayed put.

"I was a fool. I was lost. And I treated you terribly. But the thing I regret the most is not protecting you."

Her head snapped up, her gaze a laser. "What's that supposed to mean? You saw me every day. You saw her. You knew. Everything she did. And you did nothing."

"I know. And there's more. It's worse than you think."

Worse? How could it possibly be worse?

"When I had a chance to protect you, I was too selfish to let you go."

She could only blink. There were no words. Only the echo of his regret and the questions that ripped through her. They were too jumbled to speak, too vast to fully understand. So she stood like a statue, like a stupid statue, as he confessed his greatest sin.

"There was a time—you were barely five—when Justin's parents and Aretha came to me. They knew what was happening. They saw that you weren't growing like you should have been. Your skin was so pale, and you were always hungry."

"Because I was starving."

He flinched, the truth a sledgehammer.

Well, good. He deserved it.

She cocked her head, daring him to continue. But the disconnected gaze he'd always worn in her youth had disappeared. His blue eyes were bright and intense. And he didn't back down.

"They knew she was beating you."

Because her childhood had been an open book. One she'd feared no one had wanted to read.

"They wanted—" He stopped to clear his throat as the lines on his face pulled even tighter. "They offered to let you stay with them. Aretha wanted you to move into her place. You would be safe. You would be cared for. Three meals every day. Clean clothes. New clothes."

Something inside her twisted tight, but his words didn't quite make sense in her mind.

"But I said no."

It all clicked into place, and she wanted to scream. She wanted to cry. She wanted to punch her father in his lying, cheating, stealing mouth.

"How could you? How—how d-d-dare you? You!" Her hand flew from her hip, her finger waving in his face. She didn't even have time to curse her stupid stutter, so insistent was her reaction.

Forget the patrons inside the restaurant. Forget the wagging tongues of the ladies' auxiliary. Forget the scene she'd been so desperate not to make.

She'd been loved. They'd cared about her. They hadn't turned a blind eye. They'd offered refuge and hope.

And her dad had refused.

"I thought I was showing you how much I loved you by keeping you close. I thought I could make up for her shortcomings."

"Shortcomings? *Shortcomings!*" The word burst out, and she only wished she could scream it louder. "You call what she did a *shortcoming*?"

"I think she was trying. But I had hurt her—a lot. I thought

I could show you enough love to make up for it. At least I wanted to."

"You thought letting her starve me was showing me love?" She burned from somewhere deep within, a fire stoked by a pain she couldn't even call by name. Pain she'd sworn she'd dealt with that bubbled back to the surface. "You thought letting her beat me was showing me love?" Hot tears gushed forth, rolling down her cheeks. "You thought ignoring me for fifteen years was showing me love?"

He shook his head, every line on his face spelling shame. "I was selfish. I didn't know what love was. And I sure didn't know how to show it. To you or Connie."

"Don't say her name."

He flinched again.

Good.

"We were both lost. We married so young, and I hadn't been in a church since the wedding."

"And what? You want me to believe that you found God and now everything's going to be all right and we can be a family? News flash. We were never a family."

"I know it's hard to believe, but I've changed. I did find God, and I just need you to know how very, very sorry I am that I hurt you so much. You deserved better. You deserved the best. And I failed you."

Her tongue was in a knot, and her hands shook as she crossed her arms over her chest. But the tears were the worst. Unbidden and relentless. They rolled down her face and off her chin. But her hands weren't steady enough to catch them in their path.

"I know this is hard. Probably a surprise."

Probably? "I could have had a family. I could have had a mother who loved me. And . . . and you stole that from me."

His shoulders drooped and his chin dipped. "I know."

"What do you want from me?"

"I'm not asking for anything. I'm just hoping for forgiveness."

"Well, you can stop hoping. It's never going to happen." Jerking away from him, she collected herself enough to run, and then she took off.

She didn't really have any idea where she was heading as she raced away from the diner in the opposite direction of the inn, her feet carrying her faster than she'd ever run before. And then suddenly it was there, the Kanes' big white house, looming large in the wide yard. She needed to see Mama Kane, to know if it was true.

But how could it be? She'd have known, right? Someone would have told her long before now.

And they hadn't. Because it was some elaborate lie her father had concocted. Right?

She didn't knock. She never had.

Barging in through the mudroom door, she called out, gasping and stuttering and a mess of tears and hiccups. "Mama Kane! Mama K-Kane! Are you here?"

Heavy footsteps flew down the central staircase, but it wasn't Mama Kane who appeared.

Justin stopped on the last step, his hand still on the ornate wooden rail.

She slammed to a halt too, unable to look away from him.

"You talked to your dad, didn't you?"

"You knew?" Her vision flashed crimson, and she charged at him, her fists at the ready. She wasn't sure what she was going to do when she got to him, but she wanted him to hurt like she hurt. She wanted him to feel the same betrayal she did. If he could feel just a fraction of the pain that seared through her, maybe he'd understand.

But when she reached him, he reached for her. And suddenly she was sobbing in his arms. He held her so close she couldn't find a full breath or wiggle her arms, which were smashed between them. But he didn't seem to mind that her tears were feeding an ever-growing lake on the front of his plaid shirt. Or when she pressed her nose into him and left behind only God knows what.

He just held her. Every now and then a low word rumbled in his chest and made it through to her consciousness. "Okay. It's all right. Let it out."

But she was afraid if she didn't stem the flow, it would never stop. "I could have lived with Aretha. She w-wanted me." She hiccuped loudly and felt him smile where he rested his cheek on top of her head. His hand made a slow trek up her back. Then down. Then up again. Over and over it flowed, the rhythm as familiar as the waves.

"Natalie, we all wanted you."

Her breath caught. She couldn't possibly have heard him correctly. But then he said something even sweeter.

"You were practically a part of our family. When my sister comes up from Charlottetown to visit, she still says how much she misses you at family dinners."

"But I thought I was all alone. All those years. No one said anything."

One of his hands left her back, leaving a coolness in its place, and she arched against the loss and straight into him. But his hand immediately appeared on her cheek, his big thumb brushing across her chin and his fingers sifting into her curls. He held her away from him just far enough to look into her face, but she couldn't manage to get her gaze past his lips, which were dark and firm.

"Can you blame them? How could they have told you what your father had done?"

Another hiccup escaped, and his lips curved, pulling at the five o'clock shadow across his jaw. Suddenly she pulled her arm free because she had to touch that rugged line. Just once. The whiskers there were as abrasive as she'd imagined they might be. But the skin below was soft and tan.

As she reached the corner beneath his ear, she realized something had changed. "You cut your hair." It wasn't quite a question, but she wasn't sure she could believe it.

He shrugged. "Some bossy lady told me I should."

She tried for a smile, but it quaked and couldn't find its footing.

His thumb took another sweep over the apple of her cheek, and suddenly she couldn't breathe or think or do anything. A swarm of monarchs had taken up residence inside her, swooping and gliding along.

But she still couldn't tear her gaze away from his lips.

Suddenly she realized just how much she wanted him to kiss her. Or to kiss him.

She couldn't care less who instigated it. She just needed to feel his lips on hers. At least once in her life. That would be enough. Surely.

Just the one kiss.

Her entire body trembled at the very idea.

This was Justin, who she'd known forever. Justin, who had held and comforted her. Justin, who had stood up to the bullies in school and the bully in the florist shop. Justin, who suddenly wasn't just Justin anymore.

He must have felt her knees begin to give, and he tightened his hold on her. "You were never alone, you know. From that day in the lighthouse, the first time we really met. You were never alone."

Did he mean his parents had nearly adopted her? Or did he mean him? Did he mean he'd been hers forever?

She closed her eyes, and the question came out differently than she'd planned, but exactly what she so desperately needed. "Someone cared?"

"Didn't you know? Didn't you know that my mom thinks cheese sandwiches are the lowest form of sustenance, but she made them every day for you because you said they were your favorite?" His mouth twitched as though the memory was taking control.

Laughing through tears was easier than she thought, and she couldn't hold back now. "They weren't my favorite. It was just the first food I hadn't had to make for myself since I could remember."

His whole face twitched to the side, his lips pursed but grinning. "Please don't ever tell my mother that. She'll be heartbroken."

"Promise."

His hand sank into her hair, cupping the back of her head, and she couldn't find the strength anymore to hold it up. Leaning into his embrace, she nearly collapsed against his shoulder. With the tears her strength had leaked away.

"You were always welcome in this house every day and every night. I hope you knew that."

She nodded into his chest, the words coming out mumbled

against his shirt. "I did. But being welcomed and being loved are very different things. I guess I thought . . . maybe I wasn't worth it to anyone."

His entire body stiffened, and she could feel his breathing deep and measured, like he was holding back, counting to ten before he exploded. But when he spoke, his words were softer than Canada goose down. "Maybe your mom and dad were incapable of loving you, but that doesn't mean you're unlovable."

Her throat clogged with something unnamed. Fear and joy. Shame and apprehension. But there was something she had to confess. "I was afraid if I stayed on the island, I'd end up married to a man just like my dad and that I'd become just like my mom. Because no one else would ever love me."

She wanted so badly to look into his eyes, to see whatever was crossing his face as his fingers tightened in her hair and his body turned not just tense but unyielding. His heart raced below her ear, and hers flew to keep up with it. But it was too fast, an unsustainable speed.

When he finally leaned back to look at her, there were tears in his eyes too. His voice had been raked over gravel and shredded through a hay baler. "Is that the man you think I am?"

He pressed his forehead to hers, and it was warm, borderline feverish. Their breath mingling and their noses nearly touching, he stood like a statue. But he was hardly unaffected if the trembling in his hands was any indication.

Please. If he could just kiss her, it would be okay. He could make it all better.

Except a little voice in her head reminded her she wasn't free to kiss him. She wasn't free to hold him and beg him to hold her back.

She'd made a promise. And she didn't intend to end up like either of her parents.

But it was safe and warm in his embrace. Russell never had to know.

Except she'd know. And she couldn't live with herself. She still had to look in the mirror to put mascara on every day.

She closed her eyes, took a deep breath, and forced her heart to remain intact. And then she stepped out of the protection of his arms.

Just as someone behind her cleared her throat.

Heart in her stomach, she spun to face Mama Cheese Sandwich. Then the words were gushing out without thought. "I'm so sorry. I didn't know you tried to save me. I didn't know, but I shouldn't have left without thanking you."

A smile broke across Mama Kane's face and she held out her arms, so much like her son had. And Natalie tumbled into them.

18

Is that the man you think I am?

What did that even mean? Who said things like that? Of course she hadn't meant that Justin was like her father. He'd always been a good man. A kind, loyal, loving man.

So why would he think she was comparing him to her dad?

Natalie had been rolling the question over in her mind night after nearly sleepless night, and she was no closer to figuring out what Justin had meant. Which basically meant she'd spent five days walking around like a zombie, only to scare small children at the breakfast table next to hers.

The little boy who sat at the table beside hers stared at her muffin a little too long, his eyes devouring what his mouth couldn't. Even though he'd already had one of his own.

Then again, he hadn't eaten more than a bite of his breakfast sandwich on pretzel bread.

She frowned at him, and he jumped, leaning against his mother, who was consumed with caring for the littler one.

Eyeing the sweet drizzle over the tart blackberry deliciousness, she weighed her options. Caden's sweets never disappointed. But she knew what it was to be hungry. What it was to want. Something inside her melted, and she picked up the silver platter with her untouched muffin. When his mom's back was turned, she slipped the tray off her table and held it out to him.

He blinked at her with big, round eyes filled with one question. *Really?*

With a nod she gave him permission, and he snatched it up, his palm crushing the rounded dome and certainly turning his hands into a sticky mess. Not that any little boy worried about such trivialities when sweets were at stake.

After two enormous bites, he flashed a blackberry smile at her, and she matched her grin to his.

Suddenly her phone rang, and she picked it up, both praying it would be Russell and hoping it wouldn't be.

"Hi, babe." His voice was muffled, and background noise fought for dominance on the call.

"Hey." She sighed. She wanted to talk with him, to hear how the album was coming along. But neither could she deny the guilt that his voice conjured.

She hadn't done anything wrong. Not really.

But kind of.

She'd made the right decision after all. She'd stopped it—whatever *it* might have been—from happening. And she hadn't seen Justin since.

So why did it feel like shame had taken to gnawing on her stomach like a hungry dog on a steak?

Maybe if she told Russell what had happened . . .

Then what? Then he'd be hurt, and she'd feel terrible. Worse yet, it might open a Pandora's box of questions about her relationship with Justin. And why she'd left the island in the first place. And why she hadn't wanted to come back at all.

Those weren't a part of her Nashville life. They couldn't be.

She just had to get married and get back to the life that was hers for the taking. The one she'd always dreamed of.

"Natalie? Did you hear me?"

"Umm . . . I'm sorry. It's kind of noisy on your end. I missed that."

"I'm at the airport." Russell raised his voice to be heard over the shuffling of the other travelers. "I'm headed back to PEI. I got an early flight into Montreal. And I'm on the plane with Darren and Courtney."

Courtney, her bridesmaid. Courtney, whom she'd met through Russell. Courtney, who was supposed to be a friend.

Courtney, in whom she didn't dare confide.

"Oh. Great." Except it wasn't great. Their arrival simply meant that more of Russell's friends were on the way. More of Nashville would soon be on PEI. Because her wedding was right around the corner. Which only led to more of that chewed-up-steak feeling. "What time do you land?"

"About eleven. I'll get a rental car, and I'll see you at breakfast tomorrow."

"I'll wait up for you." It wasn't like she'd be sleeping anyway.

"All right. If you want to." A loud announcement in the background sounded like Charlie Brown's teachers. "They're about to board first class. Got to go. Love you."

He hung up before she could reciprocate, leaving her to stare at the screen of her phone and wonder what that had meant—she could stay up if she wanted to.

They hadn't seen each other in four weeks. Shouldn't he be so eager to see her that he'd beg her to stay up? Just for one kiss?

Maybe there was a more important question. Why wasn't she more eager to see him?

She wanted to pull out her hair or run ten miles or do anything but think about the answer to that question.

It had nothing to do with the way Justin's blue eyes had flashed like the sun across ice when he held her and looked into her eyes. And certainly the butterflies in her middle had been a result of the tumult of speaking to her father.

She'd just been so busy for the last few weeks that she hadn't had time to miss Russell.

That was definitely it. And she wasn't going to let these men and their ambiguous words keep her from getting some rest.

Except it wasn't quite time for a nap. First she had to check on a few wedding-related items. That meant a trip to see Marie.

As she pushed back her chair, it scraped along the floor, drawing the attention of the little boy licking his fingers. With a wild wave, he bid her farewell, and she shot him a smile and a low-handed wiggle of her fingers in reply.

The only boy she wanted to think about today was covered in blackberry drizzle.

That couldn't be a good thing.

At the top of the stairs to the basement apartment, she ran into Seth, whose broad shoulders seemed to fill the entire width of the hallway. He towered over her, so she had to crane her neck to look into his face. But the silver tray lined with a lace doily in his hands made him a little more approachable.

"Breakfast for the bedridden?" she asked.

He nodded, his eyes a little wild, his hair more than a little mussed. She'd seen him running his fingers through it on several occasions, which made sense. He wasn't worried only about his wife. His baby was at risk too. "She just woke up and said she wanted pancakes." He nodded at the platter in front of him, which held three fluffy, perfectly round blueberry pancakes. A little jug of syrup sat to the side. "It's the first time she's been hungry in the morning in weeks."

"So Caden made up something special for her."

"Yes."

The scent of rich fruit and sweet maple wrapped around her, and she inhaled deeply. "Mind if I follow you down? Marie said I should visit today."

He rolled his eyes, but his smile was clearly for his wife. "She's supposed to be on bed rest. But it's like she doesn't know how to rest. She's always suggesting a quick trip to Aretha's or to the store. Doesn't she know what bed rest means? When I tell her she can't, she'll do something on her computer or come up with some new advertising idea. It's like her brain has to make up for the rest of her not moving. So come on."

He led the way, not even flinching when he hit the squeaky step third from the top. When he opened the door, Natalie took a moment to wonder at the home Marie had made. The walls of the one-bedroom apartment were a soft gray, inviting and cool even in the warm summer months. And the window, though small along the top of the far wall, glowed with the sun's morning light.

Seth marched toward the bedroom, a man on a mission to get his wife whatever she wanted.

Would Russell do the same for her? Would he drop everything to care for her if she was laid up?

She tried to picture it, but the image wouldn't come. She

could see her cell phone ringing, Russell checking in to make sure she was all right. She could see him at the studio recording another track. She could see him rushing in with a bowl of soup and dropping a kiss on her forehead.

But in her imagination he always dashed away, back to his important life. Back to the things that must be done. And it made her taste something sour in the back of her throat.

"Hi, honey. I brought a visitor." Seth tiptoed into the bedroom, where Marie was propped against a mountain of pillows, her laptop in place across her legs and her fingers flying across the keyboard. She glanced up at her husband's announcement, and her teeth flashed white even in the bright room.

"Natalie. I'm so glad you're here. We have so many last-minute things to confirm." She patted the spot on the mattress beside her. "Sit down."

"Oh, you enjoy your breakfast first. I didn't mean to interrupt."

"Nonsense. You talk. I'll eat." She set her computer aside, and Seth slid the tray into place over her legs. "Thank you." She turned her lips upward, and Seth obliged with a quick peck and a gentle caress of her rounded stomach.

It was a simple kiss, but somehow it felt like she was intruding on an intimate moment, and she quickly turned her head to stare at a magazine cover on the wall. The front page of *Rest & Retreats* magazine had been framed in floating glass, and she stared at it for a long second before she realized exactly what she was looking at.

"That's Rose's Red Door Inn." She felt stupid as soon as she blurted it out. Of course it was the inn. Its big blue walls, inviting garden, and candy-apple red door couldn't be mistaken. But it was on the cover of a magazine under a headline that said "The Best-Kept Secret on the North Shore." How had she missed that?

"Yes. That's our inn." Marie glowed. Whether it was from pride or the baby was up for debate.

"How did"—she waved a hand at the picture—"that happen? That's a big travel magazine, right? Did Adam write that?"

With a chuckle, Marie shook her head. "Actually, no. But he was here when it happened. I'll tell you about it sometime. Today we have to tackle wedding things." Again she patted the spot on the bed next to her. "Have a seat."

Seth had made his way to the door but turned back one more time before exiting. "Do you ladies need anything before I go?"

Marie looked at her, and Natalie shook her head. "We're fine. Thank you, though," Marie said.

When they were alone, Natalie whispered, "Are you sure you're feeling up to this? I can take care of whatever needs to be done."

Marie cut into her stack of pancakes, loaded them onto her fork, and said, "I feel great today. I finally have my appetite back. So as long as you don't mind a few drops of syrup on my notes, let's do this."

Natalie nodded, and they dug in. Marie's lists were neat and orderly, just like the woman herself. Each page of a small notebook contained major category tasks, and the completed projects had been crossed off line by line.

Marie pointed her pen to the first page, which was labeled LOCATION. "Have you been to see the barn this week?"

Natalie almost choked on her tongue. Why did that feel

like such a loaded question? Probably because she'd been so actively avoiding said location since she and Justin had almost . . . since the last time she'd seen him. Because she didn't especially want to see him again.

Well, maybe a little. But from a good distance. With plenty of other people around. And zero temptation to kiss him.

"Um, no. I haven't. But the last time I saw it, it looked almost done. The interior has been completely stained and it looks so good. You picked the perfect color."

"It was a team effort," Marie said. It was a lie, and they both knew it. "How about the outside of the barn? Is Justin done painting it yet? Seth went over to help a couple of days ago and said there was only one wall left to complete."

She nodded. "Justin said something about painting the trim too." But that was over a week ago, so maybe it was completed already with Seth's help. After all, Justin had been avoiding her too. He'd had plenty of time to focus on getting the barn done because he hadn't been saying more vague things to her.

"Will you check on it?" Natalie's poker face must have failed her because Marie immediately added, "Or I'll ask Seth to go over there. No big deal. No need to add any pressure to the bride." She patted Natalie's hand, but it didn't help.

"No. I can do it." Besides, Russell would be back tonight. She could take him with her. Then there would be nothing to worry about. "The tables were supposed to be delivered last week. I'll make sure they're all set up."

Marie flipped a page in her book. "Perfect. The linens should be delivered on Wednesday. Did you get antiques from Aretha?"

"Yes. Well, almost. I need to go pick them up, but they're picked out."

With an easy flick of her wrist, Marie made more notes on her sheet. "Great. What theme did you go with?"

It was on the tip of her tongue, but somehow it felt like years since she and Aretha had talked. Since then she'd survived the run-in with her dad, the "event" with Justin, and too many hours of missed sleep. So the words weren't quite there. What had they decided on? "We picked a bunch of lamps and lanterns."

"Lights and shores?"

"Yes, that's it. But I don't know how we're going to make it feel like the shore."

Marie tapped her pen to her lip once, then again. Then her eyes crinkled at the corners. "Seashells by the cake. The round tables will already be full with lamps and orchids. Let's not add to them. We'll keep the shore confined to the side tables. I've got some brown burlap panels that we can use to look like sand. And when we add colorful seashells, it'll be perfect."

She checked another item off her list and added two more to-dos. With each flip of the page, they marked off another piece of the wedding puzzle.

Food? Harrison had completed a menu for the buffet-style catering. Short ribs and crab cakes and lobster rolls.

Flowers? Lois had come through with beautiful arrangements and promised to have them at the church and the barn first thing next Saturday morning.

Cake? Caden was already working on the classic white and red velvet tiers, which would be set on wooden stair-stepped cake stands handmade by Seth.

Dress? She needed to try it on one last time to make sure it still fit. Maybe she should be more worried after all the carbs she'd been eating at Caden's table. Then again, she'd done more manual labor this summer than she had in fifteen years. It should all balance out. She hoped.

"Music?"

Natalie blinked. "Um. No. I don't have a plan beyond the pianist at the church."

"Not a problem." Marie's lips tightened like it might indeed be a problem. She set her pen to tapping the paper until her eyes brightened. "Of course. This is PEI. There are a hundred *ceilidhs* and kitchen parties on this island. Surely we can drum up someone who's available on Saturday."

"As long as it's not—" She chomped into her tongue and winced against the sharp pain. She'd been about to say Justin's name. But they were supposed to be on good terms. They *were* on good terms now. So it wouldn't make any sense. There was no plausible reason why she wouldn't want him to play the music at her reception.

Except, well, it would be too much. His voice serenading her first dance with her new husband. That didn't work for her at all.

"As long as it's someone Russell likes. He's the musical one, after all."

"Of course. I'll make some calls. I've been sending guests to see the weekly show by the family at Stanley Bridge Hall for years. Maybe they'll help us out."

Marie moved on, farther into her book until her words were barely an echo, because suddenly all Natalie could think about was Justin at her wedding. Would he expect to be invited? Had Marie assumed and added him to the list? Would he even want to be there?

"So that brings us to guests. Any last-minute additions?"

"You got Mama Kane and Aretha and Jack?"

"Yes."

"And Caden and Adam were on the list."

Marie nodded. "Yes. Adam's the best man."

Right. Of course he was. "Then, I think we're good."

Marie nodded slowly, but she didn't close her book. "Aretha came by the other day. She said your dad was in town."

Natalie's whole body stiffened until she nearly fell off the edge of the bed. This could go nowhere good.

"Did you talk with him? Would you like to invite him? There's plenty of room at the barn."

Marie had gone exactly where Natalie had known she would. Right past innocuous and directly into danger. She sucked in a stabilizing breath, clasping her hands in her lap and staring at the magazine cover on the wall. "I did see him. No, I don't want to invite him."

"What did he say?"

It's none of your business. You weren't here when he made my life a nightmare and then refused to let me out of it. The words screamed through her mind, but Marie didn't deserve them. She'd never been anything but kind.

Natalie bit back the bitterness and said simply, "It doesn't matter."

"It's hard with fathers and daughters, isn't it?"

Understatement of the century. "You have no idea."

Marie's laugh was dry and humorless, and the grim line of her mouth spoke of an understanding, like she'd suffered too. "My dad's no treat. He's done everything in his power to hurt me, so I ran."

"To where?"

Her eyebrows raised in surprise, as though it should be obvious. "To here."

"Well, aren't we a pair?" Natalie wasn't too lost in her own pain to find the irony of their situation. "You came here for sanctuary, and I left here because there was none."

Marie met her gaze, her own intense and sure. But her tone was gentle. "Maybe you weren't looking in the right places. I can't seem to get away from it. Jack, Aretha, Caden, Father Chuck—they all reached out to me when I needed them most."

"Well, I wasn't so lucky. I was left with a mother who resented me and a father who betrayed me." Her breathing picked up speed, matching the pulse through her veins and the thrumming at her temples. "And then he comes back to town and apologizes, like that's supposed to make everything better. He let my mom abuse and neglect me because I was the reason she was stuck with him—stuck with a man who cheated on her and lied to us. And she hated her life so much that she did the only thing she could. She made mine miserable too. And he didn't even bother to notice. He just stayed stuck in the bottom of his bottle, and when someone tried to help, he didn't let them. He just left me to rot in that stinking house."

Her hands began to shake, but she couldn't stop. The words were flowing on their own, like a dam had been closed for too long and the truth needed to be spoken.

"And now he wants me to just forgive him? Because he's sorry? He wants me to believe he's changed. Well, I don't care anymore. I just can't. And I don't want him at my wedding!"

When her outburst finally died down, Natalie swallowed convulsively, trying to dislodge her heart, which had rammed itself into place. It didn't budge as the silence lingered for a long moment. Maybe Marie was waiting to make sure she was really done.

"For what it's worth," Marie said at long last, pushing herself up against the pillows at her back, "I'd give anything to hear my dad apologize. For anything."

"But you don't know my dad. He's the worst kind of man. He destroyed families and ruined our reputation."

Marie frowned, the sadness in her face from deep wounds. "I'm not trying to play a game of who has the worse father or in any way excuse what your dad did, but I know a thing or two about bad fathers. My dad loves money so much that he tried to leverage the very worst thing that ever happened to me for a land deal." She let out another humorless laugh. "And then he fought me tooth and nail for the trust fund my mother left me, the money I needed to keep this inn open."

Natalie blinked quickly, trying to figure out where to start with that information. The inn was in danger? Marie was a trust fund kid? Her dad was terrible!

"Is the Red Door going to be okay? W-what happened?"

"You showed up. Your booking this summer kept the doors open long enough for the judge in Boston to throw out my dad's case." A hint of a smile flitted across Marie's exhausted features, and she pressed her hand to her stomach. "I'm free to use the money in my trust fund to take care of some needed repairs. And to take care of my baby." Her pleasant expression gave way to another one of pain. "But my dad doesn't want anything to do with us now. I tried to tell him about the baby. I thought maybe . . . Well, I hoped he'd care.

If not about me, then about his grandchild. But he wouldn't even see Seth when he went to Boston to sign the paperwork."

Natalie's pulse slowed, her chest aching as she surveyed Marie. She was such a kind, warm woman. How could she have come from such an awful man? How had her goodness and gentleness survived in spite of a man who had done so many awful things?

Natalie couldn't make the puzzle pieces fit. And it poked at her, prodding her to ask questions of herself that she really didn't want to answer. If Marie had moved on, if she'd dealt with the pain, couldn't Natalie learn to let go?

"I'm not saying an apology would excuse my dad's actions— or your dad's." Marie shrugged. "I just think it's a pretty significant gesture, humbling yourself like that. Admitting to your faults and failures. And it sounds like your dad recognizes that he made some pretty big ones."

Natalie folded her arms across her stomach and nodded. "Nothing can change what he did."

"Of course not. But it doesn't mean you have to be the one to carry the weight of his bad decisions."

The back of her eyes burned, and she pressed her palm over her mouth. Some scars ran too deep.

Marie reached for her hand and gave it a soft squeeze. "It's still a bit of a mystery to me, but here's what I've learned. Forgiveness isn't reserved for the ones who deserve it. God gives it freely, and we should do the same. The one person you can set free from bitterness is you. The fact that your dad apologized is amazing. But even if he hadn't, at some point you're going to have to let go of your anger or you'll end up just like him, hurting the people you're supposed to love."

The waterworks turned on, and suddenly she couldn't keep the sobs and hiccups from following suit.

She'd done everything—*everything*—to keep from becoming her parents. And she'd still ended up just like them, wielding her anger and bitterness as a shield, trying desperately to protect herself. But it didn't work.

It never worked. It never would.

Sniffing against the flood running down her face, she said, "It took me a lot of hours of therapy to put a voice to my mom's pain. I think she was so hurt by my dad that she didn't know how to do anything but hurt me. All I knew growing up was that I didn't want to be anything like her." She curled in on herself, wrapping her arms around her stomach and wishing she could leave the island forever. Only she had to face Marie's words. "And now you're telling me I'm exactly like she was."

Marie caught her hand, tugging it free and pressing it to her knee. "I'm not saying that at all. We all deal with our disappointments and hurts differently. You don't have to be your mom or your dad. But I know that when I carried around my dad's betrayal, there wasn't room in my heart to love anyone else."

"What about Seth?" She glanced toward the door that led to the stairs, where he'd disappeared thirty minutes before. "You seem to be so in love."

Marie's face glowed, and now Natalie was sure it wasn't just the pregnancy. "We are. I love that man more than I thought was even possible. But when we met, we were a mess. We were both lugging around broken hearts, and we were afraid of what falling in love might mean." Her gaze turned distant, as though she was ten miles away and ten years ago.

"Loving someone is kind of like offering forgiveness. There's no guarantee that they're not going to hurt you again. You can't promise perfection. But you choose to love and you choose to forgive, because living in fear of being hurt again is just a facsimile of life."

Is that what her carefully crafted facade was? A facsimile of life?

But she was happy. Despite the tears currently gushing down her cheeks, she was happy.

Or are you simply safe?

No. This was happiness. A good life. A stable home. A kind man. This was what she'd always dreamed of. This was everything her childhood wasn't. This was what she wanted.

Are you sure about that?

No.

Oblivious to the argument waging inside Natalie, Marie patted her hand. "I know this is hard, but I think you should reconsider what your dad said. For your sake and for Russell's. What you don't deal with now is going to show up in your marriage." She managed a tremulous smile. "As long as your heart is still leaking, you won't be able to love Russell like he deserves."

Natalie swiped at the dampness beneath her eyes with both hands and sat up a little straighter.

She had to deal with her dad, because she couldn't jeopardize her marriage to Russell. There were too many eyes watching, waiting for her to screw this up.

Suddenly feet pounded down the stairs, the squeaky step letting out its pitiful cry. The apartment door flung open and slammed closed. Then Seth stood in the bedroom doorway, his chest rising and falling in rapid succession.

Marie was the first to catch her wits. "What's going on? What's wrong?"

He waved in the general direction of the upstairs, his breath still too fast. "Father Chuck."

"Is he all right?" Natalie asked.

"Just called. Fire at the church."

Natalie jumped to her feet, the words ringing in her ears. "Fire? Does he need help?"

"No. It's out. But the entire altar area is ruined."

"Ruined?" Marie's face turned grave. "Then where are we going to have the wedding ceremony?"

Excellent question. One Natalie didn't have an answer for.

Seth shook his head. "I don't know. But the church is no longer an option. At least not next week."

19

I can't wait to see the barn after all the work you've put into it."

Natalie nodded at Russell over breakfast the next morning to let him know she'd heard him. But she didn't have much else to offer by way of reply. Not when the wedding she was planning was turning into definitely not the wedding she'd planned.

Russell made an appreciative sound in the back of his throat as he scooped in another forkful of Caden's excellent salmon and asparagus omelet. "Have you been eating like this all summer?"

"Like what?" She eyed the cinnamon roll that she might have shared with the boy at the next table over, if his family hadn't checked out the day before. "Like three-course meals every morning from the best chef on the island? Pretty much."

"Maybe I shouldn't have left." He shoveled in another bite, savoring it just as loudly.

She knew he was referring to all the delicious breakfasts

he'd missed, but something inside her snapped. "Well, maybe you shouldn't have."

His eyebrows rose, and he wiped each corner of his mouth with his cloth napkin before setting it down again in his lap. "Is everything all right? You were acting strange last night too."

Strange like she'd spent the better part of her afternoon pulling her hair out trying to find a new venue for them to say their vows? Or strange like he'd noticed that she couldn't quite bring herself to kiss him when he arrived at the inn a little after midnight? She'd brushed it off because their friends were with him, and she hadn't wanted to make a spectacle.

But shouldn't she have missed him so much that she couldn't wait to be back in his arms?

Instead, well, she didn't know what she felt. Except that maybe something had changed while he was gone.

"I'm sorry. Yes, everything's fine. I'm just tired, I guess. It's been a long few weeks, and it's been hard to get everything done without you." That sounded like a reasonable excuse for her mutinous emotions.

"Didn't your friend help out?" He snapped his fingers twice. "Justin something-or-other."

If he only knew. "Yes. Justin helped out plenty." Helped her into this inner turmoil that was liable to sink her ship—and her chance at a future with Russell—any day now.

"So what's the problem? Too many cinnamon rolls? Your dress doesn't fit?"

Why was everyone so obsessed with her dress fitting?

Okay, that might be an exaggeration, but it sure felt like she was getting the third degree about it lately. First Marie. Now Russell. Had she gained so much weight that she *looked* like her dress wouldn't fit?

Someone put her out of her misery.

She hung her head and closed her eyes and prayed for an escape. Except that's what she always did. She ran. And she couldn't run now.

"There was a fire at the church. And now we don't have a place for the ceremony."

His forehead bunched up, and his eyes squinted. "I thought the wedding was at the barn. Isn't it?"

Seriously? Had he just admitted to not even knowing where their wedding was going to take place? Exactly how disconnected was he from her life—from their life? Was it always going to be the music and then her?

Blood boiled too close to the surface, so she pressed her hands to her cheeks and kept her head down. Her tongue was getting awfully sore from biting it, but she clamped onto it again.

Don't say anything.

But he waited for her response, his impatient fingers strumming on the table.

Taking a stabilizing breath, she licked her lips and stared straight at him. "The reception is at the barn. The ceremony was going to be at the church."

"Oh. Well, why not just move all of it to the barn? Then we won't have to travel between locations. It'll save time, and we'll get to start the party sooner."

Something about the way he said those last words made a tiny piece of her heart die. It was almost as if he was looking forward to the reception more than the marriage, to the party more than setting the tone for the rest of their lives together.

Even though she knew he didn't mean it like that, it was

hard not to read into what he said. She was marrying him for forever, and he was interested in a good party.

But she couldn't blame him for his careless words. It wasn't like he knew that she'd hoped and prayed for a marriage completely unlike her parents'. After all, she'd never told him, never spoke of the reasons why this was so important to her.

Beyond that, there was a little whisper in the back of her brain that said she didn't want to say her vows to another man on Kane property. It didn't seem right. "I don't think so. We can't just spring the entire thing on the Kanes."

"It's not any different than what you'd already planned. Besides, this will make everything easier."

"But there aren't any pews for the guests to sit in."

"So we'll bring in some more chairs." He knocked his middle knuckle against the blue tablecloth as though that settled the whole thing. And in his mind it did.

But just because Natalie had temporarily run out of valid reasons why the Kanes' barn was not the place to do this didn't mean her argument was over. Temporary hiatus was more like it. Until she could pick it back up, she was forced to follow Russell down the road to the barn to see all the hard work they'd put in.

She hadn't been quite ready.

Even from the edge of the road, the sturdy barn couldn't be missed. Justin must have mowed the grass around the structure, and against the shorter green, the white walls and blue roof gleamed beneath the sun. A touch of gray in the shingles kept it from blending into the too blue sky or the vast water that reached to the horizon. From this angle she could make out the edge of a red cliff, a narrow finger into the ocean, a testament to PEI's beauty.

She wanted to stand there for a long moment, close her eyes, and drink in the smell of wildflowers and fresh-cut grass. Her head lolled to the rhythm of the waves, and she smiled at the familiarity.

Why had she been so terrified of returning all those weeks ago?

But there was no time to consider that question as Russell grabbed her hand and tugged her across the field.

"People can park over there, I guess." He pointed to one of the plots that Justin had surely cleared. "It's nice enough. As good as the church."

Only it wasn't the same. Surely God could be as present in an old barn as he was at First Church of North Rustico. But there was something stirring, something holy, about making a vow before God in his own house.

As they reached the barn door, the gentle strum of a guitar greeted them. It wasn't showy or loud, the notes sweet and tender. Then a low, even voice joined in, and the words nearly knocked her on her backside.

"When the storm is rolling o'er the sea
And the light can't even reach the trees,
You can find a peace with me
Somewhere on this shore."

He took a breath, changed the chord, and kept going.

"If the seasons are about to change
And every hope seems beyond your range,
I will offer you a sweet exchange
Somewhere on this shore."

She didn't have any doubt. Justin had written those words for her. And she couldn't bear to stop him. Or to hear another word.

Maybe when he'd asked her if she thought he was *that* kind of man, he'd meant that *he* would have liked to be the one to marry her. And when he'd said she wasn't unlovable, did he know for sure because he had loved her?

Maybe not now. Maybe not anymore. But once.

Could someone know her so well, know all the hurts and foibles and outbursts she was prone to, and still love her?

She'd counted that cost with Russell and decided he could not.

But what if Justin was different?

She stopped breathing, an ache in her chest so searing that she couldn't move. Russell stopped for a moment too, his face shifting into music mode. His ears seemed to twitch as he listened for every transition and pitch. Justin hit them each perfectly.

He was sitting on a round table with his back to them, his foot planted on a chair and guitar resting on his knee. His hair was taller now, filled with vibrancy and life since he'd trimmed off the ponytail. It was short over his ears and at the back of his neck, and the front had been given just enough gel to add an inch to his height.

She wanted to run her fingers through it.

She pressed her hand over her mouth and closed her eyes against the traitorous thought. She had to capture these ideas intent on getting her into trouble. Capture them and dispose of them. Immediately.

She could do that. She could definitely do that.

"Didn't you say that we're still looking for a musician?"

Russell interrupted her internal pep talk and Justin's playing at the same time.

Justin found his voice first, hopping off the table and walking toward them. "I didn't hear you come in. Good to see you, Russ." He reached out to shake hands, but Russell seemed lost somewhere else.

"It's Russell." His correction was quick but not harsh. "What are you doing next Saturday?"

Justin's eyes narrowed, three little lines appearing between his eyebrows. When his gaze shifted to her, she tried to signal him to agree to nothing. But there was only so much she could do as Russell watched.

"We could use someone with your talent at the wedding and reception. And that song you just sang—maybe you could play that as Natalie walks down the aisle."

"Um . . ." Justin, so rarely at a loss for words, crossed his arms, stretching the soft cotton fabric of his shirt, and she couldn't help but recognize it as the same one she'd cried all over earlier that week. He watched her for a long second, and she shook her head quickly as Russell walked away.

"Please." She mouthed the word more than spoke it, but he couldn't miss her meaning.

"What happened to Ruth Allen? Why isn't she playing the wedding march?"

Russell tilted his head back, surely admiring the gorgeous wooden beams and the cathedral ceiling. "The church burned down."

Justin jumped. "It what?"

"Not all the way," Natalie rushed to add. "But there was a fire at the altar. The piano, stage, and cross are completely gone. We can't have our ceremony there."

"So where are you going to have it?" Even as he asked it, his face shifted into something that looked an awful lot like horror.

She cringed.

Russell noticed nothing. "Here. We can set up rows of chairs over there." He pointed to the back of the barn. "We'll say our 'I dos' and then start the party. No need to change locations. It'll be easier on everyone."

Except her and Justin.

He wiped away the abject revulsion that had been plastered across his face. With a curt nod, he forced a smile. When he met her gaze, there was a flicker of sadness in his eyes, but it didn't stop him. "I'd be happy to play your wedding. I'll call some friends, and we can have a proper party."

"Sounds great." Russell clapped Justin on the shoulder. "Ever think about doing something more professional with music?"

Justin shrugged. "Sometimes."

"We should definitely talk after the wedding."

It hit Natalie with the force of a hurricane. Her wedding would be his audition.

◆◆◆◆◆

The best part of Canada Day was the food and fireworks. So far Justin had been able to enjoy neither. The hamburgers tasted like sawdust, and the corn on the cob was even worse.

Or maybe it was him. Even the kids were devouring the potluck meal set up in the church parking lot as a last-minute fund-raiser, which they all hoped would be enough to repair the building that had been around for as long as anyone still alive.

But the repairs wouldn't come soon enough. They couldn't be done in time for Natalie's wedding.

He was going to have to go through with playing for her. At least if he performed well enough he might be able to make one of his dreams a reality. Even as he watched the other walk down the aisle toward another man.

He spit out a bite of hamburger and shoved his paper plate in the nearest trash bin, thankful for the cover of darkness. Small pockets of people from the community had gathered in their lawn chairs to thrill at the fireworks, which were about to grace the sky. But he wanted nothing to do with that. Nothing to do with any of them.

Suddenly he bumped into a beefy arm, and he jerked back. "Excuse me. I'm sorry." When he realized who he'd run into, Justin finally offered his first real smile of the day. "Harrison. Good to see you."

"Justin Kane, what are you doing wandering around out here all by yourself? You told me you were staying home."

He'd expected a greeting from the diner owner, and the high-pitched scolding caught him off guard. "Mom?"

She appeared around Harrison's far side, one hand resting on his elbow. She wagged a finger in Justin's direction. "We would've brought a chair for you if you'd told us you were coming."

We? Us? His throat suddenly felt like he'd swallowed a porcupine.

"We only brought just the two. But there's room on the ground over by the water if you want to sit with us."

So this was definitely a planned event. A . . . a . . . date? His mom was on a date with Harrison Grady. The realization rattled around as she continued jabbering, never taking her hand off Harrison's arm. Definitely possessive, like she was afraid if she let go, one of the other ladies from the auxiliary would try to take him away.

Doubtful. But maybe. After all, the man could cook. And his patch held a certain pirate intrigue.

Harrison was a friendly guy. Quiet, but everyone loved him. He was honest and loyal and worked hard to keep his restaurant the best in town. Which was why Justin and his mom had been going there for years.

But maybe she was going for other reasons too.

The couple bites of burger in his stomach suddenly hit a rough patch, and he needed to find a quiet place to digest this. All of it.

"So are you going to sit with us?" she asked.

"No thanks." He pointed toward the drink table. "I'm going to get some lemonade."

Harrison nodded. "Try one of those miniature pies that Caden made. Amazing."

With that the two slipped into the masses. If not for the way the moon reflected off Harrison's broad shoulders and balding head, Justin would have lost sight of them immediately in the darkness. But he watched the way his mother looked up and laughed, presumably at something he said. Not that Harrison was prone to making jokes.

"They make a nice couple."

He jumped again. This time at Natalie's magical appearance. "They're a couple?"

"Of course. Where have you been?"

Caught up in his own mind and worries and daydreams. Not that Natalie needed to know that. "Did she tell you that?"

"She didn't have to. It's clear to anyone with at least one working eye."

He chuckled at the lighthearted reference to Harrison's patch. But something inside him still felt sick. Had he really missed something obvious because he'd been so caught up in his own little world that seemed to revolve around Natalie?

"Is she—do you think she's happy?"

She giggled like a schoolgirl with a world of secrets. "Justin, it's been fifteen years since your dad died."

"I know. But I mean, is she happy with Harrison?"

"She's been on her own a long time. If she wasn't happy with him, she wouldn't bother with him. But look how sweet he is."

At that moment Harrison helped her into a foldable camping chair and settled her in place before sliding into the one beside her. Then he gently took her hand and held it in his own.

"I think she's happy."

Justin blinked. "All right." What else could he say? They'd grieved together for a long time. But if his mom was ready to move on, he was ready to watch her.

"Where's Russell?"

She didn't turn to look at him, instead keeping her gaze in the direction of the sea of lawn chairs. "With our friends who are here already. They set up a blanket on the edge of the water."

"Why aren't you with them?"

"Because I needed to find you."

Suddenly a loud boom pierced the night, and the accompanying red spray across the sky saved him from having to respond. There were a hundred things he wanted to say to

284

her in that moment, and only one he wanted to do. The one he'd sworn he wouldn't do again.

The crowd oohed and aahed, and she refused to look in his direction, her neck and arms stiff in the moonlight. The light was gentle on her skin, turning it to pearl, but the blues and greens of the show painted intermittent colors across her cheeks, hiding her freckles for an instant before fizzling out.

"Are you really going to do it?"

He knew what she meant, but he didn't have a ready answer, so he stalled. "Do what?"

"Play at my wedding?"

"When else would I ever have a chance to play in front of a dozen or more music industry big shots at the same time? This could be my chance for the deal I've worked my whole life for."

She sucked in a sharp breath and hugged herself like she was cold. Except it was a perfect night, warm with a gentle island breeze that felt more like a caress than an embrace. "You didn't answer my question."

No. He hadn't exactly. But she had to know she couldn't ask him to back out now.

"Are you really going to marry a man who has no idea who you are?"

An explosion seemed to shake the very ground they stood on, and she jumped. But she didn't speak.

"He has no idea about your parents or your childhood."

"So what?" Her voice was low, thoughtful. "That's not who I am anymore."

"You may not be that kid, but she sure shaped you. She's in the stutter that still comes out when you're scared or uncertain. She's in the way you try so hard to show people that you're worthy of love. She's in that sharp tongue you try so hard to hide from him. Does he even know how to volley it back at you?"

She bit the corner of her bottom lip and peeked at him out of the side of her eye. "What do you know about it?"

"Only that I've been on the receiving end of your red-headed temper more times than I can count." He paused for a quick breath but didn't dare hold off longer before continuing, lest she jump in to demonstrate exactly what he was saying. "And it's one of the things I love about you."

Her mouth was wide open, ready to argue, but his words seemed to steal the air from her balloon.

"How can he love the things he doesn't even know about? He has no idea about the little girl with stained clothes and messy hair who was picked on and bullied and overcame it all. He doesn't know how brave you were to leave this island or what it means that you got away."

When she finally answered, she dipped her chin and spoke to her shoes, perfect little flats fitting for a ballerina. She took a shaky breath that sounded strangely close to a sob. "He doesn't have to. That's not who I am."

"Or is it just not who you pretend to be?"

"I can't not marry him now. You know what'll happen if I don't."

He did. He could hear the old biddies blabbering about it already. *Rick and Connie O'Ryan's little girl couldn't even get her marriage off the ground. No one's surprised. She's just like her parents.*

"Is that a good enough reason to build your marriage on a lie?"

20

"There you are."

Justin jumped in surprise as his mother came up behind him. She rarely came into the barn. Not since he'd learned the ropes and taken over the full-time running of the farm.

But he didn't bother turning around as he ran a hand over the back of one of his heifers. "Morning, Mom." The cow let out a hard breath, and he ran his hand down her side, feeling for anything that could be causing distress and the terrible mewling that had been coming from her stall at all hours of the night. Her coat was warm and soft, and her ribs were all as they should be.

"You going to look at me? Or are you still upset about last night?"

"I'm not upset about last night." Well, not just about last night. More like everything that had been building up to that moment when Natalie had stalked off without answering his last question. Which, when he'd thought about it, was answer enough.

She was going to marry a man who didn't truly know who she was. And she was okay with that.

Maybe she'd changed more than he thought. Because she sure wasn't the woman he'd known her to be.

"Why won't you talk to me about it?" Her voice was closer, imploring, and out of the corner of his eye, he saw her rub the cow's nose.

"What is there to talk about?" He hated how surly his voice sounded. But he couldn't let it go. After all, it hadn't even been twenty-four hours. He just needed time to process. His mom usually knew when to push him where Natalie was concerned and when to let it be.

"Well, this is a big change. I thought you might have some . . . I don't know . . . thoughts about it."

"I have plenty of thoughts." The trouble was none of them worked for him. They mostly involved having that kiss he'd wanted so badly to start at the bottom of the stairs the other day, and that was out of the question. So far out-of-bounds that he couldn't even give that idea a chance to take root.

Checking the cow's hind legs, he ran a steady hand over her joints. Maybe the one nearest him was a little swollen. He squeezed it, trying to keep his grip gentle.

Bessie didn't agree on the level of pressure. She stamped her hoof on the toe of his boot, and he swallowed a scream and a word that would have gotten him a spanking if he'd said it in front of his mom as a child. Even inside his heavy-duty work boots, his toes throbbed. He was pretty sure they weren't broken, but they would probably swell all the same.

He groaned as he leaned a shoulder into the cow's side. "Not a fan of that, huh?" he crooned. "It's okay. I won't do it again."

Bessie bawled like she was waiting for some sort of guarantee. He just patted her side. "We'll let the vet handle that leg next time. But try not to step on him, okay, Bess? He charges extra when you do that."

His mom chuckled. "At least you still have a sense of humor."

Yeah, well, Natalie had stolen that from him once. He wasn't keen on letting her take it away again. "I won't let it go this time."

"This time?" His mom's forehead wrinkled, her smile fading.

"Yes. This time. We've been through this before, haven't we?"

She laughed. "Not to my knowledge. I should know. After all, I'm the one dating again."

"Dating?"

"Harrison Grady. You saw us last night. Or have you blocked that out?"

Justin rested his arm across Bessie's back and turned to look squarely at his mom. The humor of the misunderstanding was just beginning to hit him. "We're talking about you and Harrison?"

"Yes. That's why you're so upset and skipped breakfast and slammed your door three times during the night." Her voice was so earnest, so certain.

He shook his head slowly. "I'm not upset about you dating."

Her chin tipped, and her sapphire gaze turned skeptical. "You're not?"

He looked at her, really looked her over from head to toe, and he couldn't stop the smile that broke out across his face.

"Mom, I love you. And I want you to be happy. I mean, I was surprised, but . . ."

"That I'd want some companionship?"

"That you'd choose Harrison. I mean, the man barely talks, but I bet he's a pretty good listener."

The only light in the barn came through the open door at the end of the aisle, and it did a poor job of illuminating much of anything. Still, he could see the pink in her cheeks rising.

"He is. And he's so gentle. He's a good man."

He ran a hand over his hair, its short length still unusual. But he didn't regret the decision. He was going to have to start a new phase in his life whether he kept the ponytail or not. Might as well mark the change on the outside too.

Gripping the back of his neck, he tugged, hoping it might loosen the question he wanted to ask. He wasn't entirely sure what that was. "Are you . . . Is he like Dad?"

Suddenly she closed the distance between them, grabbing his free hand and pulling it into her grip. "I will never forget your father. I still love him. But I have room in my heart for more love. Like when you were born, I didn't think I could possibly ever love anyone as much as I loved you. Then your brother came along. And your sister. And I realized that my love for each of you couldn't diminish my love for the others."

He pursed his lips. "So you love him, huh? This is pretty serious. Guess I better ask him what his intentions are."

"Don't you dare, you horrid child, or I'll stop making you breakfast." But her laughter made her threat impotent.

Pulling her into his arms, he hugged her tightly. "I love you, Mom. And I'm glad that you and Harrison are happy together."

"Me too." Her posture suddenly stiffened. "But if you're

not upset about that, why all the slamming doors and pacing feet last night?"

"Sorry I kept you up."

"Apology accepted." She pulled away and stared right into his eyes. "But you didn't answer my question."

He sighed, finding a spot over her shoulder and staring at it like it held all the secrets to life.

"I suppose this is about Natalie then?"

He flinched. "What makes you say that?"

"Only two women in your life have ever made you this crazy. And you just said we're okay."

He wanted to take a deep breath, but the scents of the barn were amplified by the summer heat, and he coughed at the stench. The smell was both his livelihood and his prison, the thing that had kept him going after his dad's death and that kept him from going after Natalie and his dreams.

"She's going to marry him, Mom."

Her eyebrows rose to full mast. "And she shouldn't?"

"Come on." He waved toward the house. "You saw us the other day. That wasn't a fluke. It wasn't . . . I can't believe she's ignoring everything between us."

"But she's engaged to Russell."

He stabbed trembling fingers through his hair. "I know. But he doesn't know her. He doesn't really have any idea who he's marrying. He doesn't know about her childhood or her life here on the island. He doesn't know how funny or smart or brave she is. He probably thinks she's just like every other girl out there. Because she's too afraid to tell him otherwise." He scrubbed his face and stared at his mother through this fingers. "She's too afraid to show him the real her."

"But the real her, those are your favorite things about her, aren't they?"

He shrugged. "Pretty much."

"So why doesn't she tell him?"

Scratching at the back of his neck, he kept his head low and his voice lower. "I think she's scared. She told me . . . well, she said that she'd been afraid maybe she wasn't worth loving."

He glanced up just in time to see his mom's mouth grow tight, her arms crossing over her middle. "You told her the truth?"

"Yes." He'd told her she was special. Told her she was lovable. Because she was.

"So why not show her that Russell could also love those unique things about her?"

He blinked hard, the realization sitting like a seventy-ounce steak in his stomach. "Aren't you supposed to be on my side?"

With a laugh that was neither rich nor particularly funny, she pulled him into a quick hug. "I am on your side. If you're convinced that Natalie marrying Russell is a mistake, I only have one question. What are you going to do about it?"

True, it was only one question. But it sure packed a wallop.

All of the clichés ran through his mind. He could stand and object when Father Chuck asked if anyone would. Or he could burst in on the scene a la *The Graduate*. He could burn the barn down—then she'd really have no place for the wedding. But that seemed awfully extreme, when all he really wanted was for her to have the life she wanted.

If she thought Russell was the one, he wouldn't argue. He couldn't argue any more than he already had.

Which left him with just one painful option.

"I'm going to play at their wedding."

She let out a low whistle, astonishment heavy on her features. "When did that happen?"

"Yesterday. They had to move the ceremony to the barn because of the fire at the church."

She nodded, but the firm line of her mouth told him she had much more on her mind. "I always thought that if anyone got married on our property, in that old building, it would be you and Natalie."

Well, that sucked the air right out of the barn. "Me and Natalie? You thought about that? About us?"

"'Course I did. I always wanted another daughter, and it was clear from the first day you brought her home that there was something special between you."

"We were only ever friends, Mom. We never dated or anything."

"Oh, you don't have to date to fall in love. Your father and I didn't date. We worked together in the potato fields every summer, side by side. And one day he went from being that annoying kid with too much to say to a very handsome young man, and I couldn't take my eyes off him. Falling in love is the easy part."

And he had. Fallen in love, that is. He'd known it when they were in school, known that he wanted—needed—Natalie to be a part of the rest of his life.

And he'd done it again—fallen for her not in spite of her insecurities and temper but because of them. She brought a passion to everything she did and challenged him in a way that the pretty girls at his shows never could have.

Yet he was going to play for her as she walked toward another man and a future that didn't include him at all.

And he had no choice in the matter.

Squeezing his arm, his mom turned toward the house, then offered one quick thought before going. "Whatever you choose to do, don't let anyone else make that decision for you."

◆ ◆ ◆ ◆ ◆

"Thank you, Aretha," Natalie said as she loaded the last of the lanterns into the trunk of her car.

Aretha waved from the back door of the antique store. "Are you sure you don't want me to send Jack with you to help you unload them?"

"It's okay. I've got this."

"All right then. I'll see you tomorrow at the wedding."

Yes. The wedding was only a day away. This visit to the island, this return to her home, was almost over. And then she could go back to the life she'd been planning for.

She slammed the trunk closed and hurried to the driver's side door.

"Hello, Natalie."

The voice that had once sent shivers racing down her spine wasn't quite so intimidating now, and she turned toward her father.

"Hi, Dad."

He stood on the sidewalk, his hands stuffed in the pockets of his jeans like he'd been out for a stroll with nowhere to go. "Getting ready for tomorrow?"

This small talk was already layered with more gravitas than her last three conversations with Russell. Of course, he was off introducing his friends to his brother and taking in the harbor sights. She hadn't even tried to talk him into coming with her today. She'd even sent Courtney with him, refusing her help.

This was her last day of freedom. Her last day before everything changed. Her last day before the person she'd been could no longer be.

"Yes. What about you? What are you doing today?"

"Not much." He shrugged. "Visited Connie's grave. Left some flowers." He shuffled a foot against the cement, suddenly looking a lot older than his fifty years. "Listen, Natalie, I really am sorry. I wish there was something more I could do to show you."

"Well, you can stop apologizing. It—it grates on my nerves."

He looked up at her through one eye. "All right."

A terrible idea came to mind, and she wanted to clamp her mouth closed around it, but it popped out before it was fully realized. "And—and you can help me set up centerpieces."

His fair eyebrows lifted, the pale skin of his face shifting in confusion. "You want my help?"

No, she did not. That was a mistake. A terrible blunder. She hadn't meant to invite him at all. But the hint of a hopeful smile on his face pulled at her heart.

Could it really be that he had changed? Could God really make such a difference in a life?

Well, he had in hers, hadn't he? He'd given her hope—in the form of a friend. When she'd prayed to be rescued that day as a child in the lighthouse, she'd wanted to be saved from everything. Perhaps carried on a wave out to another island, free from her parents and the life she hated. Instead God had brought her Justin, a little boy with a smile as bright as the sun and loyalty as deep as the ocean.

And he'd saved her. He'd kept her moving and growing. He'd shared his family and taught her what love really was.

So if, in her darkest place, God had rescued her, who was to say that God couldn't rescue her dad too?

Before she could even respond to his question, he was bounding around the car, headed for the passenger door. "Anything you need, Natalie Joy."

She trembled in the face of his enthusiasm, but she motioned for him to get in. The short drive was silent, save for the hum of the tires against the pavement. Her dad sat with his hands in his lap, drinking in the sights around them. When she turned off the road down the lane Justin had cut in the grass for her wedding guests, his eyes grew large, and he seemed unable to look away from the barn.

"Is this where you're getting married?"

"Yes." She got out and met him at the trunk, where she pulled out a large box of lamps and set it in his waiting arms.

"Got another one for me?"

"I'll get the other."

He nodded and walked toward the barn door. It was closed, but he pushed his hip against it, and it swung out, flooding the entry with light. "Wow." His voice was low and filled with genuine wonder. "This is beautiful."

She entered behind him, taking a moment to bask in the beauty she'd help to create. In the last three days, she and Caden—standing in for a still bedridden Marie—had hung string after string of twinkle lights across beams and as a curtain between the ceremony and reception areas. Tables were dressed in the same colors as the orchids to come. And burlap fabric served as the shore and was covered with seashells from across the island.

Even before the lights were turned on, it was stunning.

"Want to see something cool?"

"Sure."

She set down her box, walked to the adjacent wall, and plugged in the extension cord.

The grand cathedral exploded with light, each of the thousands of bulbs shining and glowing and reaching as far as it could. All working together to build something greater. Something perfect.

"Whoa." He whistled low and long. "That's . . . that's pretty amazing. You do all this?"

She shrugged. "Most of it. Yes."

"I'm proud of you, kid."

Suddenly her eyes burned and her lip trembled, and she hated herself for wanting to hear him say it again.

This father-daughter business wasn't fair. It was supposed to be easy to hate him, to hold on to every disadvantage he'd ever forced on her. But all she wanted in this moment was to hear him say those words again, that he was proud of her.

Instead, she bit the inside of her cheek, pinched her eyes shut, and picked up her box. "Can you put one on each table? Just a little off center."

He did as she asked, saying nothing more as they walked from table to table. The kerosene lamp she'd loved at first sight found its way to the long table for the wedding party, and she set it right in the middle, between the two center seats. Tomorrow she'd be sitting on one side and Russell on the other. And they'd be married.

Forever.

Her stomach gave a gentle flop. It wasn't an entire production, just a subtle nudge that perhaps this wasn't the life she should have chosen. That perhaps she'd used the man now at her side as an excuse to ignore the one man she should have seen—really, truly appreciated.

"Do you have time for dinner tonight? I could take you to Grady's."

Ripped from her thoughts, she tried to catch up with his train of thought. But it was long gone. "Dinner?"

"I mean, I'd like to hear about your life. What have you been up to? What are you doing now? Are you happy?"

There was a hitch in the last word that tugged at her heart. "Am I happy?"

He nodded.

"I . . . I want to be." Was that the best she could offer, the only thing she could honestly say?

Oh, what a mess she'd made. What a terrible lie she'd woven into the fabric of her life. She'd lied to herself, certain how very little her past informed her present.

She'd been wrong. So incredibly wrong.

The truth was that she was moving forward with a marriage to a man she wasn't sure she really loved—a man she'd been lying to for years—because of the past. Because of what a handful of bitter old women might say.

She was so focused on Stella and Lois and their wagging tongues that she'd nearly missed the women who'd loved and cared for her in her mother's absence. Women like Aretha and Mama Kane and assorted Sunday school teachers and Justin's little sister. These women had been her surrogate mothers and siblings, the women who'd provided for and protected her.

Hanging her head, she pressed flat palms against the lavender satin tablecloth before her. Soft and cool, it did nothing to relieve the rush of heat and dread flowing through her. "I can't go to dinner tonight. It's my rehearsal dinner."

"Oh, sure."

"Dad?" She began the question but immediately lost its direction.

"Yes, Natalie?" He seemed to like calling her by her name, like he'd missed too many opportunities and wouldn't let another pass.

"Have you ever made a mistake so deep that you can't begin to fix it?"

His breath came out both stunned and mildly amused. "Do you remember who you're talking to?"

Oh. Right. Of course he had.

"So what am I supposed to do?"

He crossed his arms over his chest and tilted his head, as though inspecting each of the individual lights in the curtain that divided the sacred from the social. "I suppose you do the next right thing. You can't change the past, but staying on the same course is only going to compound the problem. No drunk ever made a better life by having one more beer. No bad father ever salvaged a relationship with his family by turning his back on them one more time."

He wasn't talking about her anymore. These were the changes he'd made, the next right things he'd done.

But could she be as strong?

"What if the next right thing will hurt people you care about?"

"I suppose that's where prayer and mercy come into play. You pray you're making the right choice, and then you beg for mercy."

◆◆◆◆◆

"And you'll stand over there."

Justin turned to look at the corner Caden had pointed to. Picking up his guitar, he trudged in that direction, all the while trying to stop the voice in his head screaming that this was the wrong decision.

But he didn't have another option. He couldn't have both. And he certainly wasn't going to get Natalie.

She'd made her choice.

When he reached his spot, he turned around to face rows of nearly empty white chairs. Adam sat in the front row, his arm draped across the back of the seat beside him. A handful of Russell's Nashville friends mingled in the back, including at least two other music industry professionals and a musician Justin had heard on the radio more than once. Russell stood next to Father Chuck in front of a makeshift cross—two beams that Justin had put together because he knew how much Natalie had wanted to be wed in the church. Lois and her special helper, Stella Burke, hunched over the last row of chairs, trying to rig up a way to hang the flowers that were supposed to be on the ends of the pews.

From her spot in the middle of the aisle, Caden directed the whole ordeal. "All right. Can I get the groomsmen up front?"

Adam and Patrick, one of the other music producers, took their spots behind Russell, slapping him on the back and joking with him while Caden's back was turned.

She pointed at Justin. "When I cue you, you'll begin. Go ahead."

Justin nodded and picked out the slow notes that wove together into "Jesu, Joy of Man's Desiring." It was the only classical piece he knew by heart, and Natalie hadn't argued for anything else. Maybe she just hadn't wanted to argue at all. Or even talk, for that matter. Their conversation about the ceremony music had lasted exactly twenty-three seconds.

Slowly the maid of honor strolled down the aisle, her hands holding an imaginary bouquet, her chin high and eyes alight.

He tried to smile, his view of her walk perfectly angled. But deep in his heart, he knew what was coming next. And he wasn't sure he was prepared. In fact, he was certain of that.

But it didn't stop Natalie from finding her place at the end of the white runner. Her head bowed slightly and brows partially furrowed, she looked uncertain. The round skirt of her navy blue sundress tipped like a ringing bell he could nearly hear. All of her fiery hair was swept up in a knot at the nape of her neck except for one waving tendril, leaving her long, slender neck on display. And he could practically feel the smooth skin there.

He'd never seen anything quite so beautiful in his entire life.

His fingers slipped as his mind wandered, and he jarred himself back into the notes of the song.

Maybe it was his mistake that drew her attention. Maybe it was something more. But when she looked up, she didn't look at Russell or Adam or Father Chuck. She looked straight at Justin.

His stomach tanked.

Her eyes were so clear, the ocean completely still. But there was a hesitancy there. A fear. As though she was begging him to tell her it was all going to be all right.

But he wouldn't do that. He couldn't. He couldn't do any of this.

He'd been so busy telling Natalie to stop lying to herself that he'd failed to notice he'd been doing plenty of that himself. His dreams weren't on equal footing. Music wasn't on par with Natalie. Not even close. He'd convinced himself that he'd be satisfied with one and not the other.

Nothing could be further from the truth.

He wanted her. He wanted their life together. He wanted her to get angry with him and see her eyes turn to ice, then to have her melt into his embrace when she forgave him. He wanted all of her passion and spice. He wanted to wake up next to her every morning for the rest of his life.

Because he just wanted her. All the things she'd tried to hide from Russell. All the things she'd tried to hide from him. All the years they'd shared and the ones they'd lost.

He wanted it all.

His heart began thudding in his ears, its tempo unstoppable and unrelenting.

This was his decision to make. And he sure as heck wasn't going to play at her wedding while she promised herself to another man.

His feet were moving before he even stopped playing, and he reached her in a few short strides. When he stopped, they were barely a foot apart. He longed to reach for her, to tell her how he really felt, but he wasn't so selfish. He'd made his decision and she'd made hers. And they'd both have to live with it.

He took a deep breath and said, "I'm sorry. I can't do this." And he did what she'd done to him fifteen years before.

He walked away.

21

Every eye in the room was trained on her. Natalie could feel the physical weight of their curiosity. All was silent except for the sound of Justin's boots marching out of the barn and the hushed whispers of Lois and Stella. The low words walked around her chest, tightening a rope there and tugging on it until her breath was gone. A cold sweat broke out across the back of her neck. They were clearly speculating on the words Justin had just whispered to her.

She was once again the favorite topic of gossip. And for good reason.

He'd said he couldn't do this. And she'd frozen. But a little voice inside her said he'd meant so much more than playing at the wedding. Maybe he couldn't watch her marry someone else because he loved her and always had.

Her heart leapt, hope a balloon that could carry her through this. It would have to carry her through. The pointed glances and rooms falling silent whenever she walked into them didn't matter. Justin had always been the answer to her prayers. And she prayed he would be again.

Do the next right thing. Her father's words echoed inside

her, the truth in them breaking the ice that had settled over her at Justin's announcement.

She stared at the whispering women, biting her lip and trying to figure out what to do with them. Shut them down or let them talk?

Either way, this story was going to make its way around town in record time. Every schoolgirl within a hundred kilometers would know how little Natalie O'Ryan had turned out to be every bit as scandalous as her parents.

She could waste time. Or she could get to doing the right thing.

"Russell," she said, reaching out a hand toward him. "We need to talk."

He loped toward her, his frown evident but not truly upset. "Where's Justin going? Patrick was just saying how good he is."

"We need to talk. Somewhere private," she added this time.

"Talk? Natalie? What's going on? We can't leave our friends." His gaze jumped toward Lois and Stella, whose disapproving glares hovered. "Can't this wait until after the rehearsal?"

She almost said yes. She almost reverted back to the way she'd always gone, the path of least resistance with him.

But that wasn't the path to being the woman she wanted to be. In fact, it led straight to the life her mother had lived. And she'd fight tooth and nail to keep from having the same fate.

Tugging on his hand, she pulled him in her wake. "Excuse us just a moment." She waved to the room filled with perplexed faces. Only Caden smiled, small but encouraging.

She could do this. She had to do this.

Outside the stars shone like a million twinkle lights just

for them. The moon too seemed intent on lighting their way, illuminating the confusion on Russell's face. "Natalie, what on earth is going on? We have guests waiting for us and a caterer setting up. What's so important that it won't wait until after the dinner?"

Smoothing her hands down the full fabric of her skirt, she took a deep breath. "I owe you an apology. I haven't been honest with you."

"What?" It came out more of a laugh than a question. "What are you talking about? We all tell white lies. It's no big deal. There's no reason for all this drama. We should go back inside before we're missed."

She shook her head hard enough to cut him off. "You don't love me."

"Of course I—"

With a wave of her hand she stopped him again. "You can't love me because you don't know me. I've been pretending to be someone that you could love for a long time."

"We've been together for three years. I think I know you."

"You don't." The back of her throat began to itch, a sure sign that tears were on their way, and she rushed to get the rest out before she completely broke down. "You can't. Because I never told you that when I was a child, my mom—"

Oh, God, help me.

This was so much harder than she'd thought it would be. Even back when she'd been too afraid to tell him the whole truth.

But Justin had called her brave for leaving on her own when she had. And she'd be brave again.

"My mom used to neglect me. And starve me. When she did pay attention to me, she beat me."

His mouth dropped open, and his eyebrows closed the gap to become one.

But she couldn't stop or the words might dry up. "And my dad was the town drunk and philanderer. He cheated on my mom for as long as I could remember. I didn't leave the island because I was looking for adventure or to get away from small-town life. I left because I was terrified that staying here would mean becoming just like them, just more fodder for town gossip. I thought that marrying you would save me from wagging tongues and speculations about my personal life. And I wasn't fair to you. I wasn't fair at all."

He blinked once, but the stunned expression on his face didn't abate. "But why didn't you tell me? You could have . . ."

She didn't let him continue for long. "I've been pretending to be someone I'm not, holding back the person I really am since the very beginning. I was so afraid you might not love me if you knew that sometimes my temper gets the better of me. It's not my best quality, but it is mine."

He interjected again. "But I've never seen you even get angry."

Her heart ached. Her head ached. Her entire body screamed for this to end. But there was more to say, more to confess. "You've never seen me angry because I've never let you. I picked the path of least resistance with you because I thought that's the type of woman you'd love. And I wanted you to love me. I thought you wanted someone poised and together, someone who could plan and host parties for your clients. Someone to put on a good face."

"Yes. You'll be great at all those things. That's why we make a great team."

"But I can't pretend to be a perfect person anymore. And I

can't marry a man who doesn't know the depth of the scars that I still carry. I mean, for heaven's sake, I never wanted to come back to this island. When you said you'd lined up our wedding here, I was so angry with you."

His confusion deepened the lines around his pursed lips. "But you never said anything. Why didn't you just tell me?"

"I know. I should have. That's on me. How could you know how much I hated my memories of this place if I never told you? But I didn't. And you don't know me. Not the real me. Not the little girl with matted hair and a stutter and hand-me-down clothes always two sizes too big. Not the teenager always afraid that some boy would think my father's reputation entitled him to take what he wanted. Not the young woman who dreamed of running away with her best friend, only to be asked to stay."

He rubbed his fingers across his forehead, stretching out the lines there, seeking some sort of clarity. "But you left."

"Yes. But I shouldn't have."

He pressed his hands to his waist and stared toward the inky sky. "I'm sorry. This is just a lot to take in."

"This is my fault." She reached for him, then pulled her hand back, unsure how much he'd welcome her touch. "I'm so sorry I didn't tell you sooner. I thought we could make it work. But it's not fair to you. And it's not fair to me."

"So, let me get this straight. You're saying you don't want to marry me?"

"I'm . . . No. I can't marry you. You deserve better than a half life with a half wife who's too afraid to speak up for fear of what people might say about her."

"But—" His gaze shifted over her shoulder, and she knew he was thinking of Lois and Stella and his friends inside, but that's not where he went. "*You're* breaking things off with *me*?" He emphasized the words that suggested this might be hurting his pride more than his heart.

"We're not a good match, Russell. I mean, you were gone for four weeks in the middle of our pre-honeymoon, and did you even miss me?"

"I was busy with the album."

She waved her hand to cut him off. "I completely understand that. But shouldn't you miss the person you're going to marry? Even when you're busy?"

"Didn't you miss me?" he asked.

Oh dear. That was a loaded question. "Not like I should have. Not like a woman who loves a man."

The lines of confusion around his face were easing, replaced with anger and something else. "But you said you loved me."

"I couldn't really love you. As long as I was lying to you, I couldn't ever give you my whole heart. I thought I could, but it was just another lie that I believed."

"But everyone in Nashville is going to talk about us." His voice rose, the anger coming out in booming notes. "They're going to talk about me."

And there it was. He was worried more about himself than he was about her.

But Justin—who knew why it bothered her so much—had made the smallest scene he could.

The gossip to come wasn't new. While it would hurt, it wouldn't burn as it once might have. She refused to be afraid of doing the next right thing just because of what others would say. People would always find something to gossip about. And eventually they'd move on.

"Let them talk." With a deep breath, she forced a trembling smile. "Isn't it better to end it now than get married under false pretenses?"

His gaze narrowed in on her, and for a split second she feared that he'd tell her he'd stay with her, that they could ride out the storm. But when he opened his mouth, he saved her from having to introduce the subject she most wanted to avoid. "Your best friend. That was Justin, wasn't it?"

Her mouth was suddenly like a desert, and she had to swallow twice before she could even get a word out. "We—we had a plan. We were going to leave together after graduation so he could pursue his music and I could get away from my parents. Then his dad died. And he had to stay. And I left."

"He's in love with you, isn't he?"

She lifted one shoulder. "I don't know."

"And you're in love with him?" His words were so detached from emotion that she wondered if he really wanted a response.

But she owed him honesty.

"Yes, I'm in love with him. Because he saw through my facade before I did."

Russell hung his head, stared at the ground for a long second, and then sighed. "There's nothing I can say to change your mind?"

She shook her head. "I really am sorry. But I promise, you don't want to marry me."

"Then I suppose this is good-bye." Without another word or even the briefest touch, he walked away into the night. His car door slammed, and headlights drifted over the grass and disappeared onto the road. She had no doubt she'd never see him again. He'd be gone from the inn when she got back, and he'd be off the island on the first plane.

She turned around, put her chin up, and marched back into the barn. This was going to be awful. There simply wasn't another word for it.

But the after, the later, might not be terrible. Because she had a sneaking suspicion right where to find Justin.

When she walked back into the barn, she ignored the tittering women in the corner and found a friendly, compassionate gaze from Caden. Despite the confusion on her face, Caden nodded, a silent encouragement to face the rest of the room.

Taking a deep breath, Natalie said, "There isn't going to be a wedding tomorrow."

◆◆◆◆◆

Justin felt like he'd lost a fight. His ribs ached and his head pounded. Even breathing hurt. Because every time he closed his eyes, he saw Natalie married to another man and the great expanse of his future dim and without direction.

He'd thrown away his chance for an album. Not a lot of music producers made their way to the island, and he'd not only walked out on Russell Jacobs, he'd walked out on the other two other producers in the barn and everyone in their circle of influence.

He wasn't sure how Nashville operated, but if people there liked to talk the way they did here, it wouldn't take long for the entire community to find out he'd walked out on a gig. His name wouldn't be worth the paper a contract would be printed on.

He'd completely blown his opportunity. His one chance. And he'd do it again in a heartbeat for the chance to be with Natalie. But she hadn't come after him. She hadn't asked him to stay.

He couldn't get past it, couldn't find anything else to hang his hope on, so he sat on the lighthouse floor, watching the light illuminate the darkness. For an instant he thought he saw two eyes—two fairies—in the secret glen. But then they vanished.

How long he sat there, stewing in his own regrets and misery, he didn't know. But the moon was high and the night deep when he heard the door below him close. His heart leapt. The squeaky rung on the ladder filled the little building. His heart stopped.

And then a red head popped through the hatch. Her eyes were narrowed against the sudden brightness of the light, but he could still make out a twinkle there. She didn't really smile, but there was a strength in her bare shoulders as she climbed the rest of the way inside.

"Fancy meeting you here," she said as she crawled to the spot right beside him. Pulling her legs up, she wrapped her arms around them and rested her chin on her knees.

He didn't know how to respond, couldn't have gotten a word around the lump in his throat anyway, so he rubbed his eyes and kept his gaze on the far-flung beam. She seemed content to do the same. As she readjusted her position, her arm brushed against his, sending sparks through him brighter than the Canada Day fireworks.

Minutes dragged by, and she said nothing. Maybe it was hours. But finally he cleared his throat.

"What are you doing here?"

"The next right thing."

"Huh?"

She slipped her hand into the pocket of her dress, and her fingers reappeared with a white slip tucked between them. "I have something for you."

He took the card she offered but couldn't read the tiny words as the light was pointed over the water. "What's this?"

"You met Patrick Weatherfield, right? One of the grooms-men."

He nodded.

"He's in A&R for a major label in Nashville. He liked what he heard tonight, and Russell had told him about the song you were playing the other day."

His tongue felt too heavy, but he forced it out. "'On This Shore'?"

"Uh-huh. Apparently Russell was impressed, and Patrick wants to hear what you've got. He asked me to give you his card."

Justin stared at the card for so long that the words ran together, making no sense. Like the words she spoke. Which couldn't be true. There had to be some mistake. "But I ruined Russell's wedding. He won't want anything to do with me."

She turned to look at him, her gaze direct and unflinching. "There's no wedding for you to ruin. I called it off."

Everything he'd been holding so tightly inside him suddenly exploded, his eyes burned, and his ears rang with the rush of blood.

No wedding. No wedding. No wedding.

His heart pumped to that rhythm, trying to make sense of it. Trying to confirm its truth.

Perhaps Natalie could read the hesitancy on his face, or maybe she needed to speak the words for herself. "You were right. I wasn't honest with him, and I wasn't being fair to him. He's a good man, but I'm not sure I ever really loved him. I loved the idea of marrying him, but maybe that was it. So I tricked him into falling in love with a woman who doesn't exist."

She squeezed her legs and hunched her shoulders. "When I realized what I'd done, I thought it was too late to tell the truth. I figured there was no way to be honest without hurting him and making myself the laughingstock of North Rustico. Stella and Lois were just waiting for me to fail, to prove them right. And I couldn't bear it. So I thought if I could just keep up the facade until after the wedding, I could make everything right."

He cleared his throat when she stopped, his voice suddenly sounding like he'd had a hundred-year nap. "What changed your mind?"

She laughed, and it rang off the metal supports, filling the tiny room. "My dad, actually. Can you believe it?" Leaning her cheek against her knee, she stared at him, her blue eyes nearly glowing. "He told me to do the next right thing. As long as I kept lying to Russell, I was only compounding the problem."

"When'd your dad get so smart?"

With a snort, she shrugged. "I have no idea. But he was right. If I'd kept going down that road, I'd have ended up ruining my life and Russell's life and hurting the man I love."

No. It couldn't be. She couldn't be talking about him. It wasn't possible that he had a chance with a Nashville label *and* a shot with the woman of his dreams.

Before he could ask her to clarify, she started up again. "I owe you an apology, Justin. I shouldn't have left. We did have a plan, and it was to stick together. But on the night before graduation, I got scared."

"Of staying with me?"

She reached for his hand, and he quickly slid his fingers between hers, holding on tight. "Never of you." She took a deep breath, and it made his heart ache and his chest hurt just to hear her struggle to find the words. "Stella Burke woke me up that night. She was pounding on the door. Mom was gone, and Dad was . . . out. When I opened it, she screamed at me. She was so angry, her face was red and splotchy, and I was sure that the whole town could hear her yelling about how my dad had had an affair with the mayor's wife—her brother's wife. It was going to ruin his political career. Her family's name was ruined. And it was entirely my dad's fault."

She winced, the memories clearly vivid in the depths of her mind. "And then she got right in my face." Natalie held up a hand five inches from her nose to demonstrate the distance. "She said, 'You're going to end up a whore just like your old man. Or you'll marry someone like him and become just like your mother.'"

He cringed. He wanted to jump to his feet and march over to Stella's perfect little house and tell her what a terrible, awful person she was. But Natalie's hold on his hand kept him rooted, kept him right beside her.

"I was afraid she was right, so I ran. That night. I packed everything I could into my duffel bag, emptied that coffee can underneath my bed, left you a note, and hitchhiked to the bus station in Charlottetown. I couldn't risk her words becoming true."

A single tear leaked onto her cheek, and he swiped at the silver track with a knuckle on his free hand.

"I realize now that it was always my choice who I would become. And I don't like the person who lies to cover scandal or fears what others say about her. I like the one who gets to be herself." Her gaze flickered away from his, then back. "With you."

He didn't have words to adequately express the firestorm inside him, so he just stared, drinking in her gentle beauty, counting the freckles across her nose.

Finally she bit into her lush pink lip. "Aren't you going to say something?"

"Like what? What would you like me to say?" Anything. He'd say anything to make her happy.

"Like that you still love me too."

His throat closed off, but he forced out the word. "Too?"

She nodded. "I have always loved you."

And then it was too much to hold back even a second longer. He brushed a loose strand of hair from her cheek, his finger dragged along the column of her neck, and her whole body seemed to tremble under his touch. Finally he cupped her face with his palm, and her lips parted. Waiting. Inviting.

Her shoulders shivered. Or it could have been him. He'd suddenly lost track of where she ended and he began. Everything inside him quaked with the force of hope and want and need. He leaned in, cutting the distance between them in half.

Their breath mingled as she sighed.

He couldn't look away. He wanted to count every single one of her freckles. He wanted to hold her as tight as he could. He wanted to make her smile every day of their lives.

Her eyes fluttered closed, her lips turned up. And he knew what she wanted. What he wanted too. He wanted it so badly that it felt like a punch to the gut.

But first, there were questions he needed to ask.

"What about your dad?"

Her eyes flew open, her perfect lips forming an angry frown. "Really? Really? You're going to ask about my dad right now?"

He dug his fingers into the silkiness of her hair, cradling her head, and despite her playfully sour words, she leaned into him.

"Well, I mean, how's that going?"

She closed her eyes, her lashes resting against her cheeks. "It's funny, bitterness. I was carrying it around like a security blanket for so long that I didn't even realize how heavy it had become. I don't think forgiveness happens all at once, but taking the first step, asking God to help me forgive him, has made that grudge so much lighter. I thought that forgiving him was somehow saying that he hadn't done anything wrong. But he and I both agree that's not the case." She lifted one pointy shoulder. "We may never be close—probably won't be. But I just feel so much lighter."

Her words filled his chest like the warmth of a fire on a cold autumn night. But she wasn't done.

"You know, it's kind of your fault."

The lazy smile that had taken up residence on his face tipped down. "Mine? What did I do?"

"You reminded me that forgiveness is so much better than the alternative."

"Sounds pretty smart of me."

She squeezed his wrist right by her ear, shooting sparks up to his shoulder and straight to his heart. "It was. I mean, when I realized I wasn't angry with you anymore, I realized how much I loved having you in my life."

"Because I am the best cake taster you know."

She giggled softly just as the light circled around, giving her a golden halo. "Because you would fork-sword fight with me. Because you make me smile. Because you held me at the hospital and didn't ask for a single thing in return except my honesty. Because you knew when I was being honest and when I wasn't. Because there's no one else I'd rather argue with. And no one else I'd rather make up with."

He slipped a little closer to her, again cutting their distance apart in half. "Is this what the making up feels like? Because I like this too."

She nodded. "Maybe more."

"What did you have in mind?" He already knew, but it was too fun not to goad her, and she gave him the pout he expected.

Before he could respond again, she closed her eyes and pursed her lips and pressed them to his.

And his entire world exploded.

Thirty-two years he'd been waiting for this kiss. Thirty-two years he'd been waiting for this moment.

Most of his life he'd denied it. When she was gone, he'd sworn it couldn't be true. But even as a teenager, he'd known. She was the one. She was his one.

Always.

Her lips were as soft as they looked. Pliant. Supple. Fierce.

And suddenly he tugged her against his side, holding her to his chest, as connected as they could be in all the ways that mattered.

Finally she pulled back, resting her head against his shoulder, her breathing deep and ragged. As it slowed, she whispered, "You were my answer to prayer when I was five. You're my answer to prayer now."

The backs of his eyes prickled like he might start crying, and he grasped for a joke, anything to lighten the mood, but all he could think about were her words. "I think you're mine too. I didn't even know how to ask for you. But someone knew I needed you. That I needed joy back in my life. That I needed my muse back."

She pulled away just enough to stare into his eyes, hers flashing bright. "That song was about me."

"They're all about you."

"Even that terrible 'Good-bye, Girl'?"

He chuckled. "Especially that one. But I'm going to have to add a new verse. The Good-bye Girl has come back."

She snuggled into his embrace, her gaze following the light to a spot past the shore. "And I'm back to stay."

His entire body stiffened. He hadn't thought. Hadn't counted on that. The sudden realization that she could have left, that her life was elsewhere, tore him open. "Are you sure? What will you do?"

"Well, as it turns out, Kane Dairy has a lovely new event facility." With a coy smile she kissed him on the cheek. "I'm thinking it's in need of a venue manager."

His stomach dropped and then did a barrel roll. "Because you're going to stay here. With me. No matter what people say?"

She didn't even tense in his arms. She just sighed, melting into him. "People will always talk about something. And if it's going to be me? Well, I'd rather they talk about how often I smile because I'm with the man I love."

"Fair enough." He kissed her again, holding her close and knowing that someday he'd get to make his mom's dream a reality. When Natalie married in the old Kane barn, she was going to marry a Kane man.

Because he wasn't going to let her go again. Ever.

His heart thudded beneath her hand on his chest, and he locked his arms around her waist, savoring the sweetness of her lips and the citrus scent around her.

When she finally pulled away to steal a ragged breath, she said, "So, you never said if you'll forgive me. I dragged you through a lot."

With a smile and another squeeze, he said, "Lady, I will always forgive you."

Epilogue

The spring air was still cool, and deep gray clouds hung low over the shoreline. But Natalie Joy O'Ryan didn't care. Not in the slightest.

Nothing could put a damper on this day. Her day.

Well, Justin's too, if she was being fair about it. But he'd told her it could be all about her. And Marie had said so too. Even Caden had agreed that the cake should be her choice.

Of course, she already knew Justin's preference. Lemon raspberry, rich enough to curl his hair. That feat wasn't so difficult, as he'd kept his hair short for almost a year. Which she didn't mind at all. It was easier to run her fingers through it. Which he didn't seem to mind either.

"Oh, Natalie!"

She froze at the cry of her name but smiled when she caught sight of Marie and Caden across the floor of the barn, Caden's hands at her cheeks.

"You look amazing!"

Natalie glanced down at the big plaid shirt she'd borrowed—actually stolen—from her fiancé before a bubble of laughter escaped. "I don't even have my dress on yet." But it didn't stop her from pressing a gentle hand to her loose updo. A few curls had been pulled free by the April breeze, and she tucked them back into place.

Marie looped a soft arm around the baby hanging from the carrier on her front, and the little one wiggled, his pajama-clad legs pushing against his mom. "You're practically glowing. Like maybe it's your special day. Like you've been waiting awhile for this day. I know someone else who has too."

A swarm of monarchs fluttered to life inside her. No one even had to say his name to set them loose, and she stared into the cathedral ceiling to keep the tears that threatened at bay. Fanning her face with her hands, she said, "You can't say things like that. Nothing sweet. Nothing kind. You'll ruin my makeup." To prove her point, she pressed a knuckle to her bottom lid, and it came away with a smudge of black. "See what you'll make me do."

Caden chuckled, reaching out her left hand, and the twinkling lights wrapped around the ceiling beams caught on the diamond there, sparking it to life with a full rainbow of colors.

"I wouldn't be so quick to laugh, missy. Your day isn't far off."

Cheeks turning pink, Caden ducked her head. "It's still a little ways away. Besides, I have to finish up the school term." She and Adam had flown back to the island from Toronto for a long weekend just for the wedding. The next time they came back, they'd be saying their own vows, celebrating their own marriage in this very barn, which had already booked an event for every weekend of the summer, most of them in conjunction with Rose's Red Door Inn.

Natalie let her gaze wander from her friend's sweet smile to the tables adorned with the kerosene lamps and lavender tablecloths she'd so loved the first time she'd decorated this space. The hanging twinkle lights and seashells were the same too. But now there were only five tables of eight—a small affair for close friends.

She didn't care how many people were here. As long as Justin met her at the end of the aisle.

"Hurry up, Kathleen."

"You hold your horses, Aretha Franklin. I'm the mother of the groom, and I won't be rushed."

"Then you'll delay your own son's wedding." Aretha looked up just as she and Mama Kane stepped inside the barn, a chagrined smile falling into place.

Natalie pressed her hand over her mouth, trying not to smudge her lipstick. But she couldn't hold back the giggle as the two women sashayed in. They each carried a box of flowers—bouquets, boutonnieres, and centerpieces—despite their official mother-of-the-bride and mother-of-the-groom dresses.

Aretha had refused to let Natalie order her flowers from Lois Bernard. "Not after the hateful things she said about . . . well, you know."

And everyone did. Lois had been quick to speculate on why Russell had left the island in such a hurry. He probably realized he wanted no connection to the O'Ryans after meeting Rick, she'd suggested to anyone who would listen. Except there weren't many people willing to listen. And she'd realized that quickly.

"But she apologized," Natalie had said to Aretha. She could never remember Lois breaking ranks, but she'd marched across the floor of Grady's Diner last fall, bowed her head, and eaten a full slice of humble pie. And what was more, Natalie had realized she wanted to forgive her. After all, if she could forgive her father, couldn't she forgive a sad, lonely florist too?

Aretha and Mama Kane hadn't been so easily persuaded, instead driving to another florist halfway across the county to pick up the flowers for the wedding.

Now Natalie hurried to their side, Marie and Caden in tow, and reached for a box, but Aretha refused to give hers up. "I'm just fine, thank you very much."

"But you have responsibilities today." Natalie gave her a hesitant smile.

Aretha nearly glowed as she hugged the cardboard box even tighter. "And I wouldn't miss them for the world. I've never gotten to be the mother of the bride before."

Those pesky tears came back in force, and Natalie had to tilt her head back, refusing to blink or risk setting them free and streaking her face.

She had been terrified to ask, afraid Aretha would think her silly. She was thirty-three years old and hadn't had a mother in a lot longer than hers had been gone.

"You might have heard . . ." Natalie had said.

"Oh?" Aretha played coy.

"Justin and I are getting married. And . . . well . . . I was wondering if you'd be the mother of the bride? My mother?"

Aretha's eyes grew wide, her tinted lips falling open. Natalie feared the dismissal that was sure to come. Why on earth did she need a mother of the bride? She steeled herself for the laughter. Instead she was swallowed in a hug that threatened to steal her breath. "Of course I'll be your mother. Anytime you want me to be. And even if you don't."

Natalie had wept into Aretha's embrace then, and the tears didn't want to stop now.

"Stay strong, girl. Or you'll have to redo your makeup." Despite her firm words, Aretha's eyes glistened with the same memory.

Natalie nodded as little Jack Sloane gave a grunt and shifted in his carrier, earning a series of quick pats on the back from his mother. "Stay asleep just a little longer," she whispered. "I need you to be ready for another nap in a couple hours. Please, sleep through the ceremony."

All the women cooed at the little guy, his upturned nose and puckered lips as cute as could be.

"I think he's more likely to delay the wedding than I am," Mama Kane said, and they all laughed before setting about unloading the boxes.

"What are you doing, Natalie?"

She looked up from where she'd placed a simple orchid arrangement beside a lamp.

Aretha motioned toward the door. "You've got to get dressed."

"But I'm the bride. Everyone will wait for me."

"And do you want to wait a minute longer than you must to marry Justin?"

Joy bubbled over inside her as she raced for the exit. "Not even a second."

◆◆◆◆◆

Two hours later Natalie took a deep breath as Jack walked her back into the barn, around the reception area, and through a veil of lights. As she stepped onto the other side to the gentle strain of Jordan's fiddle, her breath hitched and her foot caught on the hem of her white mermaid gown.

There he was, the man who knew her best and worst and loved her anyway. Justin's gunmetal suit hugged his broad shoulders, sleek and dapper, but she wouldn't have cared if he'd shown up in flannel and Levis. The longing in his eyes was all she'd dreamed of. All she needed.

Suddenly he seemed so far away, and she wasn't sure her legs could carry her all the way down the red runner. But she couldn't *not* make it.

She clung to Jack's elbow as they strolled past several church friends before reaching Caden and Adam, who offered her a true smile, assuring her there were no hard feelings. Marie and Seth sat in the same row, little Jack sleeping soundly in his dad's arms. And if Natalie didn't know any better, she'd have thought she saw a tear sliding down Marie's cheek.

Then came Mama Kane and Harrison side by side, her hands clasped around his steadying one. To her left Aretha sat beside Jack's empty seat.

And Rick O'Ryan, in his best Sunday suit, sat on Aretha's other side. His smile wide and his eyes bright, he nodded her on, as though encouraging her to make and keep the sacred vows. Each day she chose to forgive him. And while they weren't close, she was grateful for the relationship that had developed between them.

Eye to eye with Father Chuck, she couldn't risk looking at Justin this close. She couldn't risk the rush of sweet emotions that had been so near the surface all day. But when he wrapped his hand around hers, she couldn't avoid looking into his eyes. They were so sure. He was so firm.

I love you.

He mouthed the words, and they rang in her head like the sweetest refrain. A promise that he'd protect her and cherish her. Always.

As she slipped into place at the front of the aisle, her heart stuttered, then slammed against her breastbone.

She'd thought it was safe to come back to the island. She'd thought it was safe to return to these gentle shores. She'd thought it was safe to stay at Rose's Red Door Inn.

She'd been so wrong.

This wasn't safe. It wasn't easy.

It was so much better than that.

Acknowledgments

There are too many people involved in the process of creating this book to possibly thank them all. From the cashier at my local Panda Express to the guys who take care of my lawn so I can immerse myself in an always perfectly manicured island. And, of course, the readers who send notes of encouragement. You are infinitely appreciated. The few others I know by name are:

Jessica Patch and Jill Kemerer. You're the sweetest, most encouraging friends, and I'm grateful that God brought you into my life and my writing journey. Jessica, thank you for brainstorming this book with me. Mama Cheese Sandwich wouldn't have made it to the page without you.

Amy Haddock and Michelle Ule, red-pen wielders and first-draft readers. Thanks for making my book so much better than it was.

Rachel Kent, the best cheerleader, advice giver, and agent this author could ask for. I'm so glad that we met all those years ago and kept bumping into each other at the conference bookstore. I knew you had good taste in books then.

Vicki, Michele, Karen, Hannah, Jessica, and Cheryl, the incredible team at Revell. Thank you for bringing this book to life with such thought and care. I thank God that I get to work with all of you.

The whole Johnson/Whitson clan, who helped me move across the country and set up my new home while writing this book. I'd still be up to my ears in boxes and stuck on chapter 12 if it weren't for you all. Thanks for welcoming me home with open arms and such joy.

And most of all, thank you to my heavenly Father, who surprised me with another story about fathers and daughters and forgiveness. I'm so grateful to be on this writing adventure with you.

Liz Johnson fell in love with Prince Edward Island the first time she set foot on it. When she's not plotting her next trip to the island, she works as a full-time director of marketing. She finds time to write late at night and is the author of twelve novels, a *New York Times* bestselling novella, and a handful of short stories. She makes her home in Tucson, Arizona, where she enjoys exploring the area's history, attending local theater, and doting on her five nieces and nephews.

Meet
LIZ JOHNSON

LizJohnsonBooks.com

Read her
BLOG

Follow her
**SPEAKING
SCHEDULE**

Connect
with her on
**SOCIAL
MEDIA**

"The Red Door Inn took my breath away! Highly recommended!"

—**Colleen Coble**, author of *The Inn at Ocean's Edge* and the Hope Beach series

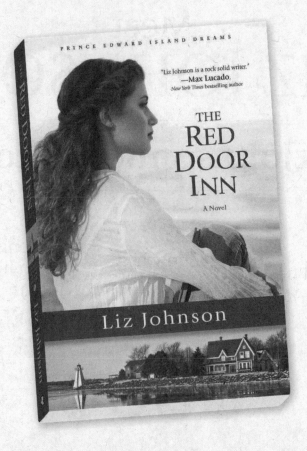

The only thing Marie and Seth agree on is that getting the Red Door Inn ready to open in just two months will take everything they've got—and they have to find a way to work together. In the process, they may find something infinitely sweeter than they ever imagined on this island of dreams.

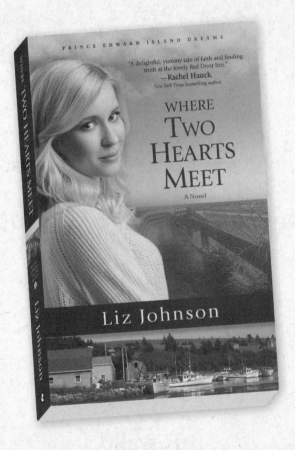